D1189545

PROLOGUE

Noah is sitting up in his bed reading the bible. He whispers a verse to himself, "*Yea, though I walk through the valley of the shadow of death, I will fear no evil: for thou art with me; thy rod and thy staff they comfort me.*"[1] He closes the bible and stares into space sorrowfully.

Franklyn just arrived at the Saint Sophia hospital to visit his brother, Noah. He wipes the snow off his coat and reads through the card rack in the gift shop, with a sarcastic smirk. He hears the clerk say, "Sir, your coffee?"

Nurse Esperanza looks at her watch and notices she still has ten minutes left for her break. She is stressed out due to all the nurses that called in sick with the canine flu virus, known as *HParvo*. She goes outside and folds her arms tight to her body to keep warm, it is extremely cold. Lighting up a cigarette, she starts swiping through her smartphone, desperately looking for a means of relief and satisfaction through social media.

Dr. Harpherd is in his office finishing up a small glass of whiskey, looking through charts with a defeated look. He mumbles to himself, "I'm running a fucking morgue, not an oncology ward," and buries his face into his hands, rubbing his tired eyes.

The cat across the hall was diagnosed with stage four lung cancer. He is the patient across from Noah's room.

---

[1] Psalm 23:4 King James Version

Noah's cat is named Nine.

Courtesy of https://pngimg.com/images/animals/cat

THE GAME WE LIVE:
A STORY ABOUT NOAH AND
THE CAT ACROSS THE HALL

INTRO:

It's December 15th, 2024; Noah Godtz is a patient, diagnosed with stage four cancer at Saint Sophia hospital, located in Canbridge, Alaska. His brother, Franklyn, will visit him soon at the hospital.

Noah is on the eighth floor, reserved for the terminally ill. His room is very plain, and there is a slight smell of urine. The beds are typical, white with steel bars on either side. There's a tray table with wheels that roll unevenly and a bedpan at the side of the bed. There's a desk drawer that has a broken steel handle that's hanging, and the bed's curtain is torn and dirty. All the windows have Venetian blinds with bent rails that hardly cover the sun from shining through. There are two solid plastic chairs on either side of Noah's bed, where you can only sit comfortably for a few minutes. The television screen is grainy with horizontal lines. There's a book titled, "_Illusions - the adventures of a reluctant messiah by Richard Bach_",[2] on the side of Noah's bed, and a laptop on his desk drawer, next to a bible. On top of the bible, there's a DVD of a movie titled "_The Game_"[3]. In his room, there's another bed but it's not taken; due to the hospital's current virus policy, you can only have one patient per room.

Noah is expecting to die soon. He is going through regret, resentment, and a guilty conscience, after choosing the military and wealth over his family and loved ones. Noah often boasts to the nurses that he dedicated twenty-six years to the military. His greatest regret is what he did to his ex-fiancé, Megan.

---

[2] https://en.wikipedia.org/wiki/Illusions_(Bach_novel)

[3] https://en.wikipedia.org/wiki/The_Game_(1997_film)

Now that Noah's days are numbered, he ventures into an emotional roller coaster, only to see that he is a victim of the game we live.

"Don't be a fool,
you don't own a fucking thing,
not even your own life."

Chapter 1: The Process meets the Conscience

Noah is sitting in bed reading the bible hoping to seek redemption from his past. He just received news from Nurse Esperanza that the hospital chaplain is out sick. Despite the upsetting news, he is excitingly waiting for his brother's arrival.

Noah hears Dr. Harpherd yelling at Nurse Esperanza in the corridor.

"This is a private hospital! Not a community hospital!" he exclaimed.

"Doctor, we have no more room for cancer patients! We are out of beds because of all the canine flu patients, and I don't know what else to do!" she replied audibly.

"That's not my job, nurse! You are the head nurse! Go do your job! And please - close my office door!" he yelled.

The door slams behind Nurse Esperanza. She stops and looks back at Dr. Harpherd's office, sighs, and marches frantically down the corridor. Noah peeks from the edge of his bed into the corridor with curiosity and sees Nurse Esperanza walk hastily past the doorway, out of sight.

The cat across the hall cries out for a nurse.

"Nurse, I need to use the bathroom! Nurse! Nurse! Nurse!"

Noah is annoyed by the cat across the hall.

"She's busy! Don't you see what's going on?! Jesus fucking Christ!" Noah yelled with contempt.

Franklyn is walking to the elevator with a coffee in hand and a bag containing a corn muffin. He's observing the patients from afar as he walks closer to the elevator. The hospital's main lobby is lined up with beds. All the beds had sick patients on them waiting to be tended to. Most of them were coughing, moaning, and complaining.

The walls of the lobby corridor are painted grey, with blotches of white where the paint had chipped; the lighting is dim and there are statues of saints placed on every corner.

There is a sizeable cross in the middle of the wall on the right by the elevator. The floor tiles are beaten up and dirty with their corners cracked, you can smell the stench of medical supplies and the sick. The elevator doors are dirty and riddled with scratches from years of wear and tear.

Franklyn hears the elevator bell and notices the light at the top of the elevator flickering on and off. The doors open and he walks in. A nurse walks in behind him smelling like cigarettes. Franklyn notices her face is completely masked with makeup. She looks at Franklyn and offers a half-smile. Franklyn grins and looks away.

"It's temporary, soon you will be sleeping," he said while looking up at the floor indicator.

The nurse nods her head in acknowledgment, offers a sarcastic smile, and continues to look down at the dirty floor. The elevator door opens on the eighth floor. Franklyn and Nurse Esperanza walk out exactly at the same time slightly bumping their elbows. They both stop to look at each other. Franklyn grins and Nurse Esperanza offers an awkward smile. She hurries down the corridor walking hastily ahead of Franklyn.

"Excuse me, nurse! Uh, nurse!" Franklyn yelled.

She turns around with an irritated look.

"Yes, sir. How can I help you?!"

"I am looking for room 8G. Do you know where that room is located?! I am looking for my brother, Noah Godtz!"

"Well, it's not behind you!" she replied contemptuously.

Franklyn looks behind him and realizes that he is at one end of the corridor. He notices the overhead light of the elevator flickering on and off.

"I guess this one is broken too," he muttered with a smirk.

Franklyn starts walking towards Nurse Esperanza and she points to the room on his lefthand side of the corridor. Franklyn smirks and nods his head acknowledging the room that Nurse Esperanza is pointing to.

"Is there anything else I can do for you, sir?" asked Nurse Esperanza.

"I got it," said Franklyn, shaking his head with a grin.

"Sure, you do," she said as she walked hurriedly towards the middle of the floor where the nurse's station is located.

Franklyn walks into Noah's room.

"Hey, Franklyn! It's good to see you, my brother!" exclaimed Noah with an exciting look.

Franklyn smiles and nods his head. He walks up to his brother, leans over, and they half-hug each other.

"How's the food in this place?" asked Franklyn.

"Terrible with a hint of stale," Noah replied.

Franklyn smiles and gestures with his eyes as if he is looking up into his brain.

"Oh... just what I'm used to."

They both chuckle.

"What's going on out there? The nurse is going crazy and there's an awful lot of commotion going on," asked Noah.

"Just an average day at a hospital. There's a bunch of canine flu patients downstairs piled up," Franklyn replied.

"Wow! It's that bad?! What the fuck!" Noah exclaimed.

"Yeah man, it's all over the news. Haven't you watched the news since you've been here?" asked Franklyn.

Noah becomes visibly frustrated.

"No, Franklyn, that television has been out of order since I got here four months ago, and the repair guy has been out sick, so no television for me. I have my laptop, so, I just watch movies."

"Well, there you go! You can read about the news online!" Franklyn exclaimed.

Noah has a sarcastic expression on his face.

"Yeah, if only the internet was working," Noah replied.

"Ha, everything is broken in this place, huh? Great way to make the patients feel comfortable," Franklyn said while faking a laugh.

"What about your phone, Noah? Can't you get internet on your phone?"

Noah sighs in frustration.

"Not really. It's an old flip phone and it takes an hour before the internet comes up. The response is really slow," Noah replied.

"Well, that doesn't help," muttered Franklyn.

Dr. Harpherd knocks briefly on the open door and races into Noah's room, dismissing Franklyn's presence.

"Mr. Godtz, are you familiar with the stage of cancer you are in?" asked Dr. Harpherd.

Noah sits up on his bed offering Dr. Harpherd his full attention.

"Yes, doctor, I am."

Dr. Harpherd looks at Franklyn and nods his head, finally acknowledging his presence.

"Mr. Godtz, our prognosis indicates that you have approximately eight days to live."

Noah's face turns pale, and he starts blinking repeatedly in shock.

"You may live passed the eight days, but we are not sure how long; we really can't say, Mr. Godtz, but I wanted to let you know what our team of specialists foresee. I will follow up with the administration on your request for a priest or chaplain to come to visit you as you asked. We've been dealing with this virus overwhelming the city and currently, resources are very low."

Dr. Harpherd starts shuffling through Noah's paperwork as he clears his throat.

"I'm sorry about this, Mr. Godtz. This is expected with stage four cancer patients."

Dr. Harpherd looks at Noah with a blank cold stare for a moment. He turns around and quickly walks out of the room.

Noah is staring into the same space Dr. Harpherd was standing in as if he were still standing there; he then looks at Franklyn with tearful eyes.

"Well, that's it, brother. I guess I'm done," said Noah with a broken voice.

Franklyn looked at his brother and puts his hand on his back offering comfort.

"Noah, eight days is enough time to find your true purpose, why you are here, and the key to life, if you really want."

Noah looks unmotivated with a half-smile on his face.

"Sure, what else do I got to lose?"

Noah really didn't understand what Franklyn meant. He is sitting silently with a blank stare on his face and Franklyn is looking at Noah, expecting him to have an emotional outburst.

"What the fuck! Where is the goddamn forgiveness in this fuckin place?! I dedicated my life to fighting for the freedom of this country and for what?! Man, I served my country! I made mistakes; I know I did! I wasn't nice to my family, my friends, or to Megan, and for that, I get to die of fucking cancer! Eight days, that's all I get! That's all that God is giving me! Eight fucking goddamn mother-fuckin' days! Fuck you, god! Fuck you!" Noah cried out in resentment.

Noah is crying hysterically while slightly hyperventilating.

Nurse Esperanza storms into Noah's room.

"Mr. Godtz, you need to calm down. This is not acceptable! You are upsetting the other patients, you know. Either you calm down or we will need to sedate you," she exclaimed.

Franklyn acknowledges Nurse Esperanza and quietly gestures for her to walk with him towards the exit door. She follows Franklyn to the door and steps out of the room into the corridor. Nurse Esperanza anxiously faces the door expecting Franklyn to speak, but Franklyn says nothing, steps back into the room, and closes the door in Nurse Esperanza's face. In the background, you can hear Noah still crying hysterically.

Nurse Esperanza stands facing the door for a moment; she rolls her eyes scornfully and then walks away.

Franklyn walks back to the side of his brother's bed staring at him.

"I think we should have a few drinks tonight, Noah, what do you think?" he asked.

Noah wipes his nose with his arm and looks at Franklyn with a puzzled look. His eyes are red and swollen from all the tears that have glossed his face.

"What? How?" Noah asked with a hoarse voice.

"I'll take care of that. Can you be calm, cool, and collected for at least one hour and write something for me?" asked Franklyn.

"What?" Noah asked with a baffled look.

"Write something for me, Noah, can you do that?"

"Yes, Franklyn, but what do you want me to write?"

"I want you to write all you can remember from childhood until today. I want you to write about anything you experienced in this life whether good or bad. I want to talk about these memories with you, Noah, can we do that?"

Noah looks confused and shrugs his shoulders.

"Ok," he replied half-heartedly.

Franklyn walks to the exit door of the room, puts on his outerwear, and turns to face Noah.

"I'll be back quickly, Noah. I'm going to keep this door closed, so go ahead and cry all you want and curse out whomever you want, even God if that makes you feel better. I'm sure he or she is used to it. If you need to scream, please scream into the pillow. We don't want nurse crappy coming in here and injecting you with any drugs to calm you. You need to let it out, brother, it is a process that begins today. *We will find your purpose, why you are here, and your key to life*; I guarantee it."

Noah nods in agreement but is still confused.

Franklyn grins, winks, and leaves the room. Noah's thoughts have taken his focus out of this world, but he distinctly hears the door close.

Noah continues to stare at the door for a few minutes, nods his head, and turns towards his desk drawer.

"He wants me to write," he mumbled.

He offers a disappointing look at the bible on his desk and opens the drawer with the broken handle. He takes out a notepad with a pen and begins to write.

Noah's story: Me versus Cancer

Childhood: Mom was an alcoholic and she was abusive to me and Franklyn. Dad was a womanizer and hardly ever home. He used the excuse of needing to work or be on the construction site. Therefore, he was hardly around. Mom used to beat me and my brother as a way of taking out her anger on Dad being a cheating womanizer. I remember when mom was drunk and tried to lure me into a hot oven because she was pissed at my dad. And I remember when she left us in the airport baggage claim area hoping we would get lost! Remember that Franklyn? I remember all the days and nights we spent in cheap hotels and staying with relatives! We were like gypsies at the young age of ten! I don't know how you did so well in school, Franklyn. We were hardly there during our younger years.

Noah pauses to laugh in a disgusted manner. He continues to write.

Middle school was a nightmare for us because we were there more frequently than in grade school. The All-American Boys military school in Chuopeka Alaska, remember Franklyn? What a great school to be in as German Italians! If I were to put a dollar for every insult and beating we took at that school we would be trillionaires!

After that, we went to the local public high school! what a joke! Remember those two girls, Franklyn? Their names were Monica and Lisa. Man, oh man, what beautiful girls they were.

They were into us, my brother, but they were scared to date us or even talk to us for too long. They were afraid of what the other students would say about them. I hated that school, Franklyn. Our biggest sports were soccer and handball! I spent most of my days smoking in the stairwell or outside by the courtyard. We had some good times with the girls there, though! Remember Sandra? Man, she was awesome. I had some good times at that high school, but we also had many fights with other students. Remember that gang called the T-Z crew? Brother, those were some mean Samoans! They cornered us in the courtyard by the main handball court.

We fought back but there were too many of them. If it weren't for that other gang that helped us, we would have been dead brothers. Yeah, I remember those guys, Rudy and Lucky. They were cool and always looked out for us. They wanted us to join their gang, but we were not into that life. But, they were still cool with that. We got lucky to have those guys as our friends. Whenever I think of our high school, it reminds me of a jail or a juvenile center, doesn't it? So many times, I had to walk out of that school with a bat in my hand or a knife in my pocket. I remember the school dean would walk around with a six-shooter off the side of his hip. Now you know that school was trouble! You know, Franklyn, the best part of my early years was having you around, man. We were always together. We are twins that don't look alike but are the same in many ways, right Franklyn? We went through some shit in our lives.

The Military: After high school, you and I went different ways. You went to the University of Alaska and then to law school; I went to the military. I'm sorry I never called you or even wrote to you, Franklyn. I got caught up with becoming an officer and working with the armored division of the military. I was obsessed with tanks and wanted to always be a tank infantry soldier. I didn't call any family members or any of our friends either. It's like I cut everyone off but not because I hated them, I just got wrapped up in myself, I guess. I did a few tours in Iraq and Afghanistan. I know I killed my share in these wars. But, I know I did this defending my country! I didn't want to do it, Franklyn, but they started with us!

Being in the military, I met some new friends and that's where I met Megan. She was a communications officer, and she was beautiful. We hit it off right away! We dated for several years, and I always thought she was the one. But I fucked that up, Franklyn. I thought about marriage, kids, and all the responsibilities and problems that come with that. I just cut her off. I didn't return her phone calls or her emails.

I gave her no explanation or closure. I regret that so much, Franklyn. That's why you are the only one visiting me. Man, I am just a bad person. This cancer is god's way of saying to me, Noah! you are a fucking asshole! Go fuck yourself and die!

During Military years: I was in the military for a long time, Franklyn. I did three tours and still wanted to do more. I was a proud E6 Tank Commander, but my tours came to an end. I was dispatched to the tank maintenance division for about six years. After that, it was just fieldwork for me for the next eight years. They had to kick me out! Lol. I could have joined the border patrol in Canada, but I enjoyed spending time around the tanks from time to time. I just couldn't stay away from them! I remember all the letters and postcards Megan sent to me, the emails and phone calls. I regret that I never replied to any of those. It's so fucked up that the only time I reached out to anyone is when I am diagnosed with stage four cancer. This is the time I chose to spend with you, Franklyn. My final days where I am the most useless to you or anyone. Life sucks and then you die. These are the words that keep going through my mind while I sit here. Franklyn, what a fucking shit show!

After an hour, Franklyn walks into the room hastily with a brown shopping bag and a plastic bag marked Pacifier's Spirits and Liquors.

"Let's celebrate!" Franklyn exclaimed.

"What?! Celebrate what?!" asked Noah with displeasure.

Franklyn walks back to the door and closes it.

"Our time together and your journey, brother! You will see how these eight days will be the most informative days of this life! Do you trust me, Noah?"

Noah gestures with a mouth shrug and a nod.

"Of course, I trust you, my brother! Shit, then, give me a drink, dammit!"

They both laugh loudly.

Franklyn hangs his outerwear. He reaches into the plastic bag and pulls out a bottle of red wine. The label read, *Screaming Eagle Cabernet 1992*, and the price tag read $525.00.

"Wow! Franklyn, you spent a lot on this one!"

Franklyn offers a big grin and winks at Noah.

"Hey man, if you're going to drink wine, might as well drink a good glass of wine," said Franklyn.

Franklyn opens the bottle of wine and pulls two wine glasses from the brown shopping bag. He gives a wine glass to Noah.

"Let's drink to a toast!" Noah bellowed.

"Ok… what do you want to toast to, Noah?"

Noah looks up and around thinking.

"Ah, fuck it! Let's just drink!" he exclaimed.

They both laugh a hardy laugh. There's a moment of silence while Noah and Franklyn are drinking their wine. Suddenly, Noah starts crying intensely.

Franklyn stares at Noah for a moment with no expression.

"My brother, if you water down the drinks in this bar, we will lose our customers!" he exclaimed with a grin.

Noah smirks, wipes his tears with the bed sheet, and takes a gulp of wine.

"Franklyn, this is really good stuff!"

They both start laughing again. Noah raises his wine glass up to the sky and chants, "Hooch! Hooch!" And Franklyn starts chanting in unison.

Franklyn grabs the bottle and pours Noah another full glass of wine.

"Oh shit, man! I was on chemo! Should I be drinking?!" exclaimed Noah.

There was a moment of silence. Noah totally forgot he was dying soon. He swallows deeply, sighs, and puts his head down as if he were on death row.

"Noah, I think we need to ask nurse crappy for details on her diagnosis."

They both start laughing loudly.

"Franklyn, this is probably the best wine I've ever had, seriously."

"Great, may I read what you wrote, Noah?"

Noah raises his glass of wine with a cheer, then passes his notebook to Franklyn.

"Sure man, here you go. Don't be too impressed!" Noah exclaimed.

Franklyn grins and starts reading Noah's notes to himself.

Several minutes go by and he breaks while reading to speak to Noah about his notes.

"Noah, mom's life was a bad one. Mom's mother died when she was an adolescent, and her father was an alcoholic. He was sickly and in bad condition, so she had to take care of him. He died shortly after her mom, so, she was left to fend for herself with local relatives. She couldn't finish middle school because of that and ended up in a neighbor's home that needed someone to tend to the chores of the house. During her years working there, she was molested, raped, and tossed back into the street as a scarred young woman."

Noah's facial expression changes from happy to angry. You can clearly see the disgust and sadness mixed in his eyes.

"How the fuck was that my fault?! Why the fuck should we pay the price for that shit, Franklyn?! She fuckin' neglected us! She tried to fucking kill me! She's a fucking bitch! A fucking bitch!"

Noah starts screaming loudly and Nurse Esperanza starts yelling from the corridor.

"Please stop screaming, you are disturbing the patients!"

You can hear her footsteps getting closer to Noah's room. Franklyn quickly grabs the bottle of wine with both glasses and puts them inside the brown shopping bag. Some of the wine spills on the bed sheets and on the floor as Nurse Esperanza storms into the room.

"What - is - the problem?!" she asked bitterly.

"We are acting out a play, nurse! It's called, *The Cat Across the Hall*. You see, Noah always wanted to be an actor, so we are acting out our characters. Sorry, it got a bit noisy, but I am trying to give my brother the opportunity to fulfill his dying wish," said Franklyn with a humble voice.

With a suspicious look, Nurse Esperanza stutters for a bit on her words.

"Oh-ok, just keep it down, please, thank you. Noah, I'll be by later to take your vitals and help you wash up."

"Nurse, I only have eight days with my brother, is it ok if we leave that for tomorrow, please?" asked Noah.

Nurse Esperanza nods and offers a slight smile as she leaves the room.

In the background, you can hear a faint voice coming from the room across the hall.

"Nurse, can you please help me?" he asked.

The voice gets louder.

"Nurse! Nurse! Nurse! I'm calling you! Can't you hear me goddammit?!" he exclaimed.

She walks up to the doorway of his room, annoyed, with her arms folded.

"I was just here helping you! I can't stay with you all day, sir! There are other patients I need to tend to!" Nurse Esperanza exclaimed with frustration.

Franklyn closes the door to Noah's room and sits back down.

"So, can we finish our drinks?" asked Franklyn.

Noah nods with grief. Franklyn avoids eye contact and changes his focus to Noah's notebook.

"Ok, Noah. So back to your point. You are right. We weren't at fault for our mother's upbringing or her relationship with our father. My point is that they are not at fault as well."

Noah is obviously flustered.

"So, what? Do we have to forgive them? That's a bowl of crap, Franklyn."

"No, we don't have to forgive them, but we don't need to blame them either," Franklyn replied.

"That doesn't make sense. Well, who do we blame then? Satan?" asked Noah mockingly.

"We don't have to blame anyone, Noah. *It is your nurtured program that compels you to blame someone or something*. Why is there a need to blame anyone? Why do you feel this somehow solves the past? By blaming mom and dad, you are only feeding your own satisfaction temporarily. How does that make sense? That satisfaction you seek doesn't last, Noah, because it is emotional and illogical. Blaming them does not reverse what you and I went through as kids. It is what they call in this game of life, emotional baggage."

"Yeah… I guess you are right about that, Franklyn, but she was still a bitch! And dad was a fucking goddamn asshole! Fuck them both! Fill my wine glass, please!" Noah exclaimed.

Franklyn grins, nods his head, and continues to read. He pauses to speak to Noah.

"That military school did suck but those kids weren't at fault, Noah."

"What?! again, Franklyn?! Are you fucking kidding me?!"

Franklyn's voice becomes firm and commanding.

"Noah, blaming them or anyone for any reason doesn't provide a solution, and it doesn't even give you closure. What happened back then was the past, brother. We defended ourselves back then and yes, we took beatings, but all of this was due to *the connection to the conscience.*"

Noah chokes slightly on his wine and offers a confused look.

"My... what the fuck? I don't get it?" Noah asked with a frown.

"You will, brother; when you are ready. Let me keep reading," Franklyn replied.

Noah shrugs his shoulders and mouth.

"Ok, it's your time wasted," he said followed by another gulp of wine.

Franklyn pauses to chuckle.

"Sandra?"

They smile at each other for a couple of minutes.

"Yes, Noah, we had some shit happen to us in our early years. All that happened in the past doesn't matter. Whether it was good or bad it doesn't matter, Noah. All this guilt does is contribute to your connection to the conscience."

Noah looks at Franklyn with a disturbed frown.

"What the fuck are you talking about, Franklyn? You sound like a wackadoo. For your information, my conscience is clear."

"Got it, Noah. So, you've heard of a guilty conscience then, correct?"

"Yeah, Franklyn, but why should I have a guilty conscience about my asshole parents or some assholes in school that hated us because we had German last names?"

Franklyn's posture becomes authoritative.

"Noah, That's not the only aspect of conscience connected that affects us. Let me keep reading your notes. We will talk more about that."

"Ok, Franklyn, but you skipped the part where I wrote, that the best part of my life was having you around. I think you missed that, brother."

Franklyn smirks while shaking his head.

"I'll stimulate your ego by kissing you on the chops after I finish reading your notes, Noah, Ok?"

Noah offers a look of disgust on his face.

"Oh no way, ha-ha, fuck you, man," Noah replied.

They both chuckle and take sips from their glass.

Franklyn continues to read Noah's notes and shakes his head in dismay.

"Noah, what are you sorry about, brother? You are sorry for doing something that satisfied you? You're sorry for something that you wanted to do? Why?"

Noah shrugs his shoulders and pauses. He takes a sip of wine and thinks about what he is going to say.

"Franklyn, I should've called Megan. I should have written back to her. I was being selfish. I was inconsiderate to her, my friends, and my family."

"Noah, that was the past, man. That doesn't matter now. What matters now is that I am here, and we are talking. That's what matters," Franklyn replied sternly.

Noah takes a deep breath gesturing relief.

"You're right, brother! Now is the time that counts! And I need a refill!" Noah exclaimed.

Noah looks uneasy while drinking his wine, and Franklyn remains expressionless.

"Ok, you got it," Franklyn replied.

He reaches over and grabs the bottle of wine from the bag. He fills both their glasses and puts the bottle of wine back down on the floor.

Noah exclaims, "Cheers!"

They both raise their glass and nod their heads.

"Noah, are you feeling guilt over the people you killed during those wars in the middle east?"

"Kind of, but not really. I think what I did was right, Franklyn. I defended this country."

"I didn't ask you why you did it, Noah. I'm asking you if you still feel guilty."

Noah shrugs his mouth, stops to think for a moment, and takes a mouthful of wine before speaking.

"I don't know."

"Noah, can we at least agree that this was the past and that it doesn't matter now?"

"Yeah, sure Franklyn. It's just hard to forget."

"Well, that's your connection to the conscience, Noah. Your connection to the conscience doesn't help you."

Noah nods in agreement, perplexed, and not really grasping what Franklyn said.

Franklyn takes another sip of wine and continues to read Noah's notes with breaks.

"Noah, whatever happened between you and Megan is…"

Noah interrupts Franklyn and says with a frustrated voice, "I know, it's the past. I know."

"Yes, exactly. And you can't change the past, Noah. Not even God can change the past or the future for that matter," Franklyn said with a grin.

Noah's body posture and tone become defensive.

"Hey man, be careful what you say in this room. I want to go upstairs when I die, not downstairs."

"I don't think there are any stairs when anyone dies, Noah."

They both chuckle and Franklyn keeps reading.

"Noah, your story is full of guilt and emotions. This is all due to your connection to the conscience. What you did or what you didn't do, that doesn't matter now. How does that help you find your purpose or why you are here? All these emotions and ego feed your connection to the conscience. Your story is like a loaded gun with a trigger and the bullets are your emotions and guilt."

Noah frowns and is visibly upset at Franklyn.

"Hey man, you asked me to write this shit, so, that's what I did. Is this why you asked me to write it? To scold me and make me feel worse than how I feel? I think you forgot, Franklyn, I am dying soon. Why did you ask me to write this crap anyway?"

Franklyn's voice becomes commanding once again.

"Because I want you to wake up. I want you to realize that your past means nothing. It's all bullshit. All this guilt and emotions trapped inside you feed your connection to the conscience! This story is full of guilt and it only sparks up your emotions.

I want you to recognize that emotions don't help you at all. The only logical statement in this letter is when you write, *Life sucks, and then you die.* In your situation, that statement is logical, Noah. *The game we live is like this on purpose."*

Noah seems troubled by what Franklyn just said.

"What the fuck are you saying, Franklyn? You are saying that *Life sucks and then you die* is all it is! And that's it!"

"Yes, Noah, that's exactly what I'm saying. Except I refer to it as the game. So, I would rephrase that to say, *the game sucks your energy and then you die."*

Noah takes two full swigs of wine and starts gasping from anger.

"Franklyn, we are all lucky you are not the hospital's chaplain. Geesh, what the fuck is wrong with you? You're like some *Frankenstein* monster."

Franklyn's tone becomes calmer but remains confident.

"Nothing is wrong with me, Noah. I'm just logical which turns out to be brutally honest for others. I pull no punches, man. You want me to tiptoe around you and tell you what you want to hear? Bullshit you by saying things like, God forgives you and you will serve penance until you are ready to go back in and play the game again? This game of life isn't like the penalty box in the game of hockey. I'm guiding you to find knowledge. *I'm introducing you to the truth about the connection to the conscience.* Not that bullshit that these religious clergymen or spiritual gurus spew unto you. *I'm using the word truth, so you can relate to what I am saying. The fact is that the word, truth, is riddled with emotion in its definition. I prefer to use the word absolute[4], however, for the sake of comprehension, I will use the word truth[5].* I'm going to tell you something else you won't like and probably will not want to accept, Noah."

"Really?..." Noah replied sarcastically followed by a sip of wine.

---

[4] https://www.etymonline.com/word/absolute

[5] https://www.etymonline.com/word/truth

"The god you pray to is a construct. A program that was installed into your brain before you were nurtured into this game we live. It is illogical brainwashing that was passed on from generation to generation through your DNA and etched into your brain. There is no god or Jesus wearing sandals sitting on a cloud somewhere between Planet Earth and bumblefuck watching over you, there is only a program called, The Conscience. And the conscience is not on your side. Wake up and smell the wine you are drinking. What you really need is to *find your purpose* and *why you are here*, Noah. If you are willing to listen and offer me the time, I will guide you to find the absolute answer to those questions."

Noah drinks the rest of his wine in one fell swoop as if he just took a hard slap to the face.

"Sure, Franklyn. No one else is here to send me off anyway. I'll listen and I'll try my best to follow you," said Noah with doubt in his voice.

"It's simple, Noah, it's either red or blue, just like your favorite song."

"Hey man, I love that song!" Noah exclaimed while singing, "*Midnight Blue,* *tara-ta-ta, oh-oh, oh-oh.*"

Franklyn and Noah keep drinking their wine and talking. They briefly discuss topics on conscience connected and the conscience, discussing the tangible, and intangible aspects of it. They discuss how nature, nurture, emotions, ego, and programming through society, television, and social media affect humanity. They go through a couple of bottles of wine until after midnight.

They both fall asleep with wine glasses in their hands, Noah sitting up in his bed and Franklyn sitting on the most uncomfortable chair.

"The game we live is
like this on purpose."

Chapter 2: Eight is not so infinite

Franklyn wakes up the next day from sleeping in his chair. He feels a sharp pain in the middle of his back.

"This chair's a killer, this body needs a new backside," mumbles Franklyn and then chuckles to himself lightly.

Noah is curled up in a fetal position hugging his pillow.

Franklyn stands up and stretches his long arms to the ceiling, looking toward the broken Venetian blinds, he sees the sunlight hitting the winter frost on the window. He puts his boots on and starts walking around the room stretching out as much as he can. The cracking of Franklyn's back is loud.

"Wow, brother! I hear your bones popping from here!" said Noah, while still curled up in bed.

"Yeah, that chair had my butt for dinner," Franklyn replied.

They both giggle.

"What's for breakfast?" asked Franklyn.

"Probably the worst food they can muster up," Noah replied.

"What do you want, Noah? I'll go downstairs and get us breakfast."

"Are you sure? I don't want to impose on you, Franklyn."

Franklyn frowns while batting his eyes.

"I don't know what that means, Noah. I was planning to get a coffee and a corn muffin anyway."

Noah is noticeably excited.

"Ok! Then, I'll have pancakes! I sure wish, *Snowflake Cafe and Cakes*, were close by! I love their pancakes, man," Noah exclaimed.

"Snowflake Pancakes on the way…" Franklyn replied.

"Really?!" Noah asked in awe.

"Sure, Noah, I'll be back."

Franklyn puts on his heavy outerwear.

"Isn't it _too cold for titties out there_!" Noah bellowed.

"My titties are covered well and good," Franklyn replied with a grin.

They both chuckle.

There's a loud knock at the door and Dr. Harpherd abruptly walks in.

Franklyn bows and speaks with a baritone voice.

"Buenos Dias, doctor parca."

Dr. Harpherd frowns with a confused look.

"Excuse me? Uh...I didn't get that?"

Franklyn grins goofily from ear to ear.

"It's Spanish for good morning doctor," he said.

Dr. Harpherd looks at Franklyn blinking his eyes with a cold stare.

"Oh,… I don't speak Spanish."

Dr. Harpherd flashes his eyebrows and looks over at Noah.

"Mr. Godtz, I have some paperwork for you to review and sign. It has to do with policies and procedures after your…" Dr. Harpherd looks uncomfortable while shuffling through the paperwork. He looks up and down, pausing as if he is at a loss for words. "Uh… last day here with us," the doctor said in a low voice.

His voice becomes abruptly louder.

"It's several forms for, do not resuscitate and arrangements for funeral or cremation, etcetera."

The doctor stops talking and takes a long glance at Noah and then at Franklyn. They are looking at him like two vampires staring at a jugular vein. Dr. Harpherd blinks nervously and continues to speak with a commanding voice.

"It's hospital protocol, Mr. Godtz, and we have no choice but to follow through accordingly."

"Doctor, may I review those documents for my brother? I will be his legal representative," said Franklyn with assertiveness.

"Oh, are you an attorney?" asked Dr. Harpherd.

Franklyn's voice is noticeably sarcastic.

"Hardly-Wardly doctor, I'm a paralegal, which unfortunately means I know the law."

Dr. Harpherd seems a bit hesitant.

"Oh, um, ok," he replied.

"Yes, contracts are my specialty, basically I advise everyone not to sign anything unless they are getting paid," said Franklyn.

Dr. Harpherd is noticeably uncomfortable with Franklyn.

"Well, I'm not sure I understand, sir," Dr. Harpherd said.

Franklyn gestures towards the exit door of Noah's room.

"I'll explain, doctor, let's please talk in your office. I'll take care of my brother's paperwork."

Dr. Harpherd points to the paperwork firmly.

"Um, there has to be a legal authorization form or power of attorney signed by Mr. Godtz, sir," the doctor emphasized.

Franklyn takes Dr. Harpherd by the arm and escorts him towards the exit door of Noah's room. He gestures with his arm towards the corridor.

"Shall we, doctor?"

Dr. Harpherd looks back at Noah and then at Franklyn confused.

"It's ok, doctor, I'm his brother. That gives me the right to speak on my brother's behalf since he is under mental duress," said Franklyn.

Dr. Harpherd becomes defensive and responds with disapproval.

"Wait! What?! That's ludicrous!"

Franklyn looks back at Noah, smiles, winks, and bellows in a robotic voice like *Arnold Schwarzenegger* in the *Terminator* movie, "*I'll be back*!"

Franklyn closes the door behind him.

Noah hears Franklyn's muffled voice saying to Dr. Harpherd, "So, doctor, is that brand of aftershave *Jim Beam* or *JW Black*?"

Noah laughs. He finds his brother highly amusing.

"Less than eight days to live," Noah whispered to himself.

He has a grim look and starts whimpering.

"Why god?! Why are you doing this to me?! Please give me another chance! Please god, please give me another chance!" he exclaimed with a low voice.

Noah pauses and looks down on his bed. He wipes his tears with his bedsheets, takes a deep breath, and speaks to himself.

"I need to say sorry, that's what I have to do! Right, god? I need to apologize to Megan, Matt, Pete, Jimmy, Andrew, John, Phil, and everyone else, right? That's what I need to do. I need to do that now!"

Noah looks up at the ceiling in his room as if he is seeing through it and into the heavens.

"God, I'm going to say I'm sorry to everyone! And you are going to forgive me and give me a second chance! I don't want to go yet, god, you hear me! I'm not going yet, I'm not ready!"

Noah slams both his hands on the bed repeatedly as if he is beating on a drum. He reaches for his notepad and begins to write.

Letter to Megan from Noah:

Hi Megan,

It's me, Noah. Megan, I'm dying of cancer. I only have less than eight days, so please read this. I'm sorry for what I did to you, Megan. I ghosted you after your miscarriage and I'm sorry about that. Megan, I need to give you closure. I know you think it was your fault you had the miscarriage, but it was my fault. I caused your miscarriage to happen. I wasn't thinking straight, and I was scared of marriage and being a father. I wasn't ready for that responsibility because I knew I needed to work on myself. I was less than perfect, and you deserve a perfect king by your side, Megan. You are the queen of perfection, and you need a king that is perfect.

I'm sorry for what I did and how I cut you off. I think God is punishing me now. I have less than eight days to live, do you believe that? I served this country for twenty-six years. It's like that doesn't mean anything.

I don't know why God is doing this to me. Anyway, I hope you are happy. I heard that you got married and you have two kids. That makes me feel good. I always loved you, Megan. You will always be in my heart.

I know you are busy with your husband and your kids so don't feel like you need to reach out. I still have that same phone number; I never changed it. I'm at Saint Sophia hospital in Canbridge on the eighth floor for cancer patients. I'm hoping that maybe they gave me the wrong prognosis and made a mistake. Maybe the paperwork got all messed up and there's a different guy named, Noah Godtz. It's possible, Megan, anything is possible, right? Megan, if I get out of here and all of this was the hospital's mistake, I would like to take you to dinner and talk about the old days. Will you give me a chance to say sorry face to face? We can be best friends. Who knows, maybe you'll get a divorce once I am out of this hospital and I'll surely marry you. We can have kids, a big house and travel. I'll be ready this time, Megan, I promise.

With love, Noah.

Noah pauses for a moment and reads his letter repeatedly several times over. He starts sobbing and whispers, "I'm sorry Megan, I'm so sorry. I was a bad person."

Nurse Esperanza knocks on the door and walks in rolling a cart. Noah quickly wipes his tears and closes the notepad.

"Good Morning, Mr. Godtz."

"Good Morning, nurse," he replied with a sad voice.

Nurse Esperanza speaks as if she is addressing a child.

"You look like you've been crying."

"A little," he replied with a sniffle.

Nurse Esperanza smiles and glances at Noah's notepad.

"What are you writing?" she asked.

"A letter to a friend," he replied.

Nurse Esperanza offers a big smile while tidying up around the bed.

"That's nice," she replied.

Noah nods in questionable agreement.

"I need to take your vitals and you need to fill out your breakfast sheet. You don't need to keep a special diet anymore, Mr. Godtz, you can have anything you want. So, what will it be?"

"A second chance," he replied pouting with sorrow.

Nurse Esperanza nods, smiles, and stares at Noah as if she is keeping a secret.

"Mr. Godtz, I see that you've been reading the Bible, is that helping you?"

Noah looks over at the Bible with a grim look.

"I don't know. It doesn't seem like it is," he replied.

"Have you ever heard of healing crystals?" she asked.

Noah stares at Nurse Esperanza with hope in his eyes.

"No. Does that stuff really work?" he replied while wiping his face.

"It cured my mother of breast cancer. She's still alive and strong today at ninety-three," she stated with glee.

Nurse Esperanza smiles while fluffing Noah's pillows.

"Really?!" he replied in shock.

She takes her phone out and shows Noah a picture of her mother.

The screen on her phone was cracked in a few places and it smelled like cigarettes. She slides through several photos of her mother.

"Wow! She looks great! What's her name?" he asked.

Nurse Esperanza replies staring at the picture on her phone with a pleasing smile.

"Elena. It means shining light."

"Really? Ain't that somethin'," he replied.

Nurse Esperanza addresses Noah like a grade school student.

"Our names mean something, Mr. Godtz, did you know that? Have you looked up your first name and surname?"

Noah shrugs his mouth and then, shakes his head.

"Let's look up your name and I can bet you it means something," she replied.

She starts searching and pauses to read from her phone.

"Noah... means peace, restful... take a look," She shows her phone to Noah.

"Well, that is a convenient name for someone that's about to kick the bucket in seven days," he replied with a smirk.

Nurse Esperanza smiles and keeps searching on her phone.

"Well, hold on… let's look up your surname... hmm... interesting. It says God or Godly. It is a derivation of guda, God, a deity, or a divine being. So, your name means peaceful god, Mr. Godtz."

Noah's expression changes to sheer wonder.

"Really? I never knew that," he replied.

"You probably have a direct connection with the higher power, and you didn't even know it. But you are not going to connect with the higher power through reading the bible or prayer," she stated with indifference.

Noah is puzzled by Nurse Esperanza's statement.

"Really? that's what I was taught in school and pretty much by my family. Why does this hospital have a chaplain?" he asked.

Nurse Esperanza replies with an arrogant tone.

"It's the protocol for this hospital to have a chaplain or a priest. We get a lot of military patients in this hospital, so, we need to have a chaplain. Sometimes we have a priest or a minister. And it's all confusing, I know."

Noah nods firmly.

"I bet," he said.

Nurse Esperanza looks at Noah while holding both hands up to the ceiling.

"So, are you interested in knowing how I connect with the higher power?" she asked with a smile from ear to ear.

"Yes, please, please tell me!" he replied desperately.

Nurse Esperanza exclaims with a strong boundless voice.

"Meditation!"

Noah frowns and looks around his room as if he was expecting a different answer.

"I've heard of that, nurse, I thought that was for helping with sleep or relaxation."

Nurse Esperanza giggles in a condescending manner.

"It's not only for relaxation, Mr. Godtz. Meditation is also for connecting with the higher power through our chakras."

Noah is pleasantly surprised.

"Oh, wow! I didn't know that…," he replied.

"Many people don't, Mr. Godtz. That's why there are so many confused lost souls out there," she said with disappointment.

Noah smiles and agrees with her.

"You're so right about that, nurse."

"I have books on my desk that will teach you how to awaken your chakras and how to meditate so you can connect with the higher power. We don't refer to the higher power as God, Jesus Christ, or the many names religion has given it. We refer to it as the higher power of consciousness. It's really beautiful once you make that connection," she said.

Noah has a glow of amazement and hope on his face.

"Nurse, when can you bring me those books?" he asked.

"I'll go get them now and bring them to you," she replied eagerly.

She looks at her watch and suddenly becomes overly concerned.

"Oh-no! I have to finish my rounds! But I'll be right back with those books!" she exclaimed.

She hurries out of Noah's room and into the corridor. Noah is sitting up in his bed in complete astonishment but with a hint of hope.

The cat across the hall starts yelling loudly.

"Nurse! Nurse! Nurse! My wife needs water! She's thirsty!"

"She's busy, dammit! Doesn't your wife have legs?! There's a water station right on this floor, man!" Noah yelled back angrily.

The cat across the hall ignores Noah and continues to yell for the Nurse.

"Nurse! Nurse! Nurse!"

Noah mumbles under his breath with anger, "What a goddamn asshole."

Franklyn walks into Noah's room and closes the door behind him. Noah's eyes light up with a big smile on his face.

"Hey, brother! You're back!" Noah exclaimed.

"I stick to my threats, and… I got pancakes!" Franklyn exclaimed.

Noah says in a vaudeville tone while pretending he's holding a cigar, "I could eat those off the ice road, Mr. Sourdough!"

They both chuckle.

"Does it smell like cigarettes in here?" asked Franklyn.

"Yes, Nurse Esperanza was just here," Noah replied.

Franklyn gestures with his index finger as if Noah made a good point. He opens the bag to pull out a foam container.

Nurse Esperanza suddenly storms into Noah's room with several books in her hands.

She says with a big smile and a divine voice, "Welcome to enlightenment, Mr. Godtz."

Noah is overwhelmed with excitement.

"Thank you, nurse. I'm so excited about this. If I have any questions, can you help me?" asked Noah.

Franklyn looks at the books with surprise, he looks at Noah and then offers a sarcastic grin to Nurse Esperanza. He continues to pull out the contents of the paper bag containing their breakfast.

"Yes, Mr. Godtz. I can answer all your questions. I've been meditating and connecting with the higher power for over ten years now. I have been a pioneer of the awakening since I was born," she replied confidently.

"Wow!" Noah exclaimed in astonishment.

"So, be aware that there are certain crystals and oils you need to buy for the meditation to be effective. It's in the book titled, *C'mon and get with your Chakras*," she replied.

Noah has a big smile as hope overcomes his face.

"Ok, nurse, this is great. How do I know which crystals to buy that will cure my cancer?" asked Noah.

He glances momentarily at Franklyn with a look of uncertainty on his face.

The nurse smiles and nods her head at Noah.

"One of the books I brought you is all about crystals and it will tell you exactly which crystals and oils you need. There's a crystal and oil shop on Pacifier Avenue. I take my break at two in the afternoon, and I always go there for relaxation and spiritual connection. I can pick up the items you will need. Just have a list ready for me at two pm... oh, and... these items are very expensive, so you'll need at least two or three hundred dollars to cover everything," she replied.

"Ok! Thank you!" Noah exclaimed.

Nurse Esperanza quickly turns to walk out of Noah's room and Franklyn calls out to her, "Nurse!"

Nurse Esperanza turns slightly toward Franklyn.

"Yes, sir," she replied.

"I see your fingernails are a bit beat up, do you bite your nails?" asked Franklyn.

Nurse Esperanza embarrassingly closes her hands into fists hiding her fingernails.

"It's a bad habit, I know," she replied with a shy voice.

She rolls her eyes and walks quickly out of the room and out of sight.

Franklyn walks to the door and says while closing the door, "She smells like an ashtray."

Noah and Franklyn chuckle.

"Franklyn, you need to be nice. She's trying to help me," said Noah with a silly reprimanding voice.

Franklyn looks at the books with a grin on his face.

"Ok, Noah, c'mon let's get with your pancakes, and after we can get with your chakras."

Franklyn passes a coffee and a foam container to Noah.

"Vessel fuel," said Franklyn.

Noah replies with a smile and bows his head.

"Thank you, sir," he replied.

After taking a big sip of his coffee, Franklyn sits down and pulls out a corn muffin from the bag.

"That's all your having?" asked Noah.

"This is enough to help me c'mon, and get with my bowels," said Franklyn with a grin.

Noah laughs aloud, then starts eating his breakfast. You can see the glow of happiness all over his face.

"Oh, these are so good," Noah stated.

Franklyn smiles, raises his coffee to gesture as if he is toasting, and continues to drink his coffee.

Time goes by as Noah looks through the books and finishes eating his breakfast while Franklyn is cleaning up.

"Franklyn, you didn't finish your muffin? It wasn't good?"

"Ah, I'll finish it later, Noah. Let's chat for a bit about your newfound enlightenment."

Franklyn pulls his chair closer to Noah's bed.

"Franklyn, I meant to ask earlier, what did you say to Dr. Harpherd in Spanish?"

"Oh, I said to him, Good Morning Dr. Grim Reaper. Parca means Grim Reaper in Spanish," Franklyn replied.

Noah laughs in a boisterous manner.

"Ok brother, tell me what you and nurse crappy talked about," asked Franklyn.

Noah chuckles and tells Franklyn about Nurse Esperanza's mother and how the crystals cured her of breast cancer. He tells him everything Nurse Esperanza had told him about meditation and crystals. Franklyn interrupts Noah while he is talking and looking through the book about healing crystals.

"Hold on, Noah! I need to find a healing crystal that I can put in my left back pocket!"

Noah has a worried look.

"Why… Franklyn? Are you having pain in your back or in your legs? Are you ok?"

"Noah, I need to heal my wallet. It's been suffering from expenses for years now."

Noah smirks with an unpleasant look.

"C'mon man, this might help me. Now's not the time to be facetious," said Noah with discontent.

"Ok, Noah. I'm just enlightening things up. Let's do some research, shall we?"

"Ok, Franklyn, thank you."

"So, what other books do we have here?" asked Franklyn.

Noah reads the titles from the three books Nurse Esperanza loaned him.

"This one is, *C'mon and get with your Chakras*, This other one we were just reading is titled, *Your Chakra, Power Stones and You.*"

Franklyn interrupts, "Sounds like a rocky love story."

Noah ignores Franklyn and continues to speak.

"And this last one is titled, *Crystals, Oils, and Sage, Oh My*."

"Oh my, that is an interesting title, it really does say too much," said Franklyn.

Noah offers Franklyn a harsh look.

"Let's look at this last one," said Franklyn with a silly grin.

"Ok! Let's see," Noah said enthusiastically.

Noah starts reading about crystals and their healing powers aloud. He continues to read about oils, then about Sage, and then about Bulnesia sticks also known as Palo Santo. While Noah is reading aloud, Franklyn falls asleep in his chair by Noah's bed.

Hours later, Franklyn awakens to a loud whisper.

"Franklyn, Franklyn, wake up!"

Franklyn wakes up startled.

"Yeah, Noah, what?!"

"I need you to go to that crystal shop and get what's on this list for me," Noah said with an assertive voice.

Franklyn is continuously blinking having a hard time keeping his eyes open.

"What? Now?" asked Franklyn with a groggy voice and a yawn.

"Yes, Franklyn, please, I need you to go now. I don't have the cash to give Nurse Esperanza and you can use my credit card."

"Ok, Noah, no problem. Just let me wash my face and wake up. I don't want to drive out there like a *Cheechako* and end up in deep ice water," Franklyn replied.

"Oh, c'mon man, there are no deep ice roads in this town," said Noah with a playful voice.

Franklyn raises his eyebrows humorously and nods his head. He stands up from his chair and stretches his hands very close to the ceiling.

"You know, with your height, you could have played professional sports," said Noah with a coveted look.

Franklyn shakes his head.

"Sure, Noah, sports were not for me."

"You didn't even try, Franklyn."

"I gave up sports after the soccer ball kicked me back," said Franklyn with a grin.

Noah laughs aloud.

Franklyn goes to the bathroom to wash up.

After several minutes, he walks out, grabs Noah's credit card, and looks at the list, front, and back.

"Geesh, all of this just to make contact with the higher power, huh?" said Franklyn jeeringly.

Noah shrugs his mouth and shoulders.

"C'mon, man, a little support, please? The address is on that paper," Noah replied.

Franklyn smiles and winks at his brother.

"Sure, Noah, I'll be back."

Franklyn grabs his outerwear and walks out closing the door behind him. He observes the cat across the hall's room, all the flowers, balloons, statues, and the big religious cross by the side of his bed. There is a woman sitting by him reading the bible with a rosary in her hand. Everyone sitting around in that room has a solemn look on their face. The woman is moving her lips but you can't make out what she is saying.

Franklyn turns to the right heading for the elevator. He presses the elevator button and waits. You can't tell whether the elevator is coming or going because the overhead light is nonfunctional.

A few minutes later the elevator doors open and out comes Nurse Esperanza as if she were running away from a gaggle of zombies.

"Mr. Godtz, I'm going to come by in a few minutes and get that list and money from your brother," she said with a big smile.

Franklyn holds the elevator doors to reply.

"No worries, nurse, I'm going there now and I have his list. I'll take care of this," he said.

Nurse Esperanza's cell phone starts ringing and she gestures to Franklyn with her forefinger to wait. Franklyn holds the elevator while she speaks on her phone.

"Mom! For god's sake, I can't talk to you now, I'm busy," she said.

She stops speaking for a moment to listen and exclaims with annoyance, "Mom! I can't! Call Nina, mom… bye… bye, mom!" she exclaimed followed by hanging up the call.

Nurse Esperanza sighs and shakes her head in frustration. She looks at Franklyn with squinted eyes as if she forgot what she was going to say.

The elevator is beeping consistently while he holds the elevator doors open. Nurse Esperanza turns quickly and walks away down the corridor.

Franklyn grins as if he just heard a good joke. He goes into the elevator and presses the lobby.

It's midnight; Noah is sitting in his bed reading, with books scattered all over. There are oils steaming from a diffuser, incense burning, and the smell of sage with burning wood that transcends throughout the room.

Nurse Esperanza knocks loudly, opens the door, and walks in.

"How is it going, Mr. Godtz?"

Franklyn wakes up from his nap but keeps his eyes closed.

"Well, I don't know. I read these three books and I think I've been meditating correctly. According to the books, I am also using the right oils and crystals for healing. I have Amethyst, Carnelian, Rainbow Fluorite, Smoky Quartz, Rose Quartz, and Rhodochrosite crystals set up here on my bed to help cure my cancer. I'm not feeling well, but, I'm really trying," said Noah.

Nurse Esperanza replies with a voice of wisdom, "I know…"

She walks around the room with her arms extended, nodding with approval as if she is seeing the great beyond.

"This is all, though, very impressive. It smells really healing in here and I can feel the energy and positive spirits. I love the crystals you have all over the room; I can smell the Eucalyptus, Lavender, and Frankincense from your diffuser. These are all very powerful for healing, Mr. Godtz. I love the _Eye of Horus_ you have on your shrine and the _Tree of Life_ combined with the _Infinite 8_. This most certainly helps with your connection to the higher power. You are definitely on the right track, Mr. Godtz," she said.

"Will this cure my cancer?" asked Noah.

Nurse Esperanza offers a nod and an assuring gesture.

"Yes, Mr. Godtz, absolutely. I'm a certified level II reiki, you know. I helped my mother cure herself of breast cancer with these same crystals. She would carry them in the middle of her chest."

Noah's eyes open wide.

"Wow! That must have been uncomfortable!" Noah exclaimed.

Nurse Esperanza giggles while covering her mouth.

"Oh-no… she kept them in a bag inside her blouse," she replied.

"How do we know these are legitimate crystals?" asked Franklyn with his eyes closed.

Nurse Esperanza replies to Franklyn with an insulted look on her face.

"*Peace & Power Crystals* does not sell fake stones or fake items, sir. The owner of that store is a well-known and respected shaman priest. I have made a strong connection with the higher power, sir. I know for sure that these crystals are legitimate and everything in these books speaks the truth."

Noah looks at both Franklyn and Nurse Esperanza with a confused smile.

"Nurse, I'm not sure I'm making a connection with the higher power," said Noah.

"Maybe he's out of office, on PTO," said Franklyn jokingly.

Nurse Esperanza and Noah glance at Franklyn in annoyance. She addresses Franklyn with a nod and stern voice.

"The higher power doesn't have a gender, sir," she replied.

"Oh, that's right! Sorry," Franklyn replied sarcastically.

Noah frowns at Franklyn with disappointment.

"Never mind him, nurse. How do I contact the higher power?" asked Noah.

"I think it only responds to post office mail," Franklyn replied with a smirk.

Noah addresses Franklyn with frustration.

"Franklyn, please. Can you stop joking around?"

Franklyn gestures with praying hands and nods affirming his brother's request.

"Mr. Godtz, sometimes it takes longer to make contact. It took me several months before I finally contacted the higher power," she said.

"Several months! I only have less than seven days, nurse!" Noah bellowed with urgency.

Nurse Esperanza addresses Noah with an assuring tone.

"Calm down, Mr. Godtz. The higher power knows you are trying to make contact. It's not going to take your life away until you have made contact. Trust me. You are doing the right thing. The higher power knows you are reaching out."

Franklyn looks at her with a smirk and then at Noah.

"Yeah, Noah, it's probably like when you call the city and it says, thank you for waiting, you are fifth on line," he said.

Nurse Esperanza and Noah disregard Franklyn's comment.

"Nurse, so does that mean that I will live past the next six days?" asked Noah.

She addresses Noah with confidence.

"Absolutely, Mr. Godtz. You must have faith and you must believe in your heart. I am sure the higher power knows you are trying to connect and will respond to you in time. I can feel its energy in this room."

Noah nods slowly in doubt.

"Have you ever listened to *Abraham Hicks* or *Alan Watts*?" she asked.

"No, who are they?" he asked.

Nurse Esperanza chuckles and shakes her head in disbelief.

"You have much to learn, Mr. Godtz. They are enlightened teachers of spiritualism and experts at connecting to the higher power. You can listen to them on _YouTube_. Just do a search for _Abraham Hicks_ or _Alan Watts_. I'll write their names down for you on this _post-it_ notepad."

Nurse Esperanza pulls the note off and hands it over to Noah.

Noah reaches out and takes the _post-it_ note looking at it with a hint of hope.

"Listen to these spiritualists I just gave to you, Mr. Godtz. They will help guide you to connect with the higher power of consciousness," she stated.

She scoffs at Franklyn, turns, and walks out of the room while saying, "Good night, gentlemen. The diffuser is fine but please shut off the burning incense, we don't need a fire in the hospital."

Franklyn smirks at Nurse Esperanza as she quickly walks out of sight.

"That… was a crock of shit…" Franklyn stated with disdain.

Noah puts his head down staring at the _post-it_ note with doubt in his eyes.

Franklyn gets up and walks to the exit door peeking to see if anyone is nearby. Noah has a grim look and fights the tears in his eyes.

"Noah, why are you doing this? What are you looking for?" asked Franklyn.

"I don't know! I'm trying, Franklyn! I'm just paperwork in this hospital waiting to be disposed of! What am I supposed to do?! I want to live! I want to live!" Noah replied with a loud crying voice.

His cries increasingly became louder.

The cat across the hall yells out insistently.

"Nurse! What's going on?! Nurse! Someone is screaming! Someone needs help!"

"Shut the fuck up! Mind your business and go back to sleep!" yelled Noah.

Franklyn stares at Noah expressionless.

"Go back to sleep you piece of shit!" Noah said with a loud sobbing voice.

The cat across the hall continues to annoy Noah.

"Nurse! Nurse! Nurse! I hear a baby crying!"

"Jesus Christ! Shut the fuck up!" Noah cried loudly.

Dr. Harpherd calls out to Nurse Esperanza.

"Nurse, please put Mr. Godtz on sedatives right now!"

Noah is crying hysterically and slamming his fists onto a pillow on his bed. Nurse Esperanza storms into Noah's room with a cart containing syringes. Franklyn addresses Nurse Esperanza calmly but with assertiveness.

"No, you will not. I will not concede to putting my brother on drugs."

Dr. Harpherd storms into Noah's room and stammers while looking around the room. He continues to yell at the nurse.

"We need to put Mr. Godtz on sedatives now, it's past midnight and he is disturbing the entire floor!"

Franklyn stands blocking Noah from Nurse Esperanza.

"Not while I'm here. He is calm now; can't you see that? Doctor, Noah needs to remain coherent during this time. Emotional breakdowns are normal. This is how humans deal with it, do they not?" Franklyn stated firmly.

Dr. Harpherd disregards Franklyn.

"Nurse, please manage this!" Dr. Harpherd wailed at her as he hastily walked out of the room.

Nurse Esperanza acknowledges Franklyn, nods her head, turns the cart towards the exit, and walks out of Noah's room.

Franklyn walks to the door and closes it gently.

He can still hear Dr. Harpherd's muffled voice yell out, "Nurse! What's going on in that room?! It looks and smells like a séance!"

Franklyn giggles and tiptoes away from the door toward Noah. He puts his forefinger to his lips and whispers, "Shhh… you need to be meditating to reach the higher power, Noah, not crying, and screaming, right?"

Noah has a look of desperation mixed with disappointment on his face. He feels his brother is correct about this spiritual stuff being bullshit, but he also feels he has no choice and must keep trying. He looks at his brother, whimpering.

"Help me, Franklyn…"

Franklyn nods and sits down.

"Let's listen to these masters of the spirits, Noah," said Franklyn.

Noah looks down at the *post-it* note and then sticks it on his forehead while giggling helplessly.

"Pull these videos up on my phone and let's listen to what they have to say," Franklyn said with a grin.

Noah finds a video presentation by _Abraham Hicks_ and starts listening. They listen for hours. Noah looks over at Franklyn and sees that he is in a deep sleep. The time on the phone says, 3:33 am.

"Not in Texas it ain't," he said chuckling to himself.

He looks around in doubt at all the crystals, oils, the *Infinite 8,* and *Tree of Life*.

Noah whispers to himself, "I have six days left to live…"

"When you are searching for truth,
there's a whole lot of bullshit
you'll need to shovel out of the way."

Chapter 3: The cat across the hall

It's 6:37 am, and the bright overhead light over Noah's bed comes on. Nurse Esperanza is holding several books.

"Good morning, Mr. Godtz! It's a beautiful morning. I have some more books for you to help you with your journey to enlightenment!" Nurse Esperanza exclaimed.

Franklyn wakes up; his eyes squinted due to the bright light.

"What's the flood light for? Is Noah being interrogated? Noah, you have the right to remain silent. Anything stupid should go through one ear and out through the other," said Franklyn sarcastically.

Nurse Esperanza seems annoyed and replies to Franklyn rudely.

"Well, good morning to you too. I guess."

Noah sits up and sets his bed in the seated position. He could hardly open his eyes even after rubbing them a few times.

"Hi nurse, it was a late night for us. We were listening to the spiritual masters you told me about," said Noah.

Nurse Esperanza was excited to hear that Noah listened to the spiritual masters.

"That is so good to hear, Mr. Godtz. I'm glad you listened to them. So, what did you think?" she asked.

"Well, the lady that talks to the ghost don't seem too convincing," Noah replied.

Franklyn chuckles with his eyes closed still sitting in the chair he slept in.

Nurse Esperanza offers Franklyn a harsh stare.

Noah glances at Franklyn with a grin and then continues speaking to her.

"She's got some interesting things to say about manifestation, vibration, the law of attraction, and success, but I'm more interested in curing my cancer," said Noah.

Nurse Esperanza nods her head sympathizing with Noah's statement.

"Mr. Godtz, _Abraham Hicks_ is a spiritual entity that exists and functions in a higher vibration than we exist as humans," she said.

Franklyn grins with his eyes closed.

Nurse Esperanza speaks with a divine aura.

"She sees death as another form of existence. To her death is a fiction and those that have passed on, exist in a spiritual realm we cannot see, touch, or smell."

Franklyn shakes his head with his eyes closed.

"Have you ever smelled a ghost fart? No…" Franklyn stated.

Nurse Esperanza flickers her eyes repeatedly showing annoyance. She takes a deep breath and opens her nostrils wide in frustration.

"In order for us to communicate with those that have transcended into the spiritual realm, we have to remove ourselves from the physical realm, and put ourselves into the spiritual realm through meditation and vibration," she stated loudly.

Franklyn opens his eyes and shakes his head in astonishment.

"I actually read somewhere, that an earthquake happens when thousands of spirits fart at the same time. Yep, it's a scientific fact," Franklyn stated jokingly.

Noah glances at his brother, chuckles, and shakes his head.

"Stop, Franklyn, please," said Noah.

Nurse Esperanza looks very annoyed and addresses Noah with a stern voice.

"Mr. Godtz, not everyone accepts the spiritual world because they are blinded by religious cults and brainwashing. The spiritual world is different. It is real and it is true. If you accept this as truth, you will be embraced by the higher power. You will heal from this cancer."

"So, can he go home then?" asked Franklyn.

Nurse Esperanza is visibly frustrated and stammers to answer Franklyn's question.

"He can go home, if he signs his release papers, uh-um, of course, he can, of course. However, it does take about two weeks to process the paperwork so that he can go home. I think it is best for him to stay here with us so that we can take care of his needs until…"

Nurse Esperanza pauses for a minute and quickly changes the topic.

"Mr. Godtz, I'll leave these books for you. I'll put them by the side of your bed and you can read them whenever you want. I need to complete my rounds now."

She looks at Franklyn with a nasty stare, turns her cart around, and walks towards the exit door of Noah's room. On her way out she says, "Have a nice day."

"Excuse me, nurse!" Franklyn exclaimed.

Nurse Esperanza turns around and looks at Franklyn.

"Yes, sir," she replied with a scornful smirk.

"You didn't finish your sentence. You said you think it's best for him to stay here so you can take care of his needs until…?

You didn't say anything after until. What were you going to say? Until what?" asked Franklyn.

Nurse Esperanza looks up and thinks for a moment. She then looks at Franklyn with a sharp stare and shrugs her shoulders.

"Until he doesn't need us anymore," she replied.

She continues to walk out hurriedly into the corridor and out of sight.

Franklyn yells into the corridor.

"Until he dies, right?! Nurse! Isn't that what you were going to say?! Until he dies! Didn't you say these crystals and junk would cure his cancer and he would live forever?!"

"Franklyn, stop! that's enough!" Noah exclaimed.

"C'mon, Noah, this is such bullshit, man. You really think all this crap she's throwing at you will cure you?" asked Franklyn.

"What else do I have?! She's trying to help me! All you are doing is making jokes and insulting her! How the fuck is that helping me?!" Noah cried out with sadness in his voice.

"Noah, do you want me to leave?"

Noah takes a deep breath and sighs uneasily, holding back the tears in his eyes.

"No, brother, I want you to stay. Franklyn, just let me try this," said Noah with a conquered look.

Franklyn looks at Noah with a blank expression.

"Ok, Noah. I'm running out to get breakfast. What may I bring back for you?"

Noah looks stressed and disoriented.

"Huh? Oh, I'm not hungry. I'm tired and I don't feel well. I feel cold, nauseous, and worn out," said Noah.

"Ok, brother, you should get some rest. I'll get breakfast and also see if I can find an air mattress. This fucking chair is eating my ass," said Franklyn while he rubbed his butt cheeks.

Noah giggles with his eyes closed. He falls fast asleep sitting up while holding a book titled, _The Secret by Rhonda Byrne._

Franklyn puts on his outerwear and quickly walks out of the room toward the elevator.

After a few hours, Noah wakes up to screams coming from the cat across the hall.

"Nurse! Nurse! Nurse! Nurse! Nurse!"

Nurse Esperanza walks into the cat across the hall's room. Noah can peek into his room if he scoots a bit to the left side of his bed. They are arguing with each other.

"I don't know where your wife is, Mr. Ansihl! How would I know that?! I'm sure she will be here soon!" she exclaimed.

Noah whispers to himself, "Oh… the cat across the hall is Mr. Ansihl."

The cat across the hall continues to yell.

"I need my wife! I'm dying! I need my wife here now, nurse. I'm dying and she needs to be here, understand?!"

"Mr. Ansihl, you are not dying right now. Your wife is on her way, I'm sure of it," she said with confidence.

"You spoke to her? On the phone?" asked Mr. Ansihl curiously.

"Yes, Mr. Ansihl. She is on her way, and she will be here soon," she replied.

Mr. Ansihl is quiet for a moment but then, starts yelling at Nurse Esperanza as she walks out of his room.

"You are a liar! A fucking goddamn liar!"

Nurse Esperanza walks through the corridor visibly angry while shaking her head.

Noah scoots back to the middle of his bed and stares up at the ceiling. He then looks at the time on his phone and it's 9:49 am.

Franklyn's voice can be heard from the corridor, "Another spiked morning breakfast, doctor? I can smell it coming out of the elevator and I know that's not aftershave."

Noah smiles. He can hear Franklyn's footsteps coming closer and finally, he walks into the room.

"Hey! You are back!" Noah exclaimed.

"Yes, I like to keep to my threats," Franklyn replied.

Noah giggles and massages his stomach.

"What did you get for breakfast?" asked Noah.

"I got some pancakes, coffee, and a couple of bottles of wine for later, of course. And I found an air mattress!" Franklyn nods concurring with himself.

He offers a silly smile at Noah.

"I also picked up some DVD movies we can watch on your laptop."

"Awesome!" Noah exclaimed.

Franklyn grins and takes out his breakfast; a foam container with delicious snowflake pancakes and a container of coffee.

Noah looks at the container of food with glossy eyes.

"Yummy… I should have placed an order," said Noah.

"I got an extra order, in case you wanted," Franklyn replied.

Noah chuckles and claps in celebration.

"Yes! Franklyn, you're the best."

Franklyn passes a foam container of pancakes with a coffee to his brother. Noah is in his glory. He starts eating immediately as if he's starving.

Suddenly, The cat across the hall starts screaming again.

"Nurse! Nurse! Nurse!" he yelled consistently without pause.

Nurse Esperanza storms into Mr. Ansihl's room.

Noah scoots over to his left and peeks into the room across the hall.

"Mr. Ansihl! You need to stop yelling! You are upsetting the other patients!" Nurse Esperanza exclaimed angrily.

Mr. Ansihl looks around his room with confusion and disregards Nurse Esperanza's comment.

"Who was that talking?! Nurse, where is my wife?!"

"She is on her way, Mr. Ansihl, please be patient."

"She's telling a dying patient to be patient. That's a double negative, cancels out," said Franklyn.

Noah laughs a big belly laugh.

All of a sudden, Nurse Esperanza is pleasantly surprised by Mrs. Ansihl's presence.

"Here she is! Mr. Ansihl! Aww… you see?! I told you she would be here."

"Ok! Get out!" Mr. Ansihl wailed at Nurse Esperanza.

Nurse Esperanza and Mrs. Ansihl ignore him and small talk for a bit. Mr. Ansihl becomes frustrated and screams at his wife.

"Margaret, where were you?! I needed you here! I'm dying! Can't you see that?!"

"I'm sorry, dear, I wasn't feeling well this morning. I'm so sorry," Mrs. Ansihl replied while caressing his head.

Mr. Ansihl calms down but yells at Nurse Esperanza.

"Nurse! Before you leave, go get a drink of water for my wife! She's thirsty! Do that now!"

Nurse Esperanza replies while bowing her head slightly.

"Sure, Mr. Ansihl. I'll be back shortly."

Nurse Esperanza walks out of Mr. Ansihl's room, never to return with that drink of water.

Noah finishes his pancakes quickly. Franklyn puts his leftover pancakes on top of Noah's desk drawer and starts drinking his coffee.

Noah takes a sip of his coffee and looks at Franklyn curiously with a question in mind.

"What do you think is the deal with that cat across the hall? You think he's dying soon?" asked Noah.

Franklyn shrugs his shoulders while sipping his coffee.

"I think all the patients on this floor are dying," Franklyn replied.

Noah scoots over to the left side of his bed, close to the edge. He starts peeking into the room of the cat across the hall. He sees multiple people sobbing as they are walking in.

"Brother, there is so much sadness in that room, you can see it and feel it from over here. That cat's surrounded by a lot of negative energy," Noah exclaimed.

"Yep and that negativity is the only thing that goes with him after he dies, not his worldly goods," Franklyn replied.

Noah stares at Franklyn as if he were just enlightened.

Nurse Esperanza comes strolling into Noah's room with a rolling cart, she looks quickly behind her and gathers that Noah is intriguingly looking into Mr. Ansihl's room.

"Mr. Godtz, would you like to meet Mr. Ansihl?" asked Nurse Esperanza.

Noah mumbles, "No," while shaking his head.

Nurse Esperanza looks at Noah with a suspicious grin.

"I need to take your vitals, Mr. Godtz. I see you already had breakfast, thanks to your brother," she said with a modest grin.

Franklyn nods while raising his hand humorously indicating that he is Noah's brother.

Noah giggles and Nurse Esperanza smiles with a sigh.

"Your brother entertains you, Mr. Godtz. That's nice, we all need entertainment in our lives." She stated, looking covetously at Noah.

Franklyn stands up from his chair and bows as though he were performing on stage.

He looks towards the corner of Noah's room, cheats out, and says, "*All the world's a stage, and we are merely players.*"[6]

Nurse Esperanza grins and says in a boorish manner, "He reads, too."

Franklyn grins and sits back down taking a sip from his coffee.

Nurse Esperanza smiles pleasantly at Noah.

---

[6] William Shakespeare's pastoral comedy As You Like It

"Your brother has a lot to learn, Mr. Godtz. Perhaps after reading these books, you can teach him about spirituality," she said.

"Oh, I've learned a lot from my brother's spiritual findings already, nurse. It culminates in his bedpan," Franklyn replied.

Noah chuckles and is red with embarrassment.

Nurse Esperanza rolls her eyes and replies with sarcasm, "Nice."

Noah diverts Nurse Esperanza's attention.

"Hey, nurse, what's the deal with Mr. Ansihl? Is he dying soon?" asked Noah.

"Yes, Mr. Godtz. This floor is for terminally ill cancer patients," she said with an assuring nod.

"How's he taking it?" asked Noah.

"Not well. But he has a lot of family members visiting him and his wife has been with him almost as much as your brother has been here with you," she replied.

Noah looks at his brother and smiles.

Franklyn grins and says, "Hello hubby."

Noah chuckles and looks at Nurse Esperanza.

"Was he in the military?" asked Noah.

"No, Mr. Godtz. He was an Oncologist," she replied.

"What's that?" asked Noah.

"He was a cancer doctor," Franklyn interjected.

Noah glances at his brother in shock.

Nurse Esperanza nods in agreement.

"That's right, your brother is correct. Mr. Ansihl was an Oncologist here at this very hospital," she replied.

"What type of cancer does he have?" asked Noah.

"We can't really discuss patient personal matters, Mr. Godtz. All I can tell you is that his lungs are not feeling well," she replied adamantly.

Nurse Esperanza turns her cart towards the door while saying, "Have a nice day, Mr. Godtz." She then nods at Franklyn with a sneer and says, "Sir," while exiting the room hurriedly.

Franklyn stands up and gestures with a curtsy. He walks towards the exit door to close it and Noah exclaims, "No, Franklyn, leave the door open! I want to see what's going on over there!"

"Looking to catch some more drama?" asked Franklyn with a grin.

"I'm just curious about what's going on with this cat across the hall. How does a cancer doctor die of cancer?" asked Noah.

Franklyn's face shows disinterest as he shrugs his shoulders.

"This place can give you cancer," said Franklyn.

"C'mon brother, seriously," said Noah in a frustrated voice.

"The nurse said lungs, right? So, he must be dying of lung cancer. Probably a heavy smoker," Franklyn replied.

Franklyn walks back and sits in his chair.

"Fuck... that really sucks," Noah said in awe.

"Dr. Harpherd drinks like a fish. You can smell the alcohol in his breath from far away," said Franklyn.

"Yeah, that's right! I smelled it when he came in that day with the paperwork! I thought it was aftershave," Noah exclaimed.

"Maybe, if he rubs his face with whiskey after he shaves," Franklyn replied jokingly.

Noah laughs aloud.

"I think when people get stressed out a lot, they become addicted to drugs, alcohol, or cigarettes. It's an emotional escape. _Carl Jung_ wrote that it is relative to subpersonalities,"[7] said Franklyn.

Noah scoots over again to the left side of his bed and peeks into the room across the hall.

"Franklyn, the lady sitting by his bed is praying. She's reading the bible and has a rosary in her hand."

"Yeah man, that's every day," Franklyn replied.

"Serious?" asked Noah in awe.

Franklyn nods affirming what he just said. He grabs a cup of apple sauce from Noah's desk.

"Noah, are you going to eat this?"

"Nah, Franklyn, you eat it."

"This connection to the conscience wants to eat something sweet," said Franklyn.

Noah stutters with a baffled look.

"What did you just say?" asked Noah.

Franklyn continues to eat the apple sauce and doesn't reply.

Noah stares at Franklyn for a moment, shrugs his mouth, and directs his attention back to the cat across the hall, observing the activities in that room.

Franklyn doses off for a few hours and wakes up to the noise of a rolling food cart. It's lunchtime.

---

[7] https://en.wikipedia.org/wiki/Subpersonality

Franklyn stands up and stretches for a bit, then sits back down.

Noah begins to eat his lunch while focused on Mr. Ansihl's room. He passes Franklyn a pudding cup from his food tray.

"Why are you so interested in the comings and goings of that room across the hall?" asked Franklyn while eating the pudding.

Noah shrugs his shoulders while chewing his food.

"I don't know. There are a lot of people in there and a priest just walked in too. There are flowers everywhere, and statues on his desk. And there's a huge cross by his bed on the wall," said Noah.

"Yep. After he dies, they will paste him up on that cross and carry him out to the main street. In seven days, he will resurrect," Franklyn replied in a revealing voice.

"Franklyn, what the fuck man! Have respect, will you?" Noah exclaimed in shock.

"Respect for what, Noah? For bullshit? Have you ever read the bible in its entirety?" asked Franklyn.

Noah has a look of humiliation.

"Well, yeah, but not completely."

"C'mon, don't bullshit me, brother. You never read that shit, admit it," Franklyn replied.

"And you did?!" asked Noah in a confrontational manner.

"Yes, of course, I did, Noah. I read and researched all that crap. I went from Catholic to Protestant, to Jehovah's Witness, to Pentecostal, to agnostic, and then to atheist. But somewhere in between, I read the _Tanakh_, the _Quran_, and _the Vedas_."

Noah is overwhelmingly astonished.

"Completely?" Noah asked.

"Yep, *the whole enchilada*," Franklyn replied.

"Did you learn to read Hebrew, Sanskrit, Aramaic, and Arabic?" Noah asked.

Franklyn shakes his head while eating.

"Uh, not exactly, there are English translations like the *Chumash* for the *Torah,* the *Taqi-ud-Din al-Hilali* English translation of the *Holy Quran,* and *The Four Vedas English translation*. All much better reads by a margin compared to the *King James Bible*," Franklyn replied.

Noah is tremendously honored by his brother's achievements.

"Really? Franklyn, I'm impressed!"

Franklyn scrapes the bottom of the pudding cup and licks the spoon.

"Uh-huh. I used the *Lexicon* to help me read the Hebrew version of the *Old Testament*. I wasted time and could've gotten the same information from the English translation. Oh, and I also read the *Qumran texts*, *Book of Kings*, *Apocrypha*, *Jubilees*, *Enoch*, *Hanok*, *Thoth*, *Daniel*, *Ezekial*, *Samuel*, *Zohar*, *Zechariah*, *The Kebra Nagast*, *The I Ching*, *The Buddha Texts*, *The Dhammapada,* and several other books, including the *Knights Templar, Freemasons – The Commandery, Kant philosophy*, and *The Kabbalah* as well," he said while nodding.

"What? How did you find time to read all these books?" asked Noah in amazement.

Franklyn smirks while continuing to scrape any remains of pudding from the bottom of the cup.

"I made time, Noah. You get to the point in this life when you are asking, *what am I doing here* and *what is my purpose?* And everyone out there has the same stupid reply."

Franklyn changes his voice to sound dimwitted.

"To seek god, to find balance, yin yang, to become a crystal, to seek the higher power, and some say to live your life with morals and principles so you can contribute to humanity, die, and end up in heaven with god on a cloud and blah blah blah."

He tosses the empty pudding cup and spoon in the garbage and bellows, "It's all bullshit!"

"I'm confused, Franklyn. How could you say that it is all bullshit? The scriptures are the foundation of society!"

"Because it is illogical, Noah. These are just *scripts* pushed by cults, and belief systems made to feed the connection to the conscience and control humanity. All of these scriptures and books have hints hidden within the text; clues that are buried within emotional manipulation using trigger words. The scriptures also imply that extraterrestrials have been around us since the inception of Adam & Eve."

"Franklyn, you say, *the conscience* as if it is a god. What are you referring to?"

"The conscience may be a program created by extraterrestrials with a higher intelligence than us humans, but I wouldn't go so far as calling it a god," Franklyn replied with a smirk.

Franklyn visibly confuses Noah.

"Franklyn, are you saying that extraterrestrials control us?"

"Something like that. But we need to talk about other things before we get into that, Noah. All these books, these crystals, these oils, and all of this junk, I also owned at one time in my life. I researched and studied all this crap that Nurse Esperanza talked to you about. I went through many religions, including *Voodooism*, *Dharmic*, and *Taoism*. I went through the spiritual path too and did all these rituals with the chakra, pineal gland, sage, Bulnesia wood, DMT, Psilocybin nonsense, including the meditations, etcetera. I spent months on retreats with shamans in Mexico, and Chile, Monks in China, and Indians on a few reservations in Arizona, Texas, and New Mexico. If it's out there I took some time to research and participate in it."

"What the fuck!" Noah exclaimed.

"Yep. If you look at the history of books on my *A-Zome Books* account, you'll see all of those stupid books that Nurse Esperanza threw here on your bed including many more," Franklyn replied.

Noah is dazzled by Franklyn's spiritual journey.

"Franklyn, I didn't know that."

"Why would you, Noah?"

Noah looks around his room, at his shrine, and at the books on his bed with disappointment.

"So, you did all this stuff? Probably more than Nurse Esperanza and you found it all to be absolute bullshit?"

"Absolutely, brother. All these belief systems work like a panacea[8]," Franklyn replied with certainty.

Noah stares down at the books with anger and resentment. He looks over at his shrine and tears start pouring from his eyes; once again feeling sad and hopeless.

Franklyn distracts Noah from his thoughts.

"Check out the order of books on my phone. This is my account, Noah. What does it say there? Read that list."

Noah grabs Franklyn's phone and reads aloud, "*The Law of Attraction: The basic teachings of Abraham Hicks*. Her actual name is *Esther Hicks*?" asked Noah.

"Yes, Noah. *Abraham Hicks* is the entity or spirit she becomes so she can bullshit everyone and take their money. The name *Casper the Ghost* was already taken. *Abraham Hicks,* the ghost, is incorporated by the way, just in case you decide to sue the ghost to acquire its bedsheet."

Noah giggles, shakes his head in awe, and continues to read the list of books,

---

[8] https://www.vocabulary.com/dictionary/panacea

"*The Chumash: The Stone Edition (English and Hebrew Edition)*, *The Torah: Haftaros and Five Megillos with a Commentary Anthologized from the Rabbinic Writings*, *The Ancient Hebrew Lexicon of the Bible*, *Ancient Hebrew Dictionary*, *The Noble Quran: Interpretation of the Meanings of the Noble Qur'an in the English Language (English and Arabic Edition)*, *Etymological Dictionary of Biblical Hebrew: Based on the Commentaries of Samson Raphael Hirsch (English and Hebrew Edition)*, *The Gnostic Bible: Revised and Expanded Edition*, *Dharma in the Hindu scriptures and in the Bible*, *The Power of the Dharma: An Introduction to Hinduism and Vedic Culture*, *Encyclopedia of Crystals Revised and Expanded*, *Crystals for Healing: The Complete Reference Guide With Over 200 Remedies for Mind*, *Heart & Soul*, *The Four Agreements: A Practical Guide to Personal Freedom (A Toltec Wisdom Book)*, *Word Magic by Pao Chang*, *The Science Book: Everything You Need to Know About the World and How It Works*, *Soul Steps: 52 Ways to Reconnect with Spirit*, *The Pineal Gland: The Eye of God*, *The Kybalion: A Study of The Hermetic Philosophy of Ancient Egypt and Greece*, *The Secret Teachings of All Ages: An Encyclopedic Outline of Masonic, Hermetic, Qabbalistic and Rosicrucian Symbolical Philosophy.*"

Noah stops reading the list and stares at Franklyn for a few minutes.

"Franklyn, this list goes on and on stemming all the way from 2010. How did you find time to read all this stuff? What time did you have to eat or use the bathroom for god's sake?"

Franklyn shrugs his shoulders with a lax expression.

"I made time, Noah. I didn't watch much television or participate in the nightlife. There were pockets of years when I did meet someone and we spent time together, on weekend getaways, etcetera, but most of my time I spent it researching and reading. That doesn't include the shrines I had, depending on what belief system I was researching at that time. I also have a large collection of PDF books, plus thousands of links to websites with articles and literature.

The last website I was reading was the *3-6-9 Forum* which consisted of junior scientists and philosophers that didn't follow a belief system, spiritualism, or esotericism. Their purpose was to share the truth about our existence and how it is in alignment with science and technology versus cult belief systems, spiritualism, and esotericism. And they emphasize that science and technology were introduced to humans by extraterrestrials with higher intelligence. The *3-6-9 Forum* was incognito, so it was kind of difficult to locate some of their articles. However, they had good information that helped answer my questions and find truth or as I prefer, the absolute."

"So, what did you do with all that stuff you accumulated?" asked Noah.

"I filed most of it in the garbage where it belonged; I still may have some literature on old USB drives. Belief systems are what they are, Noah. They are systems that are carved in our DNA through generations and molded into humans through a program. A couple of well-known trigger words for this program are *Believe* and *Faith*. Nurse Esperanza, kept telling you the same thing repeatedly. You must have faith; you must believe. Those words trigger a program. It's these programs that have been installed in humans since the beginning of humanity through *nature* and then instilled into you through *nurture*. Some people refer to these trigger words as *Word Magic*."

Noah listens intensely to Franklyn. He has a deep studious expression on his face completely blocking out all that is around them.

"There's a book in that list called *Word Magic*. Do you see it?" asked Franklyn.

Noah scrolls through the list again.

"Yes! Here it is! *Word Magic: The Powers and Occult Definitions of Words by Pao Chang*," Noah exclaimed.

"Yes, that's the book, it's a pretty good read. There's some spiritual bullshit in that book but one thing he notes that is logical is that words do have a program attached to them, which he refers to as magic. But not the way you and I grew up to understand magic. Words contain triggers that initiate a program in us. Once Nurse Esperanza said to you, you must have *faith*, you must *believe*, a program activates in your head initiated by those trigger words. Your mind was running the program installed in you to think that you must have *faith*. That this is the only way. But those words are a trick, like social engineering. They persuade you into spending energy on something that is emotional and illogical. In that book, he also had a link to a very good *Etymology* dictionary you can download. Just that alone was worth the time spent reading that book."

"What's an *Etymology* dictionary?" asked Noah.

"It's a book that gives you the origin of words; The original meaning before it was transposed or bastardized for occult purposes. The one he had was originally published quite some time ago. I think he just scanned it to a PDF, and you can download it from his website," Franklyn replied.

"Wow! Do you still have it?" asked Noah.

   Franklyn shrugs his shoulders with an aloof look.

"Maybe. I don't know."

"Wow! Franklyn, you're like an expert in this shit."

"Expert in what? There is a lot of bullshit in those books. None of that stuff matters, Noah."

"Franklyn, you could really teach Nurse Esperanza a thing or two about this stuff."

"No way, Noah, she's a certified level II reiki. There's no learning for her this time around."

   Noah chuckles aloud. He shuffles through the books on his bed for a long moment.

"Franklyn, did you read the book titled, *The Secret*?"

"The secret is there is no secret, Noah. But I can't tell you that because it's a secret," Franklyn replied jokingly.

Noah laughs a hardy laugh while massaging his belly.

"It's all bullshit, there is no law of attraction, Noah. It's more like the law of coincidence. *All belief systems created in this game we live in are hypothetical remedies.* The game has many programs in place for the purpose of control and manipulation. That's all it is, Noah. This is what you need to recognize."

Noah takes a deep breath and pauses for a moment, collecting his thoughts to formulate words.

"Franklyn, why didn't you stop me? Why did you let me spend money on these crystals, these books, this bullshit, and nonsense?"

"Because you must go through it, Noah. It's a process. If I were to tell you right off the bat that this is a game you are in and you are being manipulated by extraterrestrials that feed on your energy like vampires, you would look at me and think I'm crazy or some wackadoo like you said earlier."

"Yes, I would," Noah stated while nodding his head.

"There are extraterrestrials walking around today on our planet, are they not? They are called the Czentarians. They were announced in 2021, right after the big pandemic and now they are walking among humanity.[9] Didn't you see the interviews on the news with these aliens?" asked Franklyn.

With a look of dismay, Noah nods his head.

"These Czentarians are supposed to be super intelligent. Far more intelligent than us humans. And they are here visiting earth today, Why? Perhaps checking out their pasturage up close?" said Franklyn with a grin and look of suspicion.

"Maybe," Noah replied with a shrug.

"I'm pretty sure, Noah. And I also noticed that the constant announcements of their presence are conveniently occurring in

---

[9]   https://www.dni.gov/files/ODNI/documents/assessments/Prelimary-Assessment-UAP-20210625.pdf - https://en.wikipedia.org/wiki/UFO_Report_(U.S._Intelligence)

tandem with the canine flu."

"Is the canine flu still a big deal?" asked Noah.

"Noah, the corridor downstairs and areas all over the hospital are still full of canine flu patients."

Noah looks at Franklyn in shock.

"Really?" asked Noah.

"Yep, all over this hospital. In fact, all the hospitals are saturated with patients. And the government is demanding for the euthanization of dogs by the thousands," said Franklyn.

Noah asks with a stutter, "E-Even puppies?"

"All canines, Noah. People are hiding their pets and trying to cope with losing them. It's emotional anarchy out there."

Noah shakes his head in disbelief.

"Holy shit!"

"That's a logical statement," Franklyn replied with a grin.

The cat across the hall starts screaming out loud.

"Nurse! Nurse! I have to use the bathroom! Nurse!"

Nurse Esperanza walks to the doorway of Mr. Ansihl's room.

"Mr. Ansihl, your wife is here, she can help you use the bedpan and help you wash up," she said.

Mr. Ansihl becomes furious with anger.

"She can't do it! She gets nauseous! She's not a nurse! Do you see her wearing a white costume?! It's your job to serve me as it states in the bible!" Mr. Ansihl wailed.

Noah and Franklyn laugh aloud.

"I think she needs to give him a crystal to calm him down," said Franklyn in a jokey manner.

They are both laughing.

"Yeah, they need to burn some incense and sage, so his wife doesn't get nauseous," Noah replied while laughing.

They both continue to laugh uncontrollably.

Nurse Esperanza is annoyed and offers a nasty stare at Noah's room.

"Oh-oh, I think she heard us laugh and she looks pissed," said Noah with a timid look.

"I would be pissed as well if I had to wipe that guy's ass every two hours. That guy's a _Pez Dispenser_,"[10] Franklyn replied.

They both continue to laugh covering their mouths to muffle the laughter.

Noah pauses for a moment in deep thought.

"Franklyn?"

"Yeah, Noah."

"Can you mentor me? Can you teach me about everything you learned?" asked Noah.

"Sure," Franklyn replied.

Noah looks down at all the books on his bed that Nurse Esperanza loaned him. He looks up at Franklyn and grins.

Nurse Esperanza walks into Noah's room unexpectedly.

"Mr. Godtz, how do you like the new books I loaned you? Which one did you like the most?"

---

[10] https://us.pez.com/collections/dispensers

Noah stutters with uncertainty and says, "Um…"

Franklyn interjects.

"We are done with these books, nurse. You can take these with you. We won't be needing them anymore."

Nurse Esperanza addresses Franklyn with a stern voice, "I'm speaking to your brother, sir."

"Oh, yes, thank you nurse, but my brother is right. I think I've read enough. I'm getting more tired lately and I don't want to read anymore; I just want to rest," Noah replied.

"Yeah, we won't need your books, we have enough toilet paper for the week," said Franklyn with a grin.

Nurse Esperanza sneers at Franklyn and offers a pleasant smile to Noah.

"Mr. Godtz, just stack the books on the floor by your bed and I will pick them up later. If you change your mind, they are there for you to read."

Nurse Esperanza turns towards the door and walks out noticeably annoyed at Franklyn.

"I think you pissed her off," said Noah.

Franklyn winks, smiles, and says, "I've been having that effect on humanity these days."

"You know what brother? I wouldn't trade you for all the people in the world," said Noah with a big smile.

Franklyn disregards Noah's comment.

"Ok, let's start by taking all this shit and throwing it in the garbage," said Franklyn.

"No, Franklyn! let's just pile these books on the floor and leave this other stuff where it is. I don't want to insult, Nurse Esperanza. She was only trying to help."

"Ok, Noah. If that's what you call it. I'm sure we will throw all of this out at some point."

Noah is evidently upset.

"You know what, Franklyn? I feel cheated, disgusted, and angry. I also want to cry but I don't think I have any tears left."

"Give me a few days, Noah. You asked me to mentor you, right?"

Noah nods his head intently.

"Let's get your notepad and a pen," said Franklyn.

"Am I writing more about my life?" asked Noah.

"No, Noah. We are going to watch movies."

"Oh, that's right! You got some DVDs," Noah exclaimed.

"Yes, it's movie time," Franklyn replied.

"What do we have?!" asked Noah excitedly.

"Ok, we have, *Artificial Intelligence*, *Into the Wild*, *The Perfect Storm*, *Argo*," Noah interjects "Hey, I like *Argo*!"

Franklyn grins and continues, "*Aliens*, *Rocketman*, *The Joker*, *X-Men: Apocalypse*, *Finch*, *Gretal & Hansel*, *War of the Worlds*, and *The Mezzosopranos*."

"Hey, *The Mezzosopranos* is a funny movie, I would watch that one over and over," said Noah.

Franklyn grins and nods in agreement.

"Yeah, the movie was created after the book and the original short film was just him with a green screen, a couple of GoPro cameras, a few lights, with a laptop," Franklyn replied.

"Really?!" Noah exclaimed in awe.

"Yep, *scripts and books become movies*. This movie is very funny. So, Noah, what are we watching first?"

Noah replies with excitement, "Um… *The Mezzosopranos*!"

"Would have been my first choice as well. There's one catch though, Noah."

Noah is reluctant to ask Franklyn.

"Oh… what?"

"You are going to watch these movies with me, but I want you to write down what you observe from each character's emotions and ego. And I want you to compare 'your' life to each scenario in the movie and write down how it is similar to yours. This first movie is going to take a long time because you will be pausing the movie and writing. I will guide you along the way," Franklyn replied.

"Wait, Franklyn, but this is a comedy. How the hell am I supposed to relate my life to a comedy?"

"Noah, you will see; we will do this one together."

"How am I going to enjoy the movie, Franklyn?"

"Your connection to the conscience will, Noah, trust me. You said that you wanted me to mentor you, correct?"

Noah nods his head.

"Then let's watch the movie together, enjoy it and learn from it at the same time. We learn from watching movies because the same programming, emotions, and ego, you experience in life are present in these movies. You will realize why you are doing this exercise. And we are going to do this for every movie you watch," stated Franklyn with certainty.

"Oh… fuck," Noah replied with a loathing voice.

"Noah, Let's start watching and learning about your purpose and why you are here in this game we live."

*"All belief systems created in
this game act as a hypothetical remedy."*

Chapter 4: I now pronounce you Noah and Ego

The bright overhead lamp over Noah's bed comes on and he hears a cute female voice.

"Good Morning Mr. Goatzee. How are you this morning?"

Noah sits up on his bed, blinking his eyes repeatedly trying to make out who is speaking to him.

"Hi, who are you?" asked Noah.

"My name is Joy, and I will be your nurse today."

"Oh, what happened to Nurse Esperanza?" asked Noah.

Franklyn interjects while lying on his air mattress with his eyes closed.

"She's probably getting acquainted with her chakras."

Noah chuckles quietly.

Nurse Joy frowns with a grin and looks at Franklyn confused.

"She's off today, Mr. Goatzee. I need to take your vitals, and here is your breakfast menu. Just check off what you would like to eat today," she said.

Noah takes the menu still trying to wake up.

"I see you're not on a special diet anymore, that's so exciting," she said with an annoying high-pitched voice.

Nurse Joy looks at Noah with a smile from ear to ear.

"Uh, I won't need the menu, nurse, my brother gets breakfast for us. Thank you. And by the way, my name is pronounced Gödtz. The d is silent," said Noah.

Nurse Joy nods her head, smiles, and continues to take Noah's vitals.

Franklyn looks at the time on his phone; It's 6:35 am. He sits up on his air mattress with his long legs crossed over each other.

"Coffee? Anyone?" Franklyn announced.

Noah raises his hand like a kid in a classroom.

Nurse Joy looks intently at Franklyn with a sparkle in her eyes and a smile.

"Did you have a bad night, Mr.....?" she asked with a subtle flirtish look in her eyes.

Franklyn stands up and stretches out like a Condor for a few minutes.

"Mr. Happy," Franklyn replied.

"Oh! such a cute name! Very nice to meet you, Mr. Happy!" she exclaimed with a toothy smile.

"I guess…," Franklyn replied apathetically.

Noah laughs intensely and interrupts their conversation.

"That's my brother, Nurse Joy. His name is Franklyn."

Nurse Joy glances at Franklyn, smirks awkwardly and begins tidying up Noah's room.

"Nurse, is it ok if I stand up this air mattress against the wall?" asked Franklyn.

Nurse Joy nods, and turns her cart to the door, waving goodbye to Noah.

"Wow! She's a doll!" Noah exclaimed.

"She probably winds up from the back," Franklyn replied mockingly.

Noah disregards Franklyn's comment.

The cat across the hall starts yelling out loud.

"Nurse! Nurse! Nurse!"

Noah scoots over to peek into the room across the hall.

Nurse Joy hurries into Mr. Ansihl's room.

"Good Morning, Mr. Anse-hool. How are you?"

Noah and Franklyn laugh aloud.

"Ha-ha, she called him an asshool," said Noah.

Mr. Ansihl wails rudely at Nurse Joy.

"Nurse! Please shut the fuck up and listen! I need my wife! Can you please get my wife?!"

"Sure, Mr. Anse-hool, I'll call her right now," she said with a tense voice.

"I'm dying, nurse. I need my wife. Call her now, ok? Right now," he said with a commanding voice.

Nurse Joy is obviously nervous and submissive.

"Yes, I will call her right now."

She hurries out to the nurse's station.

Franklyn says in a monotoned voice, "He's going to eat her alive."

Noah chuckles and nods in agreement.

Franklyn walks towards the restroom to wash up.

Noah adjusts his bed and sits up. He looks at his notepad and reads what he wrote last night:

Movie compared to my life. Mezzosopranos

Mezzosopranos is a comedy, so, I really can't compare it to my life. But the movie showed that people are always emotional. Don Giaco is my favorite character because he is funny, and he is in charge. But I can see how he is egotistical and full of himself. He doesn't like anyone crossing him, lying to him, or taking advantage of him. This has to do with his ego and his emotions.

My favorite scene is when he sees his son, James Francis Jr., dancing like <u>*Michael Jackson*</u> *right before he's about to do a hit. I couldn't stop laughing. Don Giaco starts crying because he is surprised and ashamed of his son. He feels vulnerable in the eyes of Peter Paffuto. This has to do with pride, ego, and emotions. I think he also feels guilty because he raised his son to be a hitman.*

My other favorite scenes are when James Francis Jr. tries to do stand-up comedy and there are only three people in the audience. The guy that plays the owner of the comedy club is really talented and funny. He should be in more movies. James Francis Jr. doesn't care that there are three people because he already thinks he's a star. He acts like he's famous and I think this has to do with his ego as well. His father nurtured him into being this way. But James Francis Jr. is also rebellious and wants to be an entertainer not a hitman for the mob.

All the characters for all the different gangs are funny. They all try to look important and they all are fighting for attention. I guess that's the way we all are. We want constant attention. As Franklyn says, <u>*it is why social media was invented, so, that humans can express their emotions and inflate their egos.*</u>

The fact that Petie Paffuto kills Don Giaco in the end, means loyalty sometimes can be fake. Franklyn says that <u>*social engineering can mask someone's real intentions behind loyalty and friendship.*</u> *For power and money, people will kill each other. Franklyn is right.*

Jay Francis Jr. takes revenge against all the families and kills all the members of each crew. I think that Jay Francis Jr., sought revenge to get closure. Franklyn says that <u>*closure is a trigger word.*</u>

Jay Francis Jr. and his father finally bond, then Petie Paffuto kills his father. This upsets Jay Francis Jr., and he goes on a killing spree. This shows that emotions can drive a human to even kill others. As Franklyn says, Ego and Emotions are powerful programs put into human beings. They are triggered by words and human interaction.

The movie was great. It was so funny, and I would watch it again. Franklyn says, the enjoyment of the movie and finding it funny is emotional. He says that it's ok to enjoy movies but you need to recognize that your emotions are driven by your connection to the conscience. I don't know if I still understand this, but I am trying.

Franklyn is standing over Noah, drying his hands, shoulder surfing. He walks around Noah's bed to put his boots on.

Noah stares at the ceiling for a long moment and then glances at his shrine, then past his desk at the dirty wall. He looks totally lost and defeated. Franklyn puts on his outerwear and turns to face Noah.

"It's so quiet," said Noah in a low voice.

Suddenly, the cat across the hall starts screaming at the top of his lungs.

"Nurse! Nurse! Nurse! I need my wife now! I am dying! I need my wife right now!"

No one responds; Noah peeks over to eavesdrop.

The screaming becomes louder and louder.

"Nurse! Nurse! Nurse! Nurse! Nurse! Nurse!"

Nurse Joy rushes into the cat across the hall's room.

"Mr. Anse-hool! What's wrong?!"

"I need my wife! I'm dying! I need my wife now! I need my wife right now!" he exclaimed fiercely.

Noah is eavesdropping intently and Franklyn smirks at his brother.

A gentle voice says, "Hi, nurse, may I be of assistance?"

"Oh, yes, please can you speak to Mr. Anse-hool. He is really upset," Nurse Joy replied with an anxious look.

"Hello, Mr. Anse-hool. I am minister Reginald McDuffe. I come in prayer. Can we talk?"

"Who the hell are you?!" yelled Mr. Ansihl with his eyes and nostrils flared.

"I'm a minister from the _Church of latter-day saints_ on Pacifier," he replied with a gentle voice and a smile.

Mr. Ansihl throws a foam cup of water across his room.

"Get out! Both of you! Get the hell out of my room and get my wife!"

"Oh my!" Nurse Joy exclaimed in shock.

The nurse and minister hurry out of his room and into the corridor. They both look at each other in disbelief.

"Nurse! Do your fucking job and get my wife now!"

A man walks up to Nurse Joy and the minister. It's Mr. Ansihl's brother. They are whispering to each other in the corridor. Nurse Joy puts her hands on her chest breathing a sigh of relief. Mr. Ansihl cries out to his brother, "John! Come over here! Stop talking to those idiots!"

You can faintly hear some talking and complaining, followed by Mr. Ansihl's brother closing the door.

Nurse Joy quickly walks away in distress.

The minister looks around and steps up to the open doorway of Noah's room. He is holding a bible under his left arm. He knocks softly on Noah's door and offers a gentle smile.

"Good Morning, children of God."

Franklyn quickly says, "We gave at the office," simultaneously while Noah says, "We are Jewish."

The minister walks in reverse, bows his head repeatedly and with a smile, he bids farewell and is out of sight.

Noah and Franklyn giggle quietly.

Noah peeks over to the far-left side of his bed to see what's going on with the cat across the hall; he is quickly disheartened.

"Shit, the cat's door is closed."

Franklyn smirks at his brother's quest for an escape.

"Looking for drama? Watch some more movies and write some notes, Noah. I'll be back with breakfast."

Franklyn walks out of Noah's room and closes the door behind him.

Noah browses through his notes from the movie _Finch_ for several minutes but is suddenly distracted by a rolling trash container moving across the corridor. He tries to focus as he flips through pages in his notebook.

Suddenly there's a knock at the door and a janitor walks into the room.

"Garbage?" he asked.

Noah looks around and is not sure how to reply. The man walks in and starts putting the garbage together to throw out. Noah has his eyes glued to him with apprehension. The man glances over at Noah and offers him a stale smile. He walks out with a collection of garbage bags, throws them in the container, and closes the door behind him.

"That felt uncomfortable," Noah mumbled.

Noah starts reading his notes.

Movie compared to my life: <u>*FINCH*</u>

This was a good movie. I have never seen it, so, it was exciting. Franklyn says that this is emotions and that's ok because I need to recognize that it is the connection to conscience. So, before I write about a scene I like, I have to write down the emotions behind it and how it relates to my life.

Emotions: Fear, Surprise.

Finch finds out he is trapped for forty days in a superstorm, and he is scared. I have been scared of storms before. When I was a kid, I remember being on a small plane traveling with my mom and Franklyn. It was nighttime and there was a really bad thunderstorm with lightning. I thought I was going to die. I actually took a shit in my pants. That night, I took a beating for ruining my pants.

The reason for being fearful of storms is due to self-preservation. According to Franklyn, <u>human beings are programmed with survival and self-preservation; these are aspects of the nature program</u>. He says that these programs force us to survive, and we fear when our bodies and connection to the conscience are in danger. He says that this <u>fear also feeds energy to the conscience</u>. He says <u>the conscience is a creation by an extraterrestrial intelligent life force that feeds on our energy</u>.

Finch created a robot named Jeff to take care of his dog. Franklyn says dogs create emotional attachments for humans. He considers them to be a ploy of the game, a way for us to express emotions and continue to open the pandora's box of emotions. I asked Franklyn why he feels that love or happiness are bad emotions. Franklyn said that emotions are not bad for the connection to the conscience. He said our emotions are like a pandora's box. Each emotion offsets the other.

So, for example, the opposite of joy is sadness and the opposite of anger is fear. <u>The offset is the balance that causes an imbalance</u>. He says <u>in the game there have to be opposites to create balance like night and day</u>. He says, <u>in order to have balance you have to have imbalance</u>. The imbalance is what causes anarchy. He says that <u>this connection to the conscience feeding on our energy, in turn, feeds aliens</u>. He also says <u>with the pandora's box of emotions, it is all or nothing</u>.

He says <u>in the game it is impossible to have one without the other</u>. So, you can't only live in peace, happiness, or love within the experience. I'm still trying to understand this, but Franklyn makes some interesting points.

This whole world with everything going on is crazy and senseless. That thought alone stirs up emotions. The thought of <u>Joaquin Phoenix</u> being the current president of the United States, and I read in the news that he renamed NYC to Gotham City. They also refer to him sometimes as King Phoenix. That doesn't make sense. The extraterrestrials being introduced in the news from Planet Czentar and the canine virus are showing me something is wrong. Franklyn says that's the purpose of the game we live. I agree with him and I'm starting to see the big picture. I see how the game we live in is senseless and I can see how our energy is drained by everything that goes on in our lives. Franklyn says this starts with the NNP. He says <u>the NNP is nature, nurture, and societal programming</u>.

He says that this is already in place at our inception and that it is inherited from previous generations. He says that <u>our emotions, id, ego, and superego come from nature, like in our DNA, and are nurtured. That means our parents, friends, family, schools, and society continue to mold this into us</u>. He says <u>social media has been contributing to that nurturing process as well</u>. I see that clearly.

Ok, back to the movie. Finch is afraid to drive at night because he doesn't trust people. He knows that in an apocalypse or world disaster, people will turn on each other because of the programs called; survival, and self-preservation. While in the military, I didn't trust some of the soldiers in my outfit. They just looked like they would leave you stranded or become traders and give up your life to maintain their own. But this is how we are programmed. My experience has been that survival and self-preservation stir up emotions such as fear, and anger due to hate and distrust.

Noah stares at his notes and turns the page to the next movie he watched.

There's a loud bang at the door and a heavyset woman opens the door pulling in a food cart. She violently puts a plastic tray of food on top of Noah's rolling table.

"You want milk or orange juice?" she asked, breathing heavily, with a fed-up look.

Noah shakes his head with uncertainty.

"I didn't order breakfast, mam, my brother is bringing breakfast," Noah said, followed by a half-smile.

She smirks at Noah cynically and puts a container of orange juice on the tray table.

Noah unexpectedly feels like he's in a bad movie. He observes the woman turn the food cart towards the door and waddle out, slamming the door behind her. He sits there staring at the food tray in disdain.

Suddenly, Franklyn walks in and Noah's eyes light up.

"Hey, brother!" Noah exclaimed.

Franklyn has a paper shopping bag and a coffee in his hand.

"What's this?" Franklyn asked.

"The food lady came by," Noah replied.

"You ordered breakfast? I thought you didn't like this crap, Noah."

Noah shrugs his shoulders and looks at the food tray puzzled.

"I don't know what happened, Franklyn."

Franklyn takes the tray off the rolling table and places it on the floor in the corridor by the door. He walks up to Noah and offers him a foam container. Noah shakes his head and puts his hands up to stop Franklyn.

"Franklyn."

"Yeah, Noah."

"I'm not hungry. Sorry man, I'm not feeling well."

"Ok, what's going on?" asked Franklyn.

"I haven't moved my bowels in a few days, and I feel really bloated," said Noah.

"You want me to get something from the nurse's station? Though, that childlike nurse might come over and give you an enema in the butt. I'm not sure if I would trust her with that, she may end up accidentally castrating you," he replied humorously.

Noah laughs with a grimace, holding his belly tight.

"Stop with the jokes, Franklyn. My stomach hurts."

Franklyn grins and sits down in his uncomfortable plastic chair. He starts drinking a coffee and eating a breakfast burrito. Noah is rubbing his stomach and groaning while staring at Franklyn.

"These vessels are a bitch, right? What I mean is that they are so fragile. We have to contend with pain, discomfort, illness, disease, injury, etcetera. We have to clean, feed them, and keep them hydrated. They are high maintenance and require a lot of upkeep. *Then after an experience filled with sheer senselessness, the game decides to take it away from us,*" Franklyn announced shaking his head.

"Franklyn, do you hate life and who you are?" asked Noah with a smirk.

Franklyn fakes a guffaw[11] and shakes his head while chewing his food.

"No, Noah, that's emotional. I'm explaining the obvious illogical scenario we are dealing with when it comes to these vessels."

"Why do you call it vessels? Why don't you say, our body?" asked Noah.

"Sure, call it what you wish, but you don't own your body. Let me ask you a question. How do you feel now?" asked Franklyn with intent.

---

[11] https://www.merriam-webster.com/dictionary/guffaw - (a loud or boisterous burst of laughter)

"I told you; I feel like shit. I'm bloated and my stomach hurts," said Noah with disgust.

"Exactly. You feel that way and that triggers emotions of disgust, frustration, anger, and contempt. Your own body turns against you and drains your energy, directly affecting the energy within or what you would comprehend as the soul." Franklyn replied with validation.

"What? That doesn't make any sense, Franklyn."

"Really, Noah? I'm going to ask you again. What is your own body doing to you?"

"I get that, Franklyn, but it's probably due to the chemo and the medicines I took."

"So, Noah, it has nothing to do with your own body? Where did your cancer come from?"

Noah looks around his room in doubt.

"I don't know, Franklyn. Something I ate? Something I breathed in, I guess?"

Franklyn grins suspecting Noah is avoiding the obvious conclusion.

"Let's look it up, Noah."

Franklyn grabs his phone and starts swiping to locate articles on the internet.

"*Cancer is caused by certain changes to genes, the basic physical units of inheritance. Cancer is a genetic disease.*[12] Now let's see what Genetic means, Noah."

Noah stares at Franklyn with curiosity.

Franklyn continues to read from his phone.

---

[12] https://www.cancer.gov/about-cancer/understanding/what-is-cancer

"Genetic means, *Passed on from one generation to the next. Relating to genes or heredity. Relating to the origin or arising from a common origin.*[13] So, what does that tell you, Noah?"

Noah takes a moment to carefully choose his words.

"That it probably came from mom, dad, grandpa, grandma, great-grandma?"

"And that's nature, Noah. And like I told you; nature is part of the NNP, nature, nurture, and societal programming."

Noah takes a deep breath, looks down at his bed sheet, and sighs.

"So, now our bodies are trying to kill us?" asked Noah.

"Yes, Noah, but not the way you are thinking about it. *The energy within you means more than the human body.* The human body becomes dust after you die and dissolves into the earth; the energy within persists. What is important is the energy[14] or what you would comprehend as the soul. The soul; which is pure energy, is really what matters. Because the word, soul[15], has illogical references to emotions, I will be using the words, energy, and soul, interchangeably. What is within us is pure energy, frequency, and vibration; *that which guides us to the absolute.*

Death of the human body is the circle of life and a normal process that contributes to the ecosystem. It is an aspect of nature that we must accept as human beings. *However, what we are in the logical sense is a vessel with a confined soul within the brain.* *Descartes* and the *3-6-9 Forum* referred to this as the pineal gland which produces melatonin but also contains high levels of magnetite.[16] Magnetite contains pure energy contained in the pineal gland, scientifically it has been proven that it produces alternating vibration.[17]

---

[13] https://www.amnh.org/explore/ology/genetics/what-is-genetics

[14] https://www.etymonline.com/word/energy

[15] https://www.etymonline.com/search?q=soul

[16] https://www.nature.com/articles/s41598-018-29766-z,
https://www.bmj.com/content/bmj/291/6511/1759.full.pdf,
https://pubmed.ncbi.nlm.nih.gov/1715400, https://www.ncbi.nlm.nih.gov/books/NBK550972

[17] https://www.ncbi.nlm.nih.gov/pmc/articles/PMC5566001/

And these vessels are used to drain energy in order to feed an extraterrestrial intelligence."

"What the fuck! Uh… I-I don't know about that! This is too much, Franklyn!" Noah exclaimed.

"It's too much for those who are brainwashed to see what logically makes sense. They would rather be told what to think and what to do, be programmed, walk around aimlessly, and wait for some god to come down from the sky and save them. *Yet, generations have been waiting centuries for this god, and each generation dying off only to leave the same deceitful belief systems to the next generation of humans,*" said Franklyn.

Noah shakes his head bewildered while rubbing his stomach.

"I think I need to poop," said Noah.

"Well, that's a logical response," Franklyn replied.

"No, I mean I need an enema. Can you go to the nurse's station and get one?" asked Noah.

Franklyn nods and stands up with coffee in hand. He walks out of Noah's room and to the nurse's station.

Several minutes go by; Noah is thinking about what Franklyn just said.

He looks over at the bible on top of his desk drawer and the shrine. He doesn't know what to believe anymore.

Franklyn comes back with a laxative and a paper cup of water. He walks over to Noah and hands it over to him.

"The nurse said drink this and you'll be in poop heaven soon."

Franklyn walks back around Noah's bed and sits down while Noah drinks the laxative.

Noah crushes the paper cup into a ball with an anxious look on his face.

"Franklyn, do you have something against God or religion? Because honestly, religion has helped humanity, you know."

Franklyn grabs his phone and goes on *YouTube*. He pulls up a comedian named *George Carlin*.

"Noah, have you ever heard of *George Carlin*?"

"Yeah, Franklyn. That's that comedian; old guy with a ponytail."

Franklyn nods.

"Let's listen to this video, Noah, shall we?"

Noah nods his head.

They both watch the *George Carlin* video titled, *Stand Up About Religion.*[18]

Noah starts laughing loudly after George Carlin says, "*And the invisible man has a special list of ten things he does not want you to do. And if you do any of these ten things he has a special place full of fire and smoke and burning and torture and anguish where he will send you to live and suffer and burn and choke and scream and cry forever and ever 'til the end of time. But he loves you. He loves you and he needs money!*"

They both continue to listen and laugh aloud.

"Holy shit, that was funny. I get you're point, Franklyn."

Noah puts his head down, groaning with discomfort.

"Now I actually need to poop."

"*George Carlin* just saved your ass!" Franklyn exclaimed with a grin.

Noah laughs loudly while groaning and holding his stomach. He asks his brother to help him to the bathroom.

An alarm starts going off on the eighth floor. There are people

---

[18] https://www.youtube.com/watch?v=2tp0UNcjzl8

running through the corridor.

Franklyn walks to the doorway of Noah's room and sees nurses running toward him. He notices smoke at the end of the hall.

A security guard walks by and Franklyn grabs his attention.

"Hey, what's going on? Is there a fire?"

"Yes, sir, all under control. Someone threw a lighted cigarette in the garbage of the women's bathroom. All is good now," said the security guard.

Franklyn grins while thinking of Nurse Esperanza saying, "We don't need a fire in this hospital."

Noah calls Franklyn from the bathroom for help and Franklyn helps his brother back to bed.

"I heard an alarm," said Noah.

"It was nothing. False alarm," Franklyn replied.

"Teach me more, Franklyn."

Franklyn walks back around to his chair and sits down.

"Ok, Noah, get your notepad and start writing. We are going to talk about the id, ego, and superego."

"I feel like I'm back in school," Noah replied with a grin.

"Sure, except I'll tell you the truth," said Franklyn.

Noah smiles as Franklyn continues to speak.

"Let's look up the id, ego, and superego online, and then we will look this up in the Etymology dictionary as well."

Noah nods in agreement.

"Ok, Noah, here is the definition of the id, ego, and superego; I found it simply by searching in the I.AM search engine."

Franklyn reads to Noah aloud.

"[*According to Freud's psychoanalytic theory, the id is the primitive and instinctual part of the mind that contains sexual and aggressive drives and hidden memories, the super-ego operates as a moral conscience, and the ego is the realistic part that mediates between the desires of the id and the super-ego.]*[19] Now let's look at a few different definitions because comparing research is logical. Agree?"

"Agree," Noah replied with an insistent nod.

Franklyn swipes through his phone and reads another definition to Noah.

"[*The id, ego, and superego are* **three agencies that make up your personality.** *The id is the inherited part of the personality; the ego is who you are, or self; and the superego is governed by morals and societal compasses.*]"[20]

Noah interjects while Franklyn is reading.

"So, pretty much who and what I am from nature, nurture, and societal programming."

"That is correct, Noah! And a very logical conclusion. But that's only one of many aspects of the game we live."

Noah nods in agreement.

"Ok, so, let's look for the id, ego, and superego separately in the Etymology dictionary," said Franklyn.

Franklyn swipes on his phone and starts reading.

"Aha! Let's read the etymology definition of the id!"

Noah looks at Franklyn and listens intently.

"Noah, check this out. It says, [*(1923), from Latin id* **'*it*'** *(as a translation of German es* **'*it*'** *in Freud's title), used in psychoanalytical*

19 https://www.simplypsychology.org/psyche.html

20 https://study.com/learn/lesson/id-ego-and-superego-freud.html

theory to denote the unconscious instinctual force.][21] Now let's look at the dictionary definition of the word, *it*. [1. ***Used to refer to a thing previously mentioned or easily identified. 2. used to identify a person.]***"[22]

Noah nods and is momentarily in deep thought.

"So, basically, who I am, meaning; Noah Godtz and the color of my skin, hair, eyes, etcetera."

"Yes, Noah, that which is you or *it,* means *you,* the *person.*"

"Franklyn, what does unconscious instinctual force mean?"

Franklyn replies with enthusiasm.

"Let's look it up."

Franklyn types in his phone searching for more articles.

"Ok, this is one website out of many we need to read, Noah. This type of research requires focus and intent, so we can locate the facts. *When you are searching for truth, there's a whole lot of bullshit you'll need to shovel out of the way.*"

Noah nods in agreement while Franklyn continues to read from the article.

"[*The id is the primitive and instinctive component of personality. The id is a part of the unconscious that contains all the urges and impulses, including what is called the libido, a kind of generalized sexual energy that is used for everything from survival instincts to appreciation of art. The id is also kind of stubborn, for it responds only to what Freud called the <u>pleasure principle</u> (if it feels good, do it), and nothing else.]*[23] So, the impulses that are programmed into us from *nature;* then molded into us by *nurture* and *societal programming,* like school, friends, relatives, social media, and society, are what promote those impulses. *That's the unconscious instinctual force.*"

---

[21] https://www.etymonline.com/search?q=ID

[22] https://languages.oup.com/google-dictionary-en/

[23] https://www.simplypsychology.org/psyche.html

"Nature, nurture, and societal programming," Noah replied with acknowledgment.

"That makes sense, Noah. This pleasure principle aligns with moral relativism.[24] So, shall we continue on to the etymology definitions of the *ego* and *superego*?"

"Yes, Franklyn, please."

Franklyn starts typing into his phone searching for the definition of the word ego and once again exclaims.

"Aha! *the self; that which feels, acts, or thinks, from Latin ego 'I' its use is implied in egoity.*"[25]

"Conscience connected and emotions!" Noah exclaimed.

"That sounds like you got a bingo, Noah."

Noah is staring into space with an intense look like his brain is calculating a complicated problem.

"Let's look up superego," said Franklyn.

He starts typing into his phone and reads audibly.

"Superego, [*that part of the psyche which controls the impulses of the id.*][26] Logically this promotes internal conflict."

Noah is shaking his head dumbfounded.

"Huh, I didn't know that, Franklyn."

"Brother, we were taught this shit in school, but we didn't learn the real meaning because we were *distracted*. The schools teach for the purpose of contributing to the game with a job or career. They do not teach us about our purpose or why we are here, Noah."

Noah is fascinated and nods his head in agreement.

---

[24] https://en.wikipedia.org/wiki/Moral_relativism

[25] https://www.etymonline.com/search?q=ego

[26] https://www.etymonline.com/search?q=superego

Franklyn continues to explain to Noah.

"Brother, the *superego and the id are opposing programs with ego processing the result of that internal anarchy from our…*"

"*Emotions*!" Noah interjects with an exclamation.

Franklyn nods in agreement and continues to speak.

"That process in itself eats up our energy directly affecting, that which we also refer to as…"

Noah and Franklyn answer in unison.

"*The soul.*"

"Noah, I'm going to read the definition of egoist since I have it right here before me anyway, it says, *[one who maintains there is no evidence of the existence of anything but the self*, égoiste. *Meaning 'selfish person' is from 1879. Related: Egoistic; egoistical.]*"[27]

Noah is staring at his bed sheets in deep thought. Franklyn grins watching his brother assess what they are discussing.

"Let's read another one, Noah, this one is the definition of *egotize*. It pretty much is the same when someone accuses you of having a big ego or extreme self-importance, it says, *[talk overmuch of oneself.]*"[28]

Noah chuckles and points to himself.

"That's definitely me. All I do is talk about my twenty-six years in the military and how I served my country, giving myself importance over others."

"Yes, that is the program called ego," Franklyn replied.

"I am a real shithead," Noah stated.

Franklyn addresses Noah sternly.

---

[27] https://www.etymonline.com/search?q=egoist

[28] https://www.etymonline.com/search?q=egotize

"Noah, this is a program within you. Your connection to the conscience in collaboration with the NNP is what made you egoistical and act in that manner. The energy within is not responsible for these programs. This is a process that was put into place to feed on the energy within."

"Goddamnit, these fucking alien leaches! We need to kill these bastards!" exclaimed Noah with anger.

"Noah, stop. You are not grasping any knowledge by getting angry. Having an emotional rut is what helps consume your energy, making you feel drained. There is no need for vengeance or anger. *The best solution is to seek knowledge. Knowledge of why you are here and what is your purpose.*"

"Franklyn, I still don't get one thing though."

"What is it that you don't get, Noah?"

"Should I feel bad about something good, like receiving a commendation, or a compliment?" asked Noah.

"Yes and no, Noah. If you receive these awards or compliments and you let them trigger your ego and emotions, then yes. If you receive such things and logically you use it as a tool or component to play the game strategically then, no. These awards and compliments, make you feel a high level of happiness and self-admiration. This is opening the pandora's box of emotions. Noah, with emotions, it is all or none.

Then, when you experience envy or jealousy, for example, someone insults you to attack your moment in the spotlight, that attack will cause you to have an emotional outbreak. You will come crashing down from an inflated ego because of anger or disgust. This roller coaster of emotions causes an imbalance. The energy exerted through our emotions is what feeds these extraterrestrials through the connection to conscience."

Noah nods grasping what Franklyn just said.

"So, Franklyn, other people can cause you to be emotional and feed these bastards?" asked Noah.

"Noah, you need to realize that you are being emotional. We are having a logical conversation with facts. To answer your question, yes, this is what conscience connected means. *All humans connect to the conscience, but we also indirectly have a connection with those physically around us through the conscience.* The process is that other people induce emotions from us and we induce emotions from them. *The game also implements two powerful programs called tribe and family. These are derived from nature.* We normally experience stronger emotions from people that are part of our tribe or family since we are normally around them more often. But we can also experience strong emotions from people outside of our tribe or family. It depends on the situation the game creates.

However, our main focus should be that our emotions are used to feed extraterrestrials through the connection to conscience."

"Jesus fucking Christ, what is this guy like? A big *Jabba The Hutt*?" asked Noah in anger.

"Noah, I cannot say what or who it is specifically. There really aren't any facts to prove that. All we know is that there are extraterrestrials walking around among us today. I am not sure what the reason is for them being here, but I do know they are extraterrestrials with much higher intelligence and far more advanced than humans."

Noah looks confused and is trying to gather his thoughts.

"So, Franklyn, can we really accuse them of feeding on our energy?"

"No, Noah, we cannot. I do not have any concrete facts to prove they are feeding on our energy. However, I can state that those extraterrestrials are here from planet Czentar because we have seen them. I can also state that humans are not the only sentient beings at the top of the food chain. That would be illogical according to the universal ecosystem. I don't think humans are hunted by extraterrestrials the same way we hunt animals. It makes sense that extraterrestrials feed differently. I can also state the fact that there is no god that's going to save humanity. That there is no higher power. That there is nothing in this game we live that makes sense to me nor that we are here to benefit from this experience. All I see is a teeter-totter of emotions due to lies and external anarchy which creates an imbalance. They just announced this morning that a war started between India and Pakistan."

"But, Franklyn, that's been going on for centuries."

"Yes, but both the U.S. and Russia are on opposite sides. And Canada is helping India with military personnel and equipment. There are news reports all over the internet predicting a nuclear war and an apocalypse. This creates instability, Noah. The imbalance we have been talking about. The game does this on purpose to play with humanity and feed on their energy through the emotional anarchy it creates."

Noah blinks repeatedly and shakes his head in grief.

"Noah, I'm not saying that this war is the only contributor. Logically we have to realize that *if there is a better place, It definitely cannot be reached from the place we are in now. I can logically say I KNOW WHAT THIS IS and I KNOW WHAT THIS IS NOT.* That's all I need to know. I can logically state that we have been lied to and deceived from the time of our birth until now; that this is not heaven or hell nor a path to either. *This is not a place of glory, a place where we learn, grow, and transcend to become angels and beings of light.* This is not that place, Noah. *This place is a pasture for extraterrestrials, and humans are the cattle.*"

"Geesh, that's so scary and depressing," Noah replied.

"Noah, *for as long as you give in to your emotions and refuse to see the logic, the energy within you, will suffer the consequences.* Our energy does not benefit from emotions, the NNP, the id, the ego, and the superego. They are in place to keep you confused and imbalanced. *The energy within you is logical.*"

"Ok, Franklyn, I agree. I'm just trying to take all of this in."

"Noah, you've heard of the top of the food chain, right?"

"Yes, Franklyn, *humans are said to be at the top of the food chain.*"

"That's right, Noah, and humans think they are the only sentient beings at the top. We feed on animals that are less intelligent than humans and we feed on pasturage. We feed on everything that we can kill and eat, correct?"

"Yes, Franklyn. That's correct."

"Are you such an egoist to think that humans are the only sentient beings at the top and there are no other species above us except for the gods and higher powers we construct in our minds?"[29] asked Franklyn.

Noah thrusts back into his bed bewildered by Franklyn's statement.

"Whoa, Franklyn, you are making me see things I always feared or ignored, probably because I didn't care to know."

"Noah, you will see it clearer than anyone else outside of this room. You see it now because you've been told your life will be over soon. And the only thing they have to offer you is a bullshit bible full of fallacies, a chaplain or a priest that will lie to you with a smile, and a crappy nurse that is completely brainwashed. She can't see that a handful of rocks will not cure any disease. These are all ploys of the game to keep you entrenched in emotions."

"But her mother had cancer and those stones cured her, Franklyn!"

"How do you know, Noah? Were you there? Did you speak to her doctor? I spoke to Nurse Esperanza yesterday about her mother briefly and her mother was at the beginning stages of cancer. She was going through chemo along with medication; she was then cured. *These belief systems are like a panacea.* Those crystals acted as a hypothetical remedy. The fact that her mother was cured of breast cancer at the same time she was wearing those crystals was a *coincidence*. The insensible behavior stems from people just wanting to believe others or society without doing proper research and obtaining all of the facts on their own. *Humans become victims of cults and belief systems like mice become victims in a science lab.*"

Noah nods in agreement with a hint of defeat. He is breathing heavily and not looking well.

---

[29] https://www.ncbi.nlm.nih.gov/pmc/articles/PMC7340401/

"Franklyn, I need a break brother. This is mind-blowing and I need to sleep."

"Ok, Noah, I'll step out for a bit."

Franklyn gets his outerwear, walks to the exit door, and looks back at Noah.

"Now that you were properly introduced to the id, ego, and superego, know that you will experience internal anarchy."

"I KNOW WHAT THIS IS
and I KNOW WHAT THIS IS NOT"

Chapter 5: If you're feeling six...

Franklyn wakes up to the sound of laughter. It's 4:59 am and Noah is sleeping in his bed in a fetal position, hugging a pillow. The door is open to Noah's room, and he notices the light flickering intermittently in the corridor. He clearly hears the laughter of a woman and a man.

He stands up and starts walking towards the doorway of Noah's room, peeking out to the left of the corridor where the Nurse's station is located. Dr. Harpherd is half-seated on the counter of the nurse's desk talking to Nurse Joy. The doctor is smiling and holding her hand in his. It looks like they're flirting with each other.

Franklyn notices that the door to the cat across the hall's room is open, the light is out and the bed curtain is drawn. A janitor is mopping the floor by the elevator. He stops mopping and offers a harsh stare at Franklyn for a few minutes.

Franklyn turns around, walks back in, and closes the door to Noah's room. He walks back to his chair, sits down, and looks through his phone. On his phone, there are multiple websites opened on conscience, id, ego, superego, and emotions. It looks like Noah had been researching and reading articles for hours into the night.

Franklyn lays back and closes his eyes for a minute. He opens one eye, glances to his left, and sees the shrine on top of Noah's desk drawer. The bible is inside the garbage can on top of food containers. He smirks and whispers to himself, "That's a good place for it."

He lays back, closes his eyes, and murmurs, "These eyelids are filthy."

Franklyn wakes up to the faint sound of a rolling cart. Suddenly, a bright light comes on and he hears a familiar voice.

"Mr. Noah Godtz, good morning, sir. I need to take your vitals."

Franklyn opens his eyes and sees Nurse Esperanza holding a thermometer in her hand. He closes them for a moment and hears the sound of Velcro separating from the blood pressure cuff.

The time is 6:39 am and Noah is half asleep sitting up at the nurse's disposal.

Franklyn stands up tall and stretches his arms up and to the sides. The nurse smiles pleasantly and is easily distracted by him.

"You are so tall, sir, can I ask how tall you are?" she asked affably.

"You can, the question is may you ask," Franklyn replied with indifference.

Nurse Esperanza offers a slight smirk with a humbled look.

Noah murmurs with his eyes closed, "He's six foot six."

"Well, he's not a friendly giant, that's for sure," she sneered.

"Oh, I didn't know you wanted to be friends," Franklyn replied with sarcasm.

Nurse Esperanza smirks and shakes her head in disbelief.

"Mr. Godtz, do you want breakfast today or is your brother getting breakfast for you?" she asked with a pleasing smile.

"My brother will take care of it, nurse, thanks," said Noah with a tired voice.

Nurse Esperanza offers Franklyn a stale smirk.

"Sir, I am leaving these laxatives for your brother. Please keep to only one per day. If you need to use more than one, please let me know," she said.

Franklyn nods in agreement.

Nurse Esperanza turns her cart around and walks out directly into the cat across the hall's room. Noah rubs his eyes and scooches slightly to peek over.

"Get out! I'm sleeping, can't you see that?!" Mr. Ansihl wailed at the nurse.

"Mr. Ansihl, I need to take your vitals, sir, you can stay sleeping if you want," she said with a commanding voice.

His loud yell permeates the corridor.

"Get the fuck out! Get out! I'm sleeping, can't you see that?! I don't want you here! Turn off the fucking light!" Mr. Ansihl exclaimed.

Noah looks at Franklyn while giggling in a mischievous manner.

Franklyn grins and says in a gladiator's voice, "*Are you not entertained?! Are you not entertained?!*"[30]

Noah laughs aloud at Franklyn and continues to look to the room across the hall.

It's quiet for a minute.

"Ow! Ow! You hurt me! You stupid bitch! Get the fuck out of my room! Now! I'm going to sue you!" Mr. Ansihl yelled.

She tosses the menu on his bed.

"Mr. Ansihl, stop cursing at me. You are very rude! There's your menu for breakfast!" she exclaimed.

She shuts the light off and storms out of Mr. Ansihl's room, slamming the door behind her.

"Wow! She looked angry, brother," said Noah.

Franklyn replies from the bathroom through the sound of farts and running water.

"Yep, that's everywhere, brother."

---

[30] https://youtu.be/YbBiXPVKuTA?t=83

The water shuts off and Franklyn walks out drying his hands with cheap brown paper towels. His facial stubble has residue stuck from the paper towels.

Noah giggles, entertained by the cat across the hall, the door is closed, but you can still hear loud angry mumbling.

"Pancakes today, Noah?"

Noah smiles and nods his head. Franklyn acknowledges Noah and walks toward his chair to put his boots on.

"Is it still bad out there?" Noah asked.

"What do you mean, Noah?"

"You know, the weather, Franklyn."

"Regardless of the weather, it is always either good or bad out there," Franklyn replied.

Noah smirks and observes his room. Franklyn walks towards his outerwear and puts them on. He stares at Noah while buttoning his coat.

"I'll be back, Noah. If you are up to it, watch a movie and do some more writing. Try not to get distracted by drama and the game."

Noah nods in agreement.

"Be careful out there, my brother!" Noah exclaimed.

Franklyn glances at Noah and replies with a sarcastic grin.

"You are saying something that won't change the outcome of my game."

"You're right, Franklyn. That was pretty stupid to say."

"I suggest you rephrase that to, an emotional thing to say."

Noah nods his head.

Franklyn walks out of the room, and intentionally leaves the door open.

He walks to the elevator and notices the indicator light is flickering. He whispers to himself, "It's still broken." The elevator doors open; he walks in and presses the lobby.

Noah sits in his bed staring at the shrine on top of his desk drawer. He leans over to grab a plastic bag of DVD movies and looks through them for several minutes, reading the titles to himself. He decides to watch, _The Perfect Storm_. Noah positions his laptop on the side of the bed; puts the DVD in the cd tray and starts watching the movie.

Time goes by and suddenly there's loud screaming again, coming from the cat across the hall.

"Nurse! Nurse! Nurse! Get my wife now! I need her right now! I'm dying! I need my wife!"

No one tends to the cat across the hall, so, he continues to scream.

"Nurse! Nurse! Nurse! I need my wife! What the fuck?! Is anyone working today?! Doesn't anyone hear me?! Nurse! Nurse! Nurse!"

Noah can't concentrate on the movie; he starts feeling a bit angry and frustrated. He scoots over to peek into the room across the hall. Mr. Ansihl is sitting up looking straight at him with an outraged look.

He had white hair with a receding hairline, a heavy white mustache; and circle lens glasses perched on a large nose.

Noah whispers to himself in shock.

"Oh, shit… this guy looks like _Sigmund Freud_."

Mr. Ansihl looks directly at Noah with his big black eyes.

"What the fuck are you looking at?! Mind your fucking business, asshole!" he exclaimed.

Noah starts to reply with anger.

"Hey man, go fuh…," but stops himself short.

Noah realizes that this is the conscience using the connection between himself and Mr. Ansihl. The connection to the conscience induces emotions so it can feed on that energy. He smiles and decides to start acting, helping Mr. Ansihl scream for the nurse.

"Nurse! Nurse! Nurse! Mr. Ansihl needs you! Can someone please help this man?!"

Mr. Ansihl offers a momentary nasty stare at Noah. But then, he smiles and starts giggling playfully. They both start calling the nurse aloud while laughing in a brattish manner.

Nurse Esperanza quickly appears and stops between Noah's room and Mr. Ansihl's room.

"Both of you need to stop! Mr. Godtz and Mr. Ansihl. Both of you are disturbing the other patients!" she exclaimed heatedly.

Nurse Esperanza walks up to Noah's door and slams it shut. You can slightly hear her arguing with Mr. Ansihl followed by another door closing loudly.

Noah chuckles and positions his laptop to continue watching the movie.

"That was fun," he whispered to himself with a smile.

More than an hour goes by and Noah hears Franklyn's faint voice in the corridor. He pauses the movie so he can make out whom Franklyn is talking to.

"Ok, got it," said Franklyn as the door opened.

"Hey, I thought I left this door open. Who closed it?"

Franklyn closes the door behind him.

"Nurse Esperanza closed it. She was upset because I was helping the cat across the hall get her attention," Noah said with a giggle.

"Oh, that's what she was talking about," Franklyn replied with validation.

"That's who you were talking to in the corridor?" asked Noah.

"Yes. She was lecturing me about keeping the ambiance of the hospital peaceful and blah blah blah. I stopped hearing what she was saying after the first sentence," Franklyn replied.

Noah giggles.

"To me, she starts sounding like _Miss Othmar_ from the _Peanuts_ cartoon," said Franklyn.

Noah laughs a good belly laugh.

At the doorway to Noah's room, Franklyn sets a bag on the floor, shakes his coat, and slaps the snow off his hat. Snow and ice drip in and around the garbage can. After hanging his outerwear, Franklyn grabs the bag, slips off his boots, sits, and pulls out a container of food with a coffee.

"So, Noah, what movie did you pick?"

Noah replies while grabbing the coffee and container of food.

"Oh, _The Perfect Storm_."

"Cool. What did you write?" asked Franklyn.

"I didn't finish watching it. I got distracted," said Noah with a shrug.

"The cat across the hall?" asked Franklyn.

Noah nods with a shameful look.

"So, let's finish watching it now. Let's just start from where you left off," Franklyn replied.

Noah nods his head.

He starts the movie at the scene where _Captain Billy_ of the ship and his first mate _Bobby_ are trapped in the sword-fishing boat that's sinking.

Noah glances at Franklyn and speaks while chewing.

"This is a true story."

"Sure, let's keep watching," Franklyn replied with disregard.

They both continue to eat their breakfast while watching the movie.

There's a soft knock at the door and it opens quickly after. Nurse Esperanza walks in, bats her eyes at Franklyn, and looks at Noah.

"Hi, Mr. Godtz, I'm here to collect my books. Did you actually read any of them?" She asked with a critical tone in her voice.

Noah pauses the movie and smiles at her.

"Yes, nurse, I did, and they were excellent, thank you."

Nurse Esperanza takes a deep breath, sighs, and smiles proudly.

"You took a big step towards enlightenment, Mr. Godtz. I am so proud of you."

Noah nods and grins with an unsure look.

Nurse Esperanza directs a big smile at Franklyn, she gloats while grabbing her books from the floor. Rolling her eyes, she walks out of the room closing the door behind her.

"Man, she wears a lot of makeup, doesn't she? And she smells like a botanical garden that burned down," said Noah.

Franklyn yelps a loud laugh.

"Ha! She's quite the character in this game. You need them though."

"What do you mean?" asked Noah.

"They help you realize your emotional state of mind.[31] Let's finish our breakfast and the movie, then we can chat some more."

They continue to eat while finishing the movie.

Noah is writing notes about the movie.

They both are startled by a loud slam in the corridor. A woman's voice cries aloud.

"Well, fuck you, doctor!"

Nurse Esperanza storms into Noah's room with tears on her face; wearing a shoulder bag and coat.

"Mr. Godtz, I'm leaving today! I just quit this fucking job! I've had it! I came by to wish you well on your spiritual journey. May the force of the higher power bless you and heal you!" she exclaimed.

She turns around and starts walking towards the door.

"Nurse! Wait!" Franklyn exclaimed.

Nurse Esperanza turns to Franklyn with tears in her eyes and a rosy look on her face.

Franklyn points to Nurse Esperanza and sings with a rapper's voice.

"Don't procrastinate, you must meditate, oh yeah!"

He nods repeatedly while folding his arms intently; demonstrating an end to his performance.

Noah covers his face with both hands trying to muffle his laughter.

Nurse Esperanza rolls her eyes while shaking her head and leaves the room.

---

[31] https://www.ncbi.nlm.nih.gov/pmc/articles/PMC3453527/

Franklyn walks over to close the door. At a glance he sees Dr. Harpherd yelling out while walking speedily after Nurse Esperanza.

"Nurse! Come back here! It's not what you think! Please come back!"

Franklyn closes the door, looks at Noah with a grin and walks back to his chair.

"Ok, Noah, Let's chat. Read to me what you wrote down in your notes about the movie."

"Ok," he replied.

Noah puts his scraps away and starts reading his notes audibly.

"So, these guys go out on this fishing boat, and they hardly come back with any fish. The owner of the boat gives the captain a hard time and pays him and his crew crap. The captain of the fishing boat wants everyone to know, especially the owner of the boat, that he is good at catching swordfish, and he wants to show them by taking the boat back out again."

"So, how does this compare to any part of this life? Which emotions are being used to manipulate and drain energy?" asked Franklyn.

"Well, I remember one time in Afghanistan, we were on a route doing a field inspection. I misled my team and I fucked up the entire mission. I wanted to go back and do it again, but my commanding officer wouldn't let me. He said it was protocol. I felt like I needed to prove that I can do the job. I was really frustrated, angry, and disappointed in myself. The guys got together for drinks that night, but I didn't join them, I couldn't even stand the sight of myself," Noah replied.

"Well?" asked Franklyn.

"Well, what?! I felt like shit!" Noah exclaimed while he slammed the notepad on the bed.

Franklyn crosses his legs and folds his hands on his lap. He stares at Noah with a slight grin.

"These emotions still drain my energy and affect me even with just remembering my past. That's part of the id, ego, and superego, right?" asked Noah.

Franklyn nods and continues to stare at Noah.

"I always had this chip on my shoulder like I needed to prove something. I was always envious of you, Franklyn. You came out really tall and handsome. Look at me, I came out short and not so handsome. The ugly twin."

"Why does any of that matter now? And you are not short, Noah. Five-nine is not short. Also, you had more girlfriends than I had in school. But I ask again, why does that matter now?"

"It doesn't. It doesn't even make sense. It's not logical because it's emotional. But that's my NNP," Noah replied with a solemn voice.

"And that, my brother, is another bingo! Let's continue reading!" Franklyn exclaimed.

Noah nods enthusiastically, turns the page on his notebook, and continues to read aloud.

"So, Bobby's girlfriend doesn't want him to go out on the boat again. She gets angry at him because he won't listen to her. She catches a tantrum and makes him feel bad."

Noah pauses to think and Franklyn intently stares at him while sipping from his coffee.

"Sometimes Megan was like that with me too. If I didn't do something she wanted me to do, she would get angry and try to make me feel bad. This is conscience connected, isn't it?" asked Noah.

Franklyn nods with his hands folded on his lap.

Noah continues reading aloud.

"Conscience connected includes a program that causes us to incite emotions from each other to feed energy to the conscience. The act of me being insensitive to my girlfriend caused her to get angry, sad, and fearful for my safety. But that also means that I am stirring emotions in myself too. Because when I am feeling insensitive, I also experience guilt and sadness."

Noah slams his fist into the notebook in anger.

"Jesus! What a goddamn cluster fuck!"

Franklyn sits back and sips his coffee watching his brother's internal anarchy unfold.

Noah sighs and huffs heavily and repeatedly.

"Fucking emotions man! This shit ain't easy, Franklyn!"

Franklyn nods his head and distracts Noah by pointing to the notepad.

"Noah, continue reading."

Noah looks down at his notepad, breathing heavily, and continues to read audibly.

"Well, some of the guys in the crew don't want to go out again but they are all thinking about the money. So, money kind of works like a program. You need it to pay your bills and play the game of life, like that fucking goddamn game *Monopoly*, but money also works like a magnet. People are drawn to it because they want a better life, a happier life, but that's not possible because *emotions are like a pandora's box. All or none*, right, Franklyn?"

"Noah, remember, we researched the *six emotions. Fear, anger, joy, sadness, disgust, and surprise*. We need to always reference the *alchemy*[32] *of the emotions* also known as the wheel of the emotions. This reference gives us the opposite of each one so that we can recognize the balance. Four and a half of the six emotions are

---

[32] https://www.etymonline.com/word/alchemy

negative and keep in mind that, *the opposite of balance is imbalance*."[33]

Noah agrees with Franklyn and continues.

"The crew members need money but then it becomes more of a want. So, they risk their lives and draw negative emotions like sadness from their loved ones, and that's the goddamn conscience connected. That makes them feel bad, but they feel if they make more money, then, this will make things better, but it doesn't."

Franklyn shakes his head intently. Noah continues reading out loud, breathing anxiously.

"People want money because they think it's the answer to unraveling the pandora's box of emotions, but it's a trick, it's just another fucking game. Money cannot override the program of emotion. Money gets them happiness, but the pandora's box of emotions will offset that with anger or sadness. It's that yin-yang shit, right, Franklyn?"

Franklyn nods with confidence.

Noah is becoming evidently frustrated.

"Franklyn, this place is a real shitho-"

The door to Noah's room abruptly swings open. Nurse Esperanza rushes in sobbing and sits on Noah's bed facing away from Franklyn.

"Mr. Godtz, I'm sorry I came by earlier crying and complaining. That was unprofessional and I am truly sorry."

"No, it's ok, nurse, really, it's fine," said Noah.

Nurse Esperanza continues to speak with a broken voice.

"Sometimes it's so hard for me you know. I work so many hours. I get only one day off a week and Dr. Harpherd treats me like I'm his pet. I feel so insulted and used."

---

[33] https://www.thesaurus.com/browse/balance

She continues to cry while drying her eyes with a ball of used napkins.

Franklyn interjects in a commanding voice.

"Nurse!"

Nurse Esperanza peeks over her left shoulder at Franklyn.

"My brother was indeed in the military, but he was an infantry soldier, not a chaplain. Though, I suggest you speak to a therapist. Please leave this room and don't trouble my brother with your problems," Franklyn stated in a firm voice.

Noah glances at Franklyn with despair.

"No, Franklyn, don't say that to her."

Nurse Esperanza continues to cry and wipe her tears while Noah rubs her back for comfort.

"Noah, this is unprofessional and doesn't make sense. Nurse Esperanza, does this makes sense to you? Should you be crying and pouring all of your problems on a patient that's on his deathbed?" asked Franklyn with a vigorous tone.

Noah looks at Franklyn shaking his head in shock and gesturing for Franklyn to stop.

Nurse Esperanza stands up, turns, and faces Franklyn. She takes a deep breath and sighs.

"You are right, sir. This is embarrassing and I am truly sorry," she softly cried out in a sad voice.

She holds her hands to her chest and looks away slightly towards the ceiling as if she is gesturing a heartache.

Franklyn guffaws at the nurse's gesture.

"Act two, scene one is now over, go home and meditate, stick some crystals on your forehead and inhale some incense. Please do not bother my brother again or I will file a complaint with the administration office," Franklyn replied assertively.

Noah looks down at his bed sheets with embarrassment as Nurse Esperanza storms out of his room, slamming the door behind her.

Franklyn stares at Noah while taking a sip of his coffee.

Noah stares at the door for a minute and looks at Franklyn.

"Conscience connected, huh?" said Noah.

"Yet, another bingo, Noah."

There is a lot of commotion going on in the corridor. A combination of Nurse Esperanza arguing with Dr. Harpherd and the cat across the hall yelling for his wife, "Nurse! Where's my wife?!"

"Don't get distracted by the game, Noah. Let's continue our conversation."

"What the fuck is happening in this place?" asked Noah.

"Conscience Connected. Nurse Esperanza felt a strong bond with you so she decided that you would be the victim of her emotional dump," Franklyn replied.

"Why me?" asked Noah.

"Noah, you know this. She sees a common attribute between both of you. She now sees you as a member of her tribe. She feels comfortable spewing her emotions on you. Conscience connected uses that program so it can induce emotions from both of you. Why didn't she go to any other patient on this floor? Probably because they didn't share any interest in her spiritual beliefs. That automatically made you a member of her *tribe*, you know like, *friends*? The only one that has a shrine of that crap and listened to her nonsense was you."

Noah nods in agreement.

"If she would have gone to the cat across the hall with that nonsense, you would have heard him yell, 'get the fuck out of my room!' He doesn't have an interest in her problems," said Franklyn.

"Geesh," Noah replied with an uneasy look.

"Let's get back to what we were talking about," said Franklyn.

Noah nods and continues to read audibly.

"Ok, so there was a part in the movie where one of the crew members was telling his child that his mom was going to find him a new dad. I remember our dad saying something like that to us, remember?"

Franklyn nods and sips his coffee.

"Anyway, that made me feel angry, guilty, sad, depressed; like I had no control. My dad said that to me, and I felt manipulated. So, this is caused by the program of conscience connected," said Noah.

"That's a logical statement," Franklyn replied.

Noah is suddenly unmotivated and fatigued.

"I'm tired of talking. I'm not feeling well, Franklyn, please teach me about anything."

"You are writing about the movies and comparing these scenarios to your own life, that makes you the teacher and the student, Noah. This is the best way to learn. *There is no better teacher than yourself.*"

Noah offers a nod of affirmation.

"I suggest you keep discussing your notes with me and continue to watch these movies. Stick with these writing exercises, Noah. And, I am adding one more exercise for you."

"Sure, what is it?" asked Noah.

"Noah, I want you to write every night before you go to sleep everything you know, including pros and cons, about the conscience, conscience connected, the vessel, the brain, emotions, the NNP, the id, ego, and superego."

"But I'm still researching and learning, Franklyn."

"That's ok, Noah. Whatever you know and can remember is good enough."

"Franklyn, while you were speaking to Nurse Esperanza, it sounded like you were angry. You were being emotional, right?"

Franklyn grins and shakes his head.

Noah speaks as if he has solved a riddle.

"But I saw your face and the tone of your voice, you were angry, brother," he said in a confident voice.

"Noah, I know I sounded angry. I had to act that way. That's the only way to strategically play the game we live. I needed to become an actor, like an actor in a movie but the movie I'm in happens to be the game we live. I have to be strategic and make it look and feel like I'm upset, but I'm just being strategic and logical. I admit that my connection to the conscience sometimes causes me to express emotions. I'm not going to control that, but I can recognize it and implement strategic logic. *By acting as if I'm upset, I can get the same response as if I was being emotional.* Politicians do the same, except that they use it as a tool to control humanity."[34]

"So, do you bottle up your emotions inside you?" asked Noah.

"Not anymore, Noah. It took time for me to function this way in the game. It wasn't easy, I must admit that sometimes the NNP manipulates my actions and that triggers emotions that drain energy. That happens to me mostly with disgust. But I call out the connection to conscience and handle the situation strategically with logic."

---

[34] https://www.etymonline.com/word/esoteric

Noah smirks and speaks in a mechanical voice while moving his arms robotically.

"So - you – turned – yourself – into - a -robot."

Franklyn grins.

"No, Noah, I try to not allow emotions to be triggered. And when I feel it happening, I recognize it and call out my connection to the conscience. People have accused me of being cold and heartless. I am not going to follow those that are brainwashed and continue to feed my energy to the conscience blindly; that is illogical. Emotions, the NNP, id, ego, and superego are illogical."

"Just like Nurse Esperanza's emotional tantrum," said Noah.

"That's right! That whole outburst from Nurse Esperanza was illogical. Society would refer to her behavior as immature. But even the use of that word doesn't make sense. Humans are immature because they are emotional not because they are children or juveniles. However, the sensible statement would be, *Emotions are illogical because they cause irrational behavior. Carl Jung refers to this as constellated – disturbed by the complex,*"[35] Franklyn replied.

"Ain't that somethin'," said Noah.

Noah writes audibly, "*Emotions cause us to be irrational. How do we find truth or the absolute if we are illogical?*"

"Noah, do you remember your most emotional moments and the decisions you've made while being angry, sad, disgusted, or having contempt?" asked Franklyn.

"Yeah, I've made my share of fucked up decisions for sure."

"That's because when your emotions are triggered, they cause you to make illogical decisions. Your decisions are partly or entirely illogical due to your emotional state. And that is the program stemming from the NNP," Franklyn replied.

---

[35] https://www.amazon.com/Collected-Works-C-G-Jung-Psychoanalysis/dp/B01JXQXFW6/ref=tmm_hrd_swatch_0?_encoding=UTF8&qid=&sr=

"Nature, nurture, and *societal programming*," Noah stated with certainty.

"Affirmative," Franklyn replied.

"Franklyn, I've made some good decisions when I was happy and that is an emotion."

"Like what?" asked Franklyn.

"Well, I remember one Christmas, I gave Megan a diamond pendant that she always wanted. She couldn't find it anywhere and I spent a lot of time looking for it, I finally found it and gave it to her as a gift. That was a happy moment for both of us," Noah replied.

Franklyn leans over closer to Noah with his arms resting on his thighs and clasping his hands.

"Ok, so let's break this down, shall we? Christmas is a program, the act of you searching for that pendant is a program, the act of finding the pendant is a program and the act of giving it to Megan is a program. Now, tell me about the emotions behind each one. Tell me how Christmas is a program, Noah."

Noah looks up as if he is looking into his thoughts.

"Well, Christmas is a program that was probably put into us from nature and then nurtured. The purpose of Christmas is to experience joy and happiness. But that's not always the case because you experience sadness when you see others in need. The poor are living in a worse situation than us. And sometimes people are rude and mean during Christmas shopping, like *Black Friday*, and they stomp on each other just to get gifts," Noah replied.

"The rudeness and stomping on other humans rushing into stores don't occur because of Christmas but let's just stick to Christmas promotes joy and happiness for now. And of course, the opposite of joy and happiness is sadness. Happiness or joy is also balanced by anger and contempt, but let's not go into the pandora's box yet. Let's move on to the next one, How is the act of giving a gift a program?" asked Franklyn.

"So, it makes us feel good when we give a gift and that's ego for sure. When you receive a gift you feel happy, and I guess your ego gets inflated too because you feel that someone else values you. But I guess all of that is temporary because when you get into a disagreement or you start arguing, your anger progressively gets worse because you feel resentment. And I guess that's another program used to drain energy from us," Noah replied.

"Noah, what did you experience searching for that pendant?"

Noah's facial expression changes to contempt.

"Oh-brother, that was a fucking nightmare. People are just nasty and rude, Franklyn. I finally found the pendant at a store located in Ohio. They had it listed online for sale. I remember it was $1899. But when I tried to buy it online, I couldn't. The website kept giving me an error with the shopping cart. So, I called them up and they confirmed that the pendant was indeed in stock. I was relieved and happy about that. I told them that I couldn't order it from their website and asked If I could order it directly from them. And they said that phone orders included a cost of $250. Man, I was so pissed off. That asshole clerk argued with me on the phone for about an hour. Finally, I said fuck it and decided to look elsewhere. I finally bought the same pendant from a store in Canada. But then _DHL_ fucked up the shipment with customs and that was a nightmare I went through for about a month. I finally resolved everything, and I got the shipment a few weeks before Christmas with the pendant intact."

Noah feels triumphant and smiles with joy. He then looks at Franklyn like a child caught lying to their parent.

Franklyn grins and stares at Noah intently.

"That whole experience drained my energy and triggered all types of emotions," said Noah with a broken voice.

"Noah, after everything you went through to find that pendent, you felt like Megan owed you something."

"No. Why would I feel she owed me anything?"

"Noah, you didn't mention to her everything you went through to find that pendent during any of your disagreements or arguments? You had no resentment? You mentioned the word resentment before."

Noah blinks his eyes slowly with a sigh.

"Well, yeah, when we were having disagreements and arguments about me going on a second tour to Iraq; we had one last big argument and she gave the pendant back to me. That hurt my feelings badly. I thought about what I went through for that pendant and I was angry at her. I was hurt and upset, Franklyn. But that's conscience connected, and those goddamn programs in us."

"Noah, did you resent Megan? Did you resent her for something she didn't even ask you to do?"

"Yes, Franklyn! I resented her! I had expectations and I was hurt! It wasn't the same with her after I came back from Iraq! We just didn't get along anymore!"

Noah starts sobbing with anger.

"Franklyn, I made some bad decisions and I ended up with regret. I didn't mean to do any of that to her."

Noah's cries are deeper and he starts hyperventilating.

"These fucking programs, this fucking connection to the conscience, and goddamn fucking aliens! Why don't they leave us alone?! I hate this fucking place!"

Franklyn takes a deep breath and looks at his brother with an absolute blank stare.

Noah looks up at him with his face wet from tears and tosses his notebook with frustration.

"Franklyn, this is a mind fuck! This is what you are doing to me. You are just fucking my mind with this shit!"

Noah continues crying with a conquered look.

There's a loud bang at the door and a heavyset woman walks in with a food cart.

She looks at them with a frustrated look on her face. With a nasty attitude, she throws a tray of food on top of Noah's rolling table.

"Milk or Orange Juice?" she asked huffingly.

Franklyn looks at the woman with a grin.

"How about both?"

She tosses a container of orange juice and a small carton of milk on the food tray. With an arrogant smirk, she turns her cart around towards the door and exits slamming the door behind her.

"What's her problem?" asked Noah in a sobbing voice.

Franklyn shrugs his mouth and shoulders.

"She's been eating the food in this place," he replied.

Noah giggles and wipes his face with his bed sheets.

Franklyn stands up and stretches his arms in a circle.

"Noah, I'm going out to take care of some errands and get a bite to eat. I should be back in a few hours."

"Franklyn…"

Franklyn glances at Noah.

"You are helping me, Franklyn. I know that it doesn't look that way, but you are the only one helping me."

"I'm not helping you, Noah, you are helping yourself. I'm just guiding you to the information. Do you want me to bring something back for you or are you planning to eat the brick and mortar on this tray?"

Noah giggles quietly and looks at Franklyn with a childlike smile.

"I've been wanting a _Big Mac_ and French Fries."

"Ah, that stuff will kill you," said Franklyn with a grin.

"I know, but it's so good," Noah replied.

They both giggle for a minute. Franklyn puts on his outerwear and then leaves the room.

Noah stares at the closed door to his room for a moment.

He sets up his laptop and decides he is going to watch, _The Joker_.

Noah falls asleep during the movie and wakes up startled, "Franklyn! - Franklyn?!"

He sees the rolling table close to his bed with a _Big Mac_, French Fries, and an Apple Pie on top. He smiles knowing his brother was there and delivered the food he asked for. He thinks to himself, Franklyn set it all up without waking me.

Noah rewinds the movie back to where he left off and starts eating his food with a look of satisfaction. He finishes watching _The Joker_ and several other movies into the night. While intermittently looking at the time, he wonders when Franklyn will come back.

It's past midnight and Noah falls asleep after watching a movie titled, _The Game_.

"There is no better teacher than yourself"

Chapter 6: We are illogically connected

Noah wakes up to the sound of a rolling cart. The bright light comes on from the overhead lamp. His eyes hurt to open; it feels like someone threw sand in them.

"Mr. Godtz, I need to take your vitals, sir."

Noah positions his bed so he can sit up. He's a bit disoriented but he recognizes that familiar voice.

"Hi, Nurse Esperanza. What time is it?" he asked.

"It's 7:01 am, Mr. Godtz, how are you?" she asked with a smile.

Noah looks to his right and sees an empty chair and the air mattress resting against the wall. He wonders if his brother is coming back.

Nurse Esperanza smiles and glances in the same direction Noah was looking.

"Where's your brother today, Mr. Godtz?"

Noah shakes his head with uncertainty.

"Would you like to see the breakfast menu? I'm assuming you will be eating breakfast from our cafeteria today?" she asked.

Noah shakes his head and looks disoriented.

"Nurse, I just would like a coffee, if that's ok."

"Sure, Mr. Godtz."

Nurse Esperanza smiles at Noah and starts tidying up his bed.

Noah rubs his eyes and looks to the right to where his brother normally sits.

"You miss him, don't you?" she asked with a smile.

Noah looks at Nurse Esperanza with a blank expression. He is not sure if agreeing with her makes sense.

"This conscience misses him," he replied.

Nurse Esperanza frowns in confusion.

"What do you mean, this conscience? You sound like you are two different people, Mr. Godtz," she replied with a giggle.

Suddenly, Franklyn walks in through the door with a brown shopping bag and a notebook under his arm.

"Franklyn!" Noah bellowed.

Nurse Esperanza smiles bashfully as she looks at Franklyn.

Franklyn grins and hangs his outerwear by the door. He stomps his feet to remove any remaining snow and slips off his boots, he then walks to the chair where he usually sits.

"Nice to see you again, sir," she said cattily.

"Hey nurse, Noah has a gift for you by the way," Franklyn replied with a fake grin.

Noah glances over at Franklyn with a frown, surprised and confused.

"What?!" Noah exclaimed.

"Oh my god! Really?!" she said with excitement.

"Absolutely… it's this book," Franklyn replied.

He grabs a book on top of Noah's desk drawer and gives it to her. Nurse Esperanza looks at the book front and back. She reads the front cover aloud.

"_Illusions, The Adventures of a Reluctant Messiah by Richard Bach_. Wow! This is so nice, Mr. Godtz. I will be sure to start reading it today."

"It's a short read," Franklyn replied.

"Oh, yes, it's not a big book at all," she said.

Franklyn utters with sarcasm.

"That's not what I meant."

Nurse Esperanza frowns in confusion and looks over at Noah.

"He means that you'll get the message from the book immediately. It's very well written," said Noah.

"Oh, yes, I understand, Mr. Godtz. Thank you so much for this gift," she said.

She holds it to her chest and bellows, "*The gift of knowledge is what binds humanity*!"

"Did you just write that?" Franklyn asked sarcastically.

"Yes, through the higher power of consciousness which has touched me," she said with an annoyed tone.

"I guess, *The meek shall inherit the earth*,"[36] Franklyn announced.

Nurse Esperanza frowns at Franklyn confused.

"Gentlemen, have a blessed breakfast today. May the love of the higher power be with you," she said.

Franklyn sips his coffee and belches loudly.

Nurse Esperanza offers a look of disgust to Franklyn.

"Excuse him, nurse, enjoy the book, it's very good," said Noah.

Franklyn hands over a coffee and a food container to Noah. He starts eating his pancakes disregarding Nurse Esperanza. She offers a grin, turns her cart to the door, and walks out hurriedly.

---

[36] https://www.bible.com/bible/59/MAT.5.ESV, https://www.merriam-webster.com/dictionary/meek

Noah and Franklyn look at each other laughing childishly.

"Franklyn, where did you go after you left yesterday?" asked Noah while chewing his food.

Franklyn shrugs his shoulders.

"Does it matter, Noah?"

"Franklyn, I had a hard time sleeping and I think my emotions kept me looking at the time. I felt like I was anxious and hoping you would come back."

"Why?" asked Franklyn.

"I don't know. That's why I am asking you," said Noah.

Franklyn fakes a chuckle under his breath.

"Really? Noah, you don't know? You really need me to tell you?"

"I guess emotions and the NNP?" asked Noah.

"Noah, I would say that is a logical response."

Noah takes a sip of his coffee and stares at his blanket for a few minutes.

"Is this like a program within us that promotes attachment and dependency?" asked Noah.

"What do you think? What makes sense, Noah?"

Noah nods with enlightenment.

"Oh-brother… this bullshit had me tossing and turning all night. I was checking the time on my phone constantly, I couldn't sleep."

"You should have called out the conscience," said Franklyn with a grin.

"I did… but It didn't work," Noah replied with a frustrated voice.

"That's not how it works, Noah. This isn't similar to when you pray and you wait for some god to answer. This is a program within you that you need to recognize. *You just need to know that it was your connection to the conscience running its programs to induce emotions.* And that's, all that it is. You don't need to do anything else."

"Isn't it supposed to make you feel better?" asked Noah.

Franklyn shakes his head and grins with skepticism.

"Noah, I didn't say that, and you're not making sense because feeling better is associated with emotions. What is it that needs to feel better? The energy within you or your connection to the conscience? The energy within doesn't align with the conscience or its programs. The energy within is logical and in its purest form."

"I'm confused, Franklyn. Are we the conscience or is the conscience outside of us?"

"Both. *We have a conscience that is defined by spiritual theory and a connection to conscience. The connection to conscience uses the common programs we share with others in our space,*" Franklyn replied.

Noah nods with unsureness.

"Are you familiar with a mainframe, Noah?"

Noah nods with certainty while chewing his food.

"We used them in the military for advanced reconnaissance of our enemies," Noah replied.

"Sure," Franklyn said sarcastically.

Noah shrugs his mouth and shoulders.

"Think of '*The Conscience*' as a mainframe computer and think of humans as terminals with a similar likeness to, and a link to, this mainframe computer," said Franklyn.

"That makes sense," said Noah.

"So, we have a connection to the conscience just like terminals are connected to a mainframe. Since terminals are a product used for computing, they act, look, and are programmed similarly to the mainframe itself. But unlike the terminal, the mainframe handles all of the processing. The link is used to feed information from the mainframe to the terminals and vice-versa.[37] Originally, they were called dumb terminals. Hence the conscience is like a mainframe and humans are like dumb terminals. The connection to the conscience is like the link between a terminal and the mainframe. Technology had changed from mainframe to client-server, but history repeats itself in this game. Today, the cloud, much like a mainframe, is configured to manage all resources," said Franklyn.

Noah is shaking his head showing uncertainty.

"Now I am really fucking confused. Are you saying we are computers?" asked Noah.

"You are getting close, Noah. We function like computers except that humans are much more sophisticated. Nikola Tesla wrote; *The human being is a self-propelled automaton entirely under the control of external influences. Willful and predetermined though they appear, his actions are governed not from within, but from without. He is like a float tossed about by the waves of a turbulent sea*.[38] Humans go through the process of an infant to child to teenager to adulthood. Computers don't go through that process. However, *Artificial Intelligence* can very much, in fact, go through the same process humans do, becoming a *sentient being with consciousness*."

Noah interjects with enthusiasm.

"Hey, I heard about that. I read something about that search tool called I.AM. It can help you locate anything; even takes your fingerprint and offers you all sorts of things related to your DNA; things to do and things you can buy. It's like it controls what you buy and influences the choices in your life. That fucking thing even comes in android form for the purpose of companionship."

---

[37] https://www.oreilly.com/library/view/learning-dcom/9781449307011/ch01s01.html

[38] https://m.imdb.com/name/nm2410046/quotes

"Yes it does, I.AM has already reached adulthood." Franklyn replied with a grin.

"So, are humans being replaced?" asked Noah.

Franklyn shrugs his shoulders.

"That wouldn't align with the universal ecosystem. Besides, I don't know of any facts to prove that," Franklyn replied, followed by a bite.

Franklyn tosses his food container in the trash bin and syrup splatters about. He sips his coffee and continues to stare at Noah.

Noah feels a bit uncomfortable and is hesitant to ask questions.

"Franklyn, *what if we really don't have a soul, or as you say, the energy within? Maybe we are just sentient beings with consciousness, and our purpose, is only to feed these aliens through our connection to the conscience?*"

"That's possible and would support the logic of a universal ecosystem, Noah."

"So, you agree?" asked Noah.

"Yes, but there is something within me asking, *why aren't we told that this is our purpose or the reason for our existence? I don't see the logic in how humanity is being lied to, used, and preyed upon. I KNOW WHAT THIS IS, and I KNOW WHAT THIS IS NOT.* Something doesn't make sense, Noah. This is what prompted me to dig deep into my purpose and existence."

"That's a good point, Franklyn."

"Noah, I decided to find truth and be logical with my pursuit. I decided not to go with the flow of society or follow the masses. *That is the purpose of the NNP; to have humanity follow nonsense blindly.*"

"I guess I was one of those idiots that followed society," Noah replied with a guilty giggle.

"Noah, *the intention of me guiding you to open your eyes and show to you what you already know is not for the purpose of you to be emotional.* Remember, I went through this same process too."

"That's right, Franklyn. I'm still trying to control my emotions and way of thinking."

"Noah, *you can't control your emotions, nor does it make sense to control them.* Otherwise, by trying to control emotions, you are still contributing to your connection to the conscience. *You just need to call it out and recognize what it is and why it happens.* The reason you feel guilt, or the need to control your emotions is due to the NNP. All guilt does is provoke emotions."

"But how does recognizing and calling out the connection to conscience help me?" asked Noah.

"It helps you recognize how your emotions, the NNP, id, ego, and superego manipulate you, Noah. This practice also guides you to finding your purpose and recognizing why you are here. It helps you take off the blinders to actually see what's going on in this game. You will also come to understand that your soul, energy within, or whatever it is that is searching for truth, will not see how this game we live makes sense."

Noah nods with certainty.

"You just said a few days ago, *Life sucks, and then you die*, why did you say that, Noah?"

Noah looks up as if he is searching for the right words.

He shrugs his shoulders and says, "I guess because I felt incomplete as if I didn't accomplish the things I wanted to accomplish. I felt like I was cheated and not given enough time to do the things I wanted to do. I'm fifty-eight years old, Franklyn, and I wish I had more time. At least another twenty years before I die. Now with this fucking cancer, I only have a couple of days left."

"Noah, let's say you weren't in this hospital bed, and you didn't have this cancer that's ending your role as Noah. And let's say you were out there somewhere. Would you be thinking about writing a letter to Megan to say you are sorry? Would you have been thinking about your friends back at home that you disregarded? Would you be looking to accomplish these things you say you need to accomplish? Or would you be chasing some other woman, or back at the base looking for field work, perhaps admiring a tank to distract you from truth?"

Noah looks at Franklyn with a tamed look.

"I would be chasing some woman or working in the field, probably admiring a tank as you said, Franklyn. I wouldn't be thinking about anything else."

Noah looks down and stares at his bed sheets for several minutes and then glances intermittently at Franklyn with guilt.

"I'm doing all of this now because I am dying soon, Franklyn, I should have been doing this a long time ago, along with you."

"It wasn't your time, Noah. Now is your time. The past does not matter. Let's concentrate on what's happening now."

Noah nods insistently.

"Yes, Franklyn. Now is the time that counts!"

Franklyn sits back in his chair, crosses his legs, and takes a sip of his coffee. Noah looks around his room glancing at Franklyn like a lost child.

"So, this is a game we are living in and we are like sentient beings containing an energy source that feeds extraterrestrials, right? So, how did these souls, or energy within, end up in these bodies? Who or what created this?" asked Noah.

"I don't know, and I don't know if that even matters, Noah. What matters is that *I KNOW WHAT THIS IS* and *I KNOW WHAT THIS IS NOT*. If this is how life is supposed to be, then why are humans not told that from the beginning? Why the stories of a god or a higher power? Why all the misleading lies that keep humans entrenched in hopes of being saved? Why are all of the occurrences in this world, leading humanity to internal and external anarchy? Everything that happens in this experience leads every person to an emotional outbreak. *It's like a roller coaster ride that doesn't stop until the game decides when your ride is over.*"

"Death?" asked Noah.

"That's correct, Noah, *right before you die, your energy is drained by common negative emotions including surprise with a negative undertone. It's like your energy is being sucked through a straw.*"

"I think I get it, but I'm not sure," Noah replied.

"You are not ready yet. We will talk about this again, specifically the *program* called *death.* Let's get back to why you didn't sleep well and why you were anxious," said Franklyn.

Noah pauses for several minutes to think.

"Well, that was my programming that made me feel this way and of course, it's my connection to the conscience that feeds that *Jabba The Hutt* son of a bitch."

Franklyn grins and stares at Noah.

"You know, Franklyn, I feel like I'm in therapy talking to a psychiatrist. That's how you make me feel."

"I'm not the one that's being manipulated by emotions, Noah. You asked for my help and you are having expectations that are emotional. For as long as you lose focus to these distractions, you will not retain knowledge. Would it be better for you if I were talking to you from the toilet? Or standing on my head in the corner of the room?"

Noah giggles shaking his head.

"Ok, Franklyn, I get it. By the way, I need to use the bathroom, can you help me?"

"Sure," Franklyn replied.

Franklyn helps his brother to the bathroom, then walks to the exit door of Noah's room and peeks across the corridor. He notices the cat across the hall has his curtain pulled, hiding the bed from view.

Time goes by and Franklyn hears Noah calling him from the bathroom, he helps his brother back to bed.

All of a sudden, the cat across the hall starts screaming.

Noah scoots over to the left side of his bed. He peeks into the cat across the hall's room but can't see much due to his bed curtain.

Mr. Ansihl is arguing with the nurse.

"Didn't I just ask you to get my fucking wife?! Clean your damn ears and do what I asked you to do! You are supposed to serve me! Aren't you the nurse?! If you can't do your job then get Dr. Harpherd in here immediately! I'm going to call the doctor! Dr. Harpherd!"

Nurse Esperanza is frustrated and speaks loudly to Mr. Ansihl as she opens his bed curtain aggressively.

"Mr. Ansihl! I will not allow you to speak to me in this manner! Do you hear me?!" she exclaimed.

"No, I don't fucking hear you because I'm the man and you are the servant![39] Now do your fucking job and get my wife now!" he wailed loudly.

Nurse Esperanza's voice is stuttering with emotions.

"Mr. Ansihl! I-I am not your servant! I-I am the head nurse in this hospital with ha-hardly a staff and many patients to-to tend to!"

Mr. Ansihl laughs loudly.

---

[39] https://www.kingjamesbibleonline.org/Genesis-3-16/

"Rah-Rah-Rah-Right! That's not my fucking problem nurse! Shut up and get my wife now!" he replied loudly, followed by a wicked laugh.

Nurse Esperanza quickly walks to the doorway facing the corridor. She closes her eyes, gestures with a mudra; takes a deep breath, and turns around to address Mr. Ansihl.

"Mr. Ansihl! *There is no such thing as a problem without a gift for you in its hands!*"[40]

Mr. Ansihl frowns with disgust and opens his eyes wide.

"What the?!... What the fuck was that idiotic gibberish coming from your mouth?! Get out of my room! Get out now and get my wife!"

Nurse Esperanza starts sobbing and hurries out of Mr. Ansihl's room into the corridor exclaiming, "I can't take this anymore!"

Noah looks at Franklyn in astonishment.

"Did she just quote from the book we gave to her?" asked Noah.

"I think so, and it didn't help," Franklyn replied.

They both laugh a hardy laugh.

Franklyn stands up and stretches his arms out in circles, his back cracks several times. He walks to the door of Noah's room and closes it.

"Noah, no more distractions, let's get back to our conversation."

Noah nods his head. Franklyn sits back down in his chair, crosses his legs, and his hands on his lap. He stares at Noah for several minutes. Noah looks at Franklyn with a sincere look on his face.

"What should we talk about?" asked Noah.

"Conscience connected. Noah, what do you think it is?"

---

[40] https://www.amazon.com/Illusions-Adventures-Reluctant-Richard-Bach/dp/0440204887

"Another program? A program to stir up emotions from each other?" asked Noah.

"That's a good start. Keep thinking about what makes sense," Franklyn replied.

"I have a question and need to clear something up," said Noah.

Franklyn nods.

"Are we considered energy vampires? Do we feed off each other's energy as well?" asked Noah.

"How? Tell me, Noah, can you go through days, weeks, months without eating food, feeding only on energy?"

Noah looks around thinking.

"No. But isn't it possible to feed on the sun?" asked Noah.

"Absolutely not. The human body cannot function without eating food. Even those that claim to feed on the energy of the sun cannot survive without eating food. It is a proven fact that humans cannot feed on the sun as plants do. The human vessel does get some energy and nutrients from the sun. However, the vessel needs food to function," Franklyn replied.

"But we can't live without the sun!" Noah exclaimed.

"Apparently according to science, the sun is necessary to maintain these vessels. Perhaps the sun works like an oven or a microwave."

Noah laughs shaking his head in disbelief.

"Get out of here, man. You're kidding, right? You actually think humans are food, like a rack of ribs?"

"Noah, again, I ask you; *Are you so egoistic to think that we are the only sentient beings at the top of the food chain? Egoism* is emotional and produces ignorance which in turn produces illogical thinking."

"No, Franklyn, I don't think that at all. You are right, there is no way humans are the only ones at the top of the totem pole," Noah replied with certitude.

"Absolutely Noah. I found this article on the internet explaining the *ecosystem*. Take my phone and read that article while I use the bathroom."

Noah grabs Franklyn's phone and starts reading about the ecosystem.

There's a soft knock at the door and it is a young pretty woman dressed in white. She pushes in a food cart and offers a beautiful smile.

"Hello, sir, how are you today? It's the most beautiful day today, sir. We have a lovely selection for lunch today. We have steak and potatoes! Yummy… and we have fish and chips. This is all courtesy of the restaurant across the street as a gift for the holy days."

Noah is mesmerized by the pretty young woman; he feels he has just seen an angel.

Franklyn yells from the bathroom.

"Fish and Chips!"

Noah glances over his shoulder to the bathroom and smiles.

The woman smiles and giggles cutely as she quickly glances toward the bathroom.

"May I have one order of the fish and chips for my brother as well, hun?" asked Noah.

"Of course! It's Christmas time! I will put two orders on your rolling table, sir, have a blessed day and enjoy your lunch," she replied with a pleasant smile.

The bathroom toilet flushes loudly as Franklyn walks out of the bathroom. He stands at the bathroom door drying his hands and staring expressionless at the pretty woman.

She looks at Franklyn with a smile and turns the food cart around leaving the room.

Franklyn walks over to the exit door of Noah's room and closes it firmly.

"You will like their Fish & Chips, I've had it before and this connection to the conscience enjoyed it," said Franklyn.

"I'm glad you enjoy something in this world," Noah replied.

"My connection to the conscience enjoys several things in this game, but that's attributed to the NNP," said Franklyn as he winked at Noah and rolled the tray of food closer to the bed.

Noah has a nauseous look and is rubbing his gut.

"Not now, maybe later. I am feeling a bit drained and my stomach feels terrible. I feel like I got a basketball stuck in my stomach that wants to shoot a three-pointer out of my butt," said Noah.

Franklyn grins and grabs one plate of fish and chips.

He sits down in his chair, crosses his long legs, and starts eating with the plate sitting on his lap.

"Noah, you can take a nap and I'll finish eating and then tend to some errands."

Noah shakes his head and with a gasp says, "I want to learn more. Let's keep talking."

"You sound out of breath, are you sure?" asked Franklyn.

Noah nods with certainty.

"Ok, we were talking about conscience connected," said Franklyn.

"Right," Noah replied.

"Noah, Conscience connected is misinterpreted. Hipsters and new age worshipers of the light or higher consciousness look at this as humans uniting for the greater good or living in love. They believe that at some point, good will conquer evil and love will conquer hate but that is illogical. The fact is that the attributes of everything in the game must have opposites to function. This is how it produces balance and in turn how it produces the opposite of balance which is imbalance."

Puzzled by Franklyn's reply, Noah interjects.

"So, conscience connected can also be a bad thing?"

"Yes, Noah. In fact, I think that conscience connected is illogical overall even when joy or a positive surprise is the initial emotion."

"Why is that?" asked Noah.

Franklyn explains while chewing on his food.

"Because you are still experiencing emotions. And when you experience emotions you use energy. And that energy feeds the extraterrestrials through the connection to conscience."

"But the connection I have with you now is a good connection, Franklyn. I don't see how that's bad."

"It's a balancing act, Noah. It's good because you are learning something from me. But you also feel an attachment and a dependency. You feel anxious when I'm not around and joyous when I am here. I didn't show up purposely yesterday and last night to give you the experience of attachment and dependency. These programs are characteristics of *family* and *tribe*, especially in *children*. I didn't show up on purpose and you experienced emotions because of that. You realized what was happening to you due to dependency and attachment. That realization came with a cost because you still experienced illogical emotions which drained your energy. The knowledge that I share with you comes with the cost of emotional outbursts. This is known as internal anarchy. Logically, this has to occur because it is part of the deprogramming process."

"So, you being here, sharing this knowledge with me, helps me with my path to truth, but comes with the cost of emotional anarchy," said Noah with confirmation.

"That's correct," Franklyn replied.

Noah looks around the room in thought.

"Franklyn, how about my relationship with anyone else other than my family, friends, or loved ones? How does that work?"

"A relationship with a stranger doesn't have to be intimate as with family or tribe, Noah. A relationship can function without love or admiration because it still utilizes similar programs through the NNP."

"I don't get it, Franklyn."

"Take for example the woman that walked in with the food cart dressed in white, did you love her or consider her your friend?" asked Franklyn.

"Well, no, she was pretty and very nice so I found her attractive," Noah replied.

"Noah, did you feel a bond with her like you feel with a family member or a close friend?" Franklyn asked with a grin.

"No, I just met her," Noah replied with a frown of defiance.

"Really, Noah? You didn't feel attracted to her? You didn't feel like she was nice? She didn't make you feel good?"

"Well, yes, I said she was attractive and she did make me feel good. But that was because she was a nice person and she was pretty. Just because I felt that way doesn't automatically make her my friend, Franklyn."

"Noah, it doesn't matter. You just said she made you feel good. The program initiated an exchange of emotions between both of you, in turn, you and that woman individually initiated the feeding process."

Noah frowns in confusion.

"Ok, I get it Franklyn, but that exchange of emotions didn't feel like someone took a bite off me like I'm a cheeseburger."

"Ha! That's funny, Noah. No, it may not, but tell me, what is the opposite of happiness? What is the opposite of feeling good? What is the opposite of joy? Emotions are like a pandora's box, you will experience the opposite of positive emotions because logically it must have balance. *Your connection to the conscience tricks you to experience positive emotions, so you must experience the negative ones as well. Since there has to be a balance with emotions, conversely there is an imbalance. This process is up and down repeatedly, like a teeter-totter or a heartbeat.*"

"I don't follow, Franklyn."

"Noah, In these times we are living in, humanity has been experiencing more negative emotions like fear, anger, sadness, disgust, and surprise with a negative undertone. *Your vessel may not feel like a cheeseburger that's been gnawed, but I bet you feel drained after an emotional outburst. That drained feeling doesn't affect the vessel or your connection to the conscience, Noah, it - affects - the – energy within you.*"

Noah nods, though uncertain about Franklyn's statement.

"I think I get it. But I felt good when she was here, I didn't feel bad, Franklyn."

"Yes, but you were attracted to her and she isn't here now. You probably won't see her again since you are expecting to die. How does that make you feel?"

"Like fucking shit, now that you bring it up," Noah replied with contempt.

"Noah, I didn't bring it up to initiate emotions from you. I brought it up to show you that there is clearly an opposite of feeling good. And that is how the balance of emotions works."

"So, the emotional experience needs to be balanced, and in turn that creates an imbalance," said Noah.

Franklyn nods and points at Noah with certainty.

"That's correct, Noah."

Noah lays still and closes his eyes for a very long moment.

Franklyn stands up, stretches his arms out, twists, and turns until his back cracks. He walks over to his outerwear and starts putting on his coat.

"Where are you going, Franklyn? We are not done yet, sit down. I have another question and then I'll take a nap."

Franklyn puts his boots on, walks over, and sits down. He rubs his hands on his knees and takes a deep breath.

Noah glances over at Franklyn with glossy eyes and a serious look.

"Franklyn, I don't have any kids, or even nephews for that matter, so, how do children fit into this whole conscience-connected thing?"

"Noah, I don't want to distract your process, because, we are making significant strides, but you do have two nephews."

Noah's eyes are wide open in amazement, he sits up slightly higher.

"What?! I have two nephews, your boys?!"

Franklyn calmly nods his head.

"How come you didn't tell me this until now?" asked Noah.

"Why – does – that – matter?" Franklyn asked.

Noah nods his head and lays back slightly uneasy but in thought.

Noah murmurs, "Conscience connected."

He stretches his neck side to side and looks at Franklyn with a grin.

"Franklyn, It doesn't matter now. But can you answer my question on children and conscience connected at least?"

"Sure, Noah. It's a sensitive subject, but *logically, children feed the process of the game. If humanity would cease to have children, the cycle of feeding the extraterrestrials through the conscience comes to an end, and these higher intelligent extraterrestrials cannot feed. Children are the inception of the game, just like the two humans referenced in the bible. You know, Adam and Eve from the Garden of Eden."*[41]

"So, having children is a bad thing?" asked Noah.

"I don't see that as a logical statement, Noah. There are emotions in that statement, you should rephrase it. But let's research and see what I.AM says."

Franklyn searches on his phone, while Noah scribbles in his notebook.

"I found this interesting article, Noah. [*Is having children meaning of life? Reproduction and genetic survival may be the meaning of Life, but it is not inescapably the meaning of your life. So, in the end, the full answer is no – we do not bestow having babies as the sole guardians of life's meaning.*][42] But, I am sure the holy scriptures contradict this article for reasons I do not have to mention."[43]

"So, having children is illogical because it keeps the universal ecosystem going and feeding the extraterrestrials," said Noah.

"That's correct," Franklyn replied.

"Whoa, I don't think that would sit well with humanity," said Noah.

"You mean the ones that have betrayed their energy within? And

---

[41] https://www.etymonline.com/word/eden

[42] https://blogs.scientificamerican.com/guest-blog/is-the-meaning-of-your-life-to-make-babies/

[43] https://en.wikipedia.org/wiki/Be_fruitful_and_multiply

the ones that serve the extraterrestrials that control humanity and the game we live? The answer then, is yes, Noah, it would not sit well with them."

"Do you regret having children, Franklyn?"

"Again, Noah, I must point out that your question is illogical because it induces emotion. *Logically, the connection to the conscience promotes children and the idea of children, family, and tribe because it maintains the cycle of life.* Hence, my connection to the conscience doesn't regret children, but any contribution to the NNP is illogical."

Noah closes his eyes for a moment.

"It's hard to accept because we are influenced by the NNP, but that makes sense," Noah said confidently.

Franklyn gestures in agreement.

"Franklyn, one more question."

Franklyn nods his head while looking at the case of the movie, *The Game*.

"Why do you refer to the tool you suspect is used for feeding on us as the conscience and not consciousness?" asked Noah.

"*It's six of one and half dozen of the other,*"[44] Franklyn replied.

Noah scowls and looks confused.

"Noah, I noticed you watched this movie, *The Game*. What did you think?"

"It was good. I liked it. I saw many similarities to the game we live in. Actually, I wrote down a question about a scene I saw in the movie," Noah replied.

Noah is looking through his notes.

---

[44] https://en.wikipedia.org/wiki/Six_of_One

"Noah, did you purposely buy this movie?"

"No, Franklyn, it is from the hospital library. I just borrowed it."

Noah locates the question he had in his notes.

"Ok, so, in one part of the movie, one of the guys in the members-only club says to Nicholas, "*Whereas once I was blind, now I can see*.[45] It's a verse from the bible, *John Chapter 9 Verse 25*. How much truth is there in the Bible?"

"Well, that's not the exact verse that's in the Bible, Noah. The verse is, *Whether he be a sinner I know not: one thing I know, that, whereas I was blind, now I see*.[46] Though the meaning of that verse has been transposed in the movie. For the objective of your research, that parable means; you are taking off the blinders. By removing distractions and deception, you will find your true purpose and the reason why you are in this game. That's why the movie, *The Game*, had written it differently.

Regarding your question about how much truth there is in the bible, I suspect that it was written by the esoteric, so there is some truth in there but most of the bible was written to manipulate and brainwash humanity. Nevertheless, I recommend reading these scriptures and related information as part of the process. You should be able to identify truth easily within the lies. Anything that is written with the intention of manipulating emotions through your NNP, id, ego, and superego is a red flag."

"Franklyn, I heard that verse and thought about our conversations. I remember that you said we need to research our purpose and seek knowledge."

Franklyn nods in agreement.

Noah pauses for a moment and looks down at his notebook. He takes a deep breath, sighs, and looks at Franklyn with bloodshot eyes.

"This body needs to sleep now. We will talk again."

---

[45] https://en.wikipedia.org/wiki/The_Game_(1997_film)

[46] https://biblehub.com/kjv/john/9-25.htm

"We will, Noah. I will write down some website links in your notepad. Read these articles when you wake up from your nap. At some point, we will talk about the dissimilarity and factual similarities between conscience and consciousness."

Franklyn looks at the time and puts his phone on Noah's bed. He walks to the door, looks over at Noah, and sees he is fast asleep.

The sound of the door closing is all you can hear on the eighth floor.

The cat across the hall is laying down in his bed sleeping, his wife holds his hand while reading the bible. She looks momentarily at Franklyn and offers a sad smile. Franklyn remains expressionless, looks to his right, and starts walking to the elevator.

An hour goes by and Noah wakes up startled at the sound of Nurse Esperanza's voice.

"Mr. Godtz, you didn't eat your food? Do you want me to warm it up in the microwave?"

Noah shakes his head.

"Nurse, I'm really thirsty. May I have some water?"

"Sure, Mr. Godtz. Is there anything else I can get for you?"

"I would like some chocolate pudding and apple sauce if you have any."

"Sure, Mr. Godtz. I'll be back momentarily."

Nurse Esperanza walks out of Noah's room.

Noah looks around and notices Franklyn is not back yet. He looks at the time on Franklyn's phone and it is 6:01 pm. He searches on the internet for the articles Franklyn noted and reads them. An hour goes by and Franklyn has yet to return.

Noah grabs the bag of movies Franklyn brought to him and he chooses, _Into The Wild_. He watches the movie and then writes notes about it.

Movie: Into The Wild

Program: Status

The parents want to buy him a new car so that he is climbing socially along with others. This introduces a few other programs like competition and conforming to society.

Program: Power

The parents strive for power and consider money and status to be more important than their own experience. They influence their children into making choices aligned with their principles. The feeling of power helps them go through the game and play it for success regardless of how it affects their children.

Program: Attachment/Ownership

The parents try to find their son and keep searching for him as if they are hunting down something they own.

Program: Authority

The police will not allow Christopher McCandless to paddle down the river without a permit. Christopher does it anyway displaying a right to freedom, which is like a double-edged sword with the conscience as it is a display of disobedience as well, which promoted fear, anxiety, and anger.

Program: Power

Christopher McCandless decides to live off the land without a dependency on his family or society. But when he eats the poison berries, he feels powerless and scared. So, in turn, he continues to feed the conscience. His experiences with others, through conscience connected, were all emotional. <u>I think people try hard to live in harmony, with love and joy only. But that's not the way the game works because there needs to be balance. And that balance has an opposite as well, which is imbalance.</u>

Noah looks at the time and it is 9:35 pm. He is thirsty and a bit hungry. Nurse Esperanza has not returned with water or with the snacks he asked for.

Suddenly Franklyn walks in and Noah's eyes light up.

"Hey man, it's good you are back. I need your help," said Noah.

Franklyn hangs his outerwear, turns to Noah, and nods in acknowledgment.

"I asked Nurse Esperanza for water and a couple of snacks and she has not returned. Can you at least get me some water? I'm really thirsty," said Noah.

"Nurse crappy, huh? Sure man, I'll be right back," Franklyn replied.

He walks out of the room, only to return moments later with several snacks on hand and a few bottles of water.

Noah is relieved and grabs a bottle of water. He drinks it nonstop for several minutes.

Franklyn places a few snacks on Noah's tray table.

"The diner across the street is still open. Do you want me to get you a sandwich?" asked Franklyn.

"I can't. My stomach is not well," Noah replied.

Franklyn nods, slips off his boots, and sits.

"What movie did you watch?" asked Franklyn.

"*Into the Wild*," Noah replied.

"Cool, Noah, may I read what you wrote?"

"Yeah, Franklyn. Here you go."

Franklyn grabs Noah's notepad and starts reading as Noah eats his pudding. He stops eating for a moment and glances at Franklyn.

"Franklyn, I have a question."

"Sure, shoot," Franklyn replied.

"Let's say humanity was to change and live differently among each other. Do you think we can turn the tables on these extraterrestrials by living without negativity? You know, live only in love and peace."

"Ha! That's funny, Noah. We just talked about the energy of all emotions and the rules of balance. Are you asking if humanity can get together and recreate this game? I don't think so."

Noah smiles in humiliation.

"Yeah, I guess," Noah replied.

"Noah, I can't even fathom how that would be logical."

Noah grins and shrugs his shoulders.

"Franklyn, I just considered the thought but I see how it is illogical. You can't have positive without negative, or good without bad, and it's like that on purpose due to balance."

"That's a very logical statement, Noah."

"So, my purpose here is to find out that I am food for extraterrestrials; I die at some point in the game, and then it's all over," said Noah with disappointment.

"You speak as if you know what happens to the soul or energy within, after the vessel dies, Noah. *Did you forget that there is a part of you that is being consumed for reasons that you may not know? Perhaps it is not called the soul, possibly it is a source of energy that is trapped in the sentient being that is you. Maybe, the energy within us is utilizing consciousness to seek the absolute. Whatever it is, it is fact, that something in you is searching for knowledge and for truth.* You ran into some obstacles and some bullshit along the way, but now you are on track. *Whatever it is that's in you, is searching for truth that's inhibited by the NNP.* Perhaps, there is another game outside of this game as well, which involves the energy within you, consciousness, and these extraterrestrials. *Nonetheless, you want to leave this experience with knowledge, recognizing the emotions that are trying to consume you, level like a straight line, and in alignment with the truth that is within you. Death is only the end of your role and consciousness, not the soul within.* Noah, I refer to the experience and the game interchangeably. *The experience is a game and the game is an experience.* Death is just another program within the game, and that topic we have to cover in detail. There's much to learn about the program called death."

Noah nods agreeing with Franklyn.

"I'll be there soon, so, I need to learn about that one, Franklyn."

Franklyn nods and starts eating one of the snacks he brought back from the nurse's station.

Noah momentarily looks through his notes to gather his thoughts.

"I'm going to watch another movie, Franklyn; Do you want to watch one with me?"

"Sure, brother."

Noah chooses *Rocketman*. They watch the movie and fall asleep after it ends. Noah falls asleep sitting up on his bed and Franklyn sitting on his chair.

Nurse Esperanza walks in quietly and tucks in Noah. She shuts off the overhead lamp and stares at Noah for a few minutes with a smile on her face. With both hands to the ceiling, she brings her head down for several minutes, saying a prayer as if she is communicating with a higher power.

Franklyn farts loudly in his chair and mumbles a few words in his sleep.

Nurse Esperanza says with an expression of disgust, "Eww."

She walks quickly out of Noah's room and closes the door gently behind her.

*"Are you so egoistic to think
that we are the only sentient beings
at the top of the food chain?"*

Chapter 7: Where is your god now?

Noah wakes up to the sound of a rolling garbage bin. He opens his eyes slightly and sees the janitor walk into his room.

The janitor is getting the garbage together. He pushes Franklyn's chair out of the way and walks around to the garbage can by the desk.

"What the fuck is this!?" he murmured loudly.

The janitor slams Noah's bible on top of the desk drawer causing crystals to spill all over the floor. This startles Noah and Franklyn.

Noah opens his eyes with shock overcoming his face. He sits up to look over at his desk and sees the bible partially covered in pancake syrup. The janitor is looking at him with a flare of anger in his eyes, shaking his head. He slams the door closed as he walks out of Noah's room.

Franklyn sits up on his air mattress.

"Was that Jesus?" asked Franklyn.

Noah chuckles while staring at the door to his room.

"Maybe," Noah replied.

Franklyn stands up and extends his arms out in circles and stretches his sides and back. He yawns out loud, concealing the sound of his bones cracking.

"This vessel needs coffee!" he announced loudly.

Noah raises his hand gesturing that he agrees.

Franklyn props his air mattress against the wall and walks over to his chair to put his boots on.

"This place is like a senseless movie," he murmured.

He walks over to his outerwear and puts them on. While buttoning his coat, he looks over at Noah.

"Noah, do you want something to eat with that coffee?"

"I'll see how my stomach does with a corn muffin," Noah replied.

"The stomach is still affecting you?" Franklyn asked.

Noah nods, massages his belly, and says, "*The NNP.*"

There's a knock at the door and it opens right after. Noah is captivated by a familiar sweet smile.

"Well, hello sunshine, how – are – we - today?"

"Hi, Nurse Joy," Noah replied smitten.

"I'm here to take your vitals and to give you today's breakfast menu, Mr. Goatzee."

"Thank you, nurse, but my brother is getting breakfast for us today."

"Well-well-well, how nice are we?" she replied with a childish high-pitched voice.

Franklyn raises a brow and shakes his head.

"I would throw up but I don't have any food in this stomach," he muttered.

Nurse Joy is concerned about Franklyn and talks to him as if she is addressing a child.

"Oh no, would you like an antacid for your tummy, sir?"

Franklyn shakes his head walking out of Noah's room quickly and out of site.

Noah hears him yelling in the corridor, "Hey, hold the elevator!"

Nurse Joy and Noah lock eyes on each other, both smiling cheerily.

"Mr. Goatzee, I pray for you every day."

Noah offers a half-smile and nods his head with a sparkle in his eyes.

"Nurse, you are very pretty."

Nurse Joy holds her hands to her chest and looks away momentarily with a big smile.

"O-M-G, You just made my day, Mr. Goatzee," she replied with a big deep happy sigh.

"In my younger years, I would have asked you to have dinner with me," said Noah.

"Oh stop! Mr. Goatzee, you are making me blush. You are such a rascal!" she exclaimed.

They both giggled and then shared a moment of silence.

"Mr. Goatzee, you are a very handsome man and I would have been honored to have dinner with such a noble man," she said.

Noah smiles from ear to ear, captivated by Nurse Joy's beauty and her perfumed aroma.

Nurse Joy walks around Noah's room tidying up and abruptly exclaims, "Oh no! your bible is drenched with syrup! That's so terrible, Mr. Goatzee! I will hurry and get you another one!"

She takes the bible to the bathroom to wipe it down.

Noah hears her talking aloud through the running water.

"Oh my god, Jesus, Mary, please forgive us."

She walks out of the bathroom hastily and places the bible in her cart.

"Mr. Goatzee, I will be right back with that bible for you."

"It's ok, nurse. I have another one inside my desk drawer. That one must have fallen from the top of my desk and I didn't notice."

"Ok, Mr. Goatzee. I'm going to clean this one and make it nice in case you want it back."

She turns her cart around, walks out the door, and greets Mrs. Ansihl in the corridor.

"Well, hello, Mrs. Ansihl. You are here early."

She closes the door to Noah's room and continues to speak to Mrs. Ansihl in the corridor.

Noah hears Nurse Joy say his name. He becomes curious and starts eavesdropping.

"Yes, I know. It's so sad. He's such a nice man," said Nurse Joy.

"God's shining light will come down upon him and bless him," Mrs. Ansihl replied.

Noah knew they are talking about him and that the last day of his life was tomorrow. He takes a deep breath, stares at the shrine on his desk for several minutes, shrugs his shoulders, and smirks.

Noah grabs his notebook and starts reading his notes.

Movie: Rocketman - Elton John is one of my favorites.

Program: resentment, sadness, anger, disappointment

Scene: Elton's mom is resentful to his dad; he doesn't pay attention to Elton or to her.

He is a cold man riddled with emotions behind a wall he built. Our dad was a bit like that too. He would disappear for days, spending time with his other wife, children, and lovers he had on the side.

I watched a video online from this guy that seemed to be a bit drugged up. But he made sense talking about a man's penis. He said that the man's penis was like a horn. And that's where the word "horny" comes from, which makes sense. He said that the penis is evil because it contributes to procreation under the influence of being horny, which often causes a negative situation, like an unwanted pregnancy. Most of the time, the dad are deadbeats and the women have to fend for themselves. It's not easy to find a good man out there that will tend to their children. Last night, I asked Franklyn about his two boys. Franklyn said he was there for them consistently. He and his boys spent time together on weekends and during summer vacations mostly. He never missed a child support payment. I asked him why he left his ex-wife and he said, "Conscience connected." The conscience used him and his ex-wife to torment each other. Fucking conscience.

Program: Attachment, Ego

Elton wants to feel important and wants to feel good. He does everything he can to get his dad to notice him, hug him, and show affection. As a kid, Elton tries to listen to music with his dad but his dad ignores him. This eats Elton up even after he is rich and famous. He never recovers from this, not even after all the fame and wealth he collected.

Scene: Elton tries connecting to his dad after he became famous. He bought him a watch. I too have done things to obtain the reward of affection, like buying Megan that pendant. You can't buy love or affection because it doesn't last. There needs to be a balance, and positive emotions come with their negative counterparts. This up and down like a heartbeat leads to imbalance. It's this fuckin' game we live.

Program: Love, Faith, Attention

Scene: In most scenes, Elton is looking for love and attention. But all of the other characters are exactly the same except that the movie is focused on Elton so, you see more of it in his life. He believes that he will find love. With finding love, you often find its opposite as well. I too was looking for love, faith, and attention throughout my life.

It was so hard to find, so I distracted myself by joining the military. I loved the military because it is structured. And this connection to the conscience loves structure. The military was good to me and kept me busy. I wasn't good to many women, especially Megan. I just needed attention.

I would go to church whenever I felt like I was lost. But I wasn't only lost, I was uninformed because of the connection to the conscience and NNP.

Program: Status, Ego

Elton tries hard to become a rock star so he can obtain the love and attention he wasn't getting from his father. I too always wanted to be admired by those around me. I had a big ego and was a bit pompous, again, because of the NNP.

I lost track here because I was getting into the movie. Elton feels alone. He gets into relationships that are positive at first but have a negative outcome and this causes him to overdose on drugs. He finally finds someone he marries and continues playing the game we live. Can anyone only find the positive aspects of this game we live? Franklyn says, absolutely not, because there has to be balance and the opposite of positive is negative. He says that was done on purpose because the extraterrestrial intelligence that is at the top of the food chain feeds off energy. And just like cows are food for humans, humans are food for something else. That's logical according to the universal ecosystem.

Time goes by; Noah sits back with his notes in hand, he sees clearly how things didn't make sense in this game we live. He thinks about the words his brother said, *I KNOW WHAT THIS IS* and *I KNOW WHAT THIS IS NOT.*

"It's making sense," he whispered to himself while looking around his room, thinking about how tomorrow will be his last day in this game.

He exclaims loudly, "I am ready!"

Franklyn opens the door and walks into Noah's room carrying a brown paper bag and a plastic bag from a department store.

"Ready for what?" Franklyn asked.

Noah ignores the question.

"What's in the department store bag?" Noah asked.

"The best Bluetooth speaker money can buy," Franklyn replied.

Noah gestures with his head displaying curiosity.

"Why did you buy a Bluetooth speaker, Franklyn?"

"So, we can listen to music and entertain our chakras!" Franklyn exclaimed.

"Ha!… Ok, sure, brother," Noah replied shaking his head.

Franklyn hangs his outerwear and leaves his boots by the door. He walks over to Noah and gives him a muffin with a coffee.

Franklyn announces, "Muffin with a coffee, light and super sweet, sir."

"Thanks, brother," Noah replied.

Franklyn grabs Noah's rolling table and pulls it closer to the side of his bed.

"What are you thankful for, Noah?"

"Nothing. This connection to the conscience has me saying senseless shit for so many years now."

Franklyn grins while nodding.

"Noah, apply acting for social interactions and playing the game. You don't need to use these social expressions with me. Once you have found truth and your purpose, you will discover these social expressions are senseless anyway."

Franklyn takes a corn muffin and coffee out of the paper bag for himself and sits down.

"You got the same thing to eat?" asked Noah.

"Yep, but I only drink black coffee, sweet, no milk. The milk makes this vessel fart," Franklyn replied.

Noah laughs aloud while enjoying his corn muffin.

"May I see your notes from last night's movie?" asked Franklyn.

Noah nods as he passes his notebook to Franklyn.

Franklyn starts reading while nodding his head showing approval. Noah looks at him concerned that he is bound to find a mistake. After several minutes, Franklyn stops reading and passes the notebook back to Noah.

"Did you read the links I wrote down?" asked Franklyn.

Noah nods with certitude.

"Franklyn, how come you said that conscience and conscious are really the same?"

"Because they come from the same source. I'm going to read you this simple definition and then I will read from an article published by the *Journal Of Medicine*. The first simple definition is that both words come from the Latin word *conscius*; this word's element means *with* and *to know*.

Now let's read parts of the article from this journal: [*While consciousness has been examined extensively in its different aspects, like in philosophy, psychiatry, neurophysiology, neuroplasticity, etc., conscience though it is an equally important aspect of human existence, which remains an unknown to a great degree as an almost transcendental aspect of the human mind. It has not been examined as thoroughly as consciousness and largely remains a 'terra incognita' for its neurophysiology, brain topography, etc. Conscience and consciousness are part of a system of information that governs our experience and decision-making process. Consciousness is the function of the human mind that receives and processes information, crystallizes it, and then stores it or rejects it with the help of the following:*

1. The five senses
2. The reasoning ability of the mind
3. Imagination and emotion
4. Memory

The five senses enable the mind to receive information, then imagination and emotion process it, reason judges it, and memory stores or rejects it. We must remember that the mechanisms of 'consciousness' are complex and intricate, whereas the workings of 'conscience' are much simpler. The concept of 'conscience', as commonly used in its moral sense, is the inherent ability of every healthy human being to perceive what is right and what is wrong and, on the strength of this perception, to control, monitor, evaluate and execute their actions. Such values as right or wrong, good or evil, just or unjust, and fair or unfair have existed throughout human history but are also shaped by an individual's cultural, political, and economic environment.][47] I only read specific parts of this journal, Noah, and you had already read this entire article, right?"

Noah offers a nod of affirmation.

"Then, we can agree that these two words derive from the same source. Anyone can look up in their search engine, *Journal of Medicine* and *conscience + conscious* and locate this article," said Franklyn.

"What does *transcendental* mean?" asked Noah.

"It means spiritual, divine, or heavenly. What a more perfect way to confuse the shit out of humanity," Franklyn replied with a grin.

Noah blinks his eyes slowly and shakes his head.

"So, Noah, we will talk more about the conscience but for now, let's watch a movie. Which one do you want to watch?"

Noah pauses to think while looking down at his bed sheets.

"*Argo*!"

"Ok, let's watch *Argo*," Franklyn replied.

Noah places his coffee and corn muffin on the tray table by the side of his bed and starts looking through the bag of movies. He grabs the movie, *Argo*, and starts playing it on his computer. They watch the movie intently. Noah grabs his notepad, flips to a clean page, and starts writing.

A couple of hours go by and there is a soft knock at the door.

---

[47] https://www.ncbi.nlm.nih.gov/pmc/articles/PMC3956087/

It opens slightly and an elderly woman's face peeks around the door.

"Hello, may I come in?" she asked with a smile.

She had grey hair and was wearing rounded glasses.

"That all depends, who are you?" asked Franklyn with an annoyed tone.

Noah pauses the movie.

The elderly woman walks in holding a bible in her hand and with a shaky voice introduces herself.

"My name is Mrs. Margaret Ansihl. I am Mr. Ansihl's wife. My husband is the patient across the hall from your room, Mr. Godtz."

Franklyn looks at Noah in confusion.

"I think she's a hundred but I'm not sure," said Franklyn.

Noah looks at Franklyn with a frown, gesturing for him to stop making jokes.

"Hello, Mrs. Ansihl, very nice to meet you. I'm, Noah Godtz."

"I'm so sorry to trouble you boys but I wanted to come by and meet you, Mr. Godtz, and…", she nods at Franklyn unsure as to what to say.

Franklyn bows his head and exclaims with a divine tone.

"I am Jesus of Alaskareth!"

Noah interjects with a slight chuckle.

"My brother, Mrs. Ansihl, that's my brother, Franklyn Godtz."

Mrs. Ansihl disregards Franklyn's reply and smiles at Noah nodding her head as a sign of greeting.

"May I sit down, Mr. Godtz?" she asked.

She grabs a plastic chair and struggles to drag it closer to Noah's bed.

Noah looks at Franklyn and mutters, "A little help, brother?"

"Looks like she's got it," Franklyn replied.

Noah shakes and frowns in disappointment.

"Frown on you, they need the exercise!" Franklyn whispered loudly.

Franklyn continues to sip on his coffee and offers a blank stare at Mrs. Ansihl.

She sits down and takes a deep breath as if she just finished a long workout. She pulls a bible out from her purse with a rosary and touches Noah's arm with a smile.

"I would like to say a prayer for you, Mr. Godtz, if that's ok," she asked.

"We are Jewish!" Franklyn exclaimed boisterously.

Mrs. Ansihl is trembling with embarrassment.

"Oh, I am so... so sorry, please forgive me."

Noah frowns at Franklyn.

"We are reformed, Mrs. Ansihl, it's ok. Please go ahead and say your prayer," Noah replied.

"Are you sure it's ok, Mr. Godtz?" she asked.

Franklyn replies with sarcasm, "He's dying soon, so make it quick."

Mrs. Ansihl looks at Franklyn slightly annoyed with a frown.

"Excuse me?!" she exclaimed in a harsh manner.

Noah glances at Franklyn and mouths the word, stop.

"Don't pay him any mind, Mrs. Ansihl, please go ahead," Noah replied.

Mrs. Ansihl offers Franklyn a look of contempt and with a huff, starts flipping through pages in her bible. She has bookmarks sticking out various sections of the bible. Several minutes go by in silence and she unexpectedly exclaims with a fist in the air.

"Oh, yes! This one!"

She points eagerly to a page in her bible.

"God has just spoken to me, Mr. Godtz. This is the verse sent from the holy father for you."

She smiles and starts reading with an intense voice.

"Now there was a Pharisee, a man named Nicodemus who was a member of the Jewish ruling council. He came to Jesus at night and said, "Rabbi, we know that you are a teacher who has come from God. For no one could perform the signs you are doing if God were not with him…"[48]

As she continues to read, Franklyn's facial expressions change comically. Her voice becomes louder and more dramatic with each verse. And with a fist in the air, she cries:

"For God so loved the world that he gave his one and only Son! that whoever believes in him shall not perish but have eternal life! For God did not send his Son into the world to condemn the world, but to save the world through him. Whoever believes in him is not condemned, but whoever does not believe stands condemned already because they have not believed in the name of God's one and only Son. This is the verdict: Light has come into the world, but people loved darkness instead of light because their deeds were EVIL!"[49]

Mrs. Ansihl pauses to sneer at Franklyn with a frown. She looks over at Noah and changes her expression to a pleasant smile, puts her head down, and finishes reading the verse.

---

[48] https://www.bible.com/bible/compare/JHN.3.1-21
[49] https://www.bible.com/bible/compare/JHN.3.1-21

Noah looks at Franklyn with shock in his eyes while Franklyn shrugs and smirks.

"Would you like me to do a rosary prayer for you, Mr. Godtz?" she asked.

"Uh… uh, no, It's ok, Mrs. Ansihl, you-you should be with your husband," Noah replied with a stutter.

Mrs. Ansihl's face becomes obviously tense with a cold stare.

"He - is - sleeping," she uttered harshly.

She smiles and nods her head at Noah asking for permission. Noah looks at Franklyn with indecision.

Franklyn shrugs his mouth and shoulders.

"She must be bored," said Franklyn.

Mrs. Ansihl opens her eyes wide and points at Franklyn with a sneer.

"Sir, you are overtaken by Lucifer and his evil ways! You need to pray so that God can release you from this curse!" she exclaimed.

"What I need right this second is a lobotomy," Franklyn replied.

Noah looks at his brother shocked with embarrassment.

"Franklyn! Stop, brother!" Noah muttered.

While addressing Noah, Mrs. Ansihl tilts her head slightly with a firm stare at Franklyn.

"No need to worry, Mr. Godtz. I have the word and the will of God here in my hands," she said.

Franklyn disregards Mrs. Ansihl and focuses on his phone.

Mrs. Ansihl offers an intent stare at Franklyn holding her bible up in one hand. She rolls her shoulders back with her chest thrust out.

"I have dealt with the imps of Lucifer many times in my life!" she exclaimed.

"Since the Roman empire, right? Pontius Pilate? You met him?" Franklyn interjected with a smirk.

"I have a prayer for you, disciple of Lucifer, that will cast you out this window and out from this room!" she exclaimed.

Franklyn thrusts back firmly into his chair while yelling.

"Ouch!"

She gestures to Franklyn with anger in her eyes.

"This prayer will protect, Mr. Godtz from you, sir, and will help keep him in the light of God!"

"Oh… goodie," Franklyn replied sarcastically.

There is a pause for several minutes as Mrs. Ansihl skims through her bible. Noah is looking down at his bed sheet in discomfort.

Mrs. Ansihl notices the grim look of embarrassment on Noah's face. She pauses to tap on his arm expressing comfort.

"Don't worry, Mr. Godtz. I have dealt with the evil of Lucifer directly. I have the power of Christ within me," she said with a confident nod.

Mrs. Ansihl scoffs at Franklyn with disgust. Franklyn smirks and continues looking through his phone, ignoring Mrs. Ansihl.

She puts her hand on Noah's hand, comforting him, and addresses Noah with a calm, divine voice.

"Mr. Godtz, your first name, and last name are derived directly from the bible. Did you know that?"

Franklyn interrupts.

"No, it is not. The last name Godtz is not in the bible at all, in fact, the only derivation of that name is Götz, which is German, and that name is not in the bible either."

Mrs. Ansihl takes a deep breath in frustration.

"Sir! I thought I had expelled you! The name Godtz is indeed in the bible as I am holding it here in my hand as proof. This is the word of God!" she exclaimed.

"Our last name is not spelled G-O-D. It is Godtz, which is of German origin. You won't find it in that book you are holding," Franklyn replied firmly.

Mrs. Ansihl bats her eyes in frustration.

"Sir, I said I will find it and indeed will show you," she said with a poised voice.

Mrs. Ansihl starts flipping through pages in her bible.

A few minutes go by and Franklyn says, "I just searched on the internet through my phone, and the surname, Godtz, is not found in the bible, lady."

Mrs. Ansihl chuckles, clears her throat, sits back, and offers a strong stare at Franklyn as if she could beam a laser right through his head.

"The internet, sir, is full of evil and was created by the devil," she replied.

Franklyn smirks and says with a muttering voice, "Two very intelligent handsome devils named Larry and Sergey, so that's right."

Noah continues to glance back at Franklyn anxiously.

Mrs. Ansihl rubs Noah's arm offering comfort.

"Pray, Mr. Godtz. Pray every day for you and your brother. He is a lost cause you know. This room has evil in it! These pictures you have on your wall, these stones, and this incense. These are the tools of Lucifer!" she exclaimed.

Franklyn exclaims in a childish manner while shaking his head.

"Uh-Uh, Nurse Esperanza gave that to us and she's a certified level two reiki."

Mrs. Ansihl points at Franklyn and utters loudly with contempt.

"Oh, I see! That woman is lost you know! She's always upsetting my husband! She's rude and immoral!"

Franklyn smirks and looks down at his phone as if he's reading an interesting article.

Mrs. Ansihl puts her hand back on Noah's hand and speaks to him with a serene tone.

"Mr. Godtz, Nurse Joy has told me that tomorrow is your last day with us."

She starts gesturing as if she is crying, wiping her eyes but there were no tears.

Noah nods with a slight frown. She just reminded him that tomorrow is the day that Dr. Harpherd said he would die.

"Mr. Godtz, keep in prayer and know that your time of death is remarkably close to the birthday of our savior, Jesus Christ. That is very special and divine you know."

Franklyn interjects again.

"Actually, the day Jesus Christ was born was not on December 25th. There is research and facts that prove Jesus Christ was born sometime in the middle of June because the bible states in _Luke 2:7-8_,[50] that the shepherds were tending to a flock which only occurred during warmer months, not in December."

Mrs. Ansihl closes her bible firmly, sounding a loud clap.

---

[50] https://www.newsweek.com/december-25-really-day-jesus-was-born-what-bible-says-1270667

"Says the disciple of Satan!" she yelled.

"That's right! It means I was there! so, ha!" Franklyn exclaimed.

"Sir, the birth date of Jesus Christ is clearly in the bible. The power of God is not limited by the cold winter in December. The truth is in this book which you loathe so clearly," she replied.

"The proof is in the pudding. You need to read outside of that book and taste the facts," said Franklyn.

Mrs. Ansihl opens her bible and reads a verse.

"I will read a verse for you, wicked man."

She points at Franklyn with a sneer.

"Behold, I have given you authority to tread on serpents and scorpions, and over all the power of the enemy, and nothing shall hurt you!" [51]

She slams her bible shut, opens her eyes and nostrils wide, staring directly at Franklyn.

Franklyn massages his chest as if he were experiencing pain.

"Oh-no!"

Noah is frozen looking straight down at his bedsheets and he is clearly uncomfortable.

Franklyn addresses Noah firmly.

"Did you know that Christmas is actually a pagan holiday? Yep, it was the day the pagans celebrated Yule. You know, like the Christmas song that says, *make the yuletide gay…*"

Franklyn continues to speak to Noah glancing at Mrs. Ansihl intermittently.

"Yep, Every winter, Romans honored the pagan god Saturn, the god of agriculture, with Saturnalia, a festival that began on December 17, and

[51] https://www.bible.com/bible/compare/LUK.10.19

*usually ended on or around December 25, with a winter-solstice
celebration in honor of the beginning of the new solar cycle.*[52] Christmas
is actually a day celebrated by pagans and disciples of Satan, right,
Mrs. Ansihl? Wait a minute… are you a pagan, Mrs. Ansihl?"
asked Franklyn while staring at her suspiciously.

Mrs. Ansihl looks away quickly, opens her bible, and starts
whispering verses to herself.

"Did you know that the word Christmas is not in the Bible?[53] Yep,
not a chance in hell," Franklyn announced.

She continues to murmur a prayer.

Suddenly the voice of Mr. Ansihl saves her.

"Nurse! Nurse! Nurse! Where's my wife?! Get my wife now!"

Mrs. Ansihl stands up uneasily and stutters saying goodbye.
She touches Noah's arm, offers a warm smile, and starts walking
hastily while saying, "God be with you."

As she approaches the doorway, she glances back as if she was
going to say something else, but gestures to them with disregard
and quickly walks out of Noah's room.

Noah stares at Franklyn in disbelief, Franklyn shrugs his
shoulders and grins.

The cat across the hall is yelling loudly.

"Margaret! Where were you?! Ok, shut up and get me cold water!
I'm thirsty, can't you see that?!"

Franklyn says with a smirk, "The voice of god saved her."

Noah shakes his head in disbelief and chuckles with a timid
look.

"Noah, did you not realize all the gibberish and nonsense that

---

[52] https://www.history.com/this-day-in-history/christ-is-born

[53] https://thinkaboutsuchthings.com/facts-about-the-birth-of-jesus/

woman was talking?"

Noah nods his head and sighs.

"Franklyn, bear with me, I'm trying to adjust to this new way of thinking."

"Adjust to logic?! Adjust to the absolute?! Everything I pointed out to her was fact, Noah, but she wouldn't listen. These bible thumpers want to continue wearing blinders believing some bullshit that's not even true. They only continue to believe in a book full of lies because it gives them an excuse. When the shit hits the fan for them, they open their bible and depend on some god to fix their problems or save them. They take no responsibility for themselves. They don't research anything or try to seek knowledge. They depend on spiritual leaders to tell them what to do. Nurse Esperanza and Nurse Joy are two perfect examples brother, can't you see that?"

"I see it, Franklyn," he replied with fatigue.

"Noah, don't take my word for it, here's my phone and read those articles I just quoted from. Do your own research. Depend on yourself for knowledge, not on others."

Franklyn stands up and walks towards the exit door to Noah's room.

"How do we know these websites are writing facts?" asked Noah.

Franklyn closes the door firmly to Noah's room and turns to answer him.

"Good point, Noah. The author has all of the chapters and verses noted, including additional research with links cited in the article. The author of these articles took time to locate facts. And you should be doing the same."

"But I don't have much time left for research, Franklyn," said Noah with a defeated voice.

"That's true, but If you have doubt or a question on something specific, look it up. The information is within reach, all it takes is effort. You can use my phone since it's easier to surf the internet. Noah, the information and facts are out there if you want to find them. Just know that you have to read past the bullshit."

"Franklyn, how do I know what is bullshit and what is not?"

"The bullshit is usually masked with rhetoric, emotions, and trigger words. This is how humans are deceived, Noah."

Noah nods in agreement.

"Franklyn, can you help me to the bathroom, after that, I need you to help me back, so, I can get some sleep."

Franklyn nods, helps him to the restroom, and then back to bed. Noah falls asleep quickly. He closes the laptop, places it on the rolling table, then heads over to put on his boots and outerwear.

Franklyn walks out to the nurse's station to retrieve water and some snacks for Noah.

Noah wakes up momentarily; through his squinted eyes, he sees Franklyn leave his room. Noah hears the door close as he falls back asleep.

A few hours go by and Noah wakes up to the sound of Nurse Joy's voice.

"Well, hello, sunshine. I missed you," she whispered loudly.

Noah smiles like a kid that just got a reward.

She asks, "Are we having lunch today? Looks like the lunch lady came by and you were in a deep sleep. She left your lunch at the nurse's station. Are you hungry?"

"I would love to have a lunch date with you nurse; that would be my dying wish."

"Of course, Mr. Goatzee. I'll get your lunch warmed up and I have a sandwich for myself in the fridge. We will sit and have lunch together. That would be nice."

"Wow! That would be nice," Noah replied excitedly.

Nurse Joy hurries out of sight into the corridor.

Noah takes a deep breath and stares at his bed sheet for several minutes. He uses Franklyn's phone as a mirror to fix himself up and cover his bald spots as much as possible. He realizes he's acting illogically and whispers to himself, "Conscience connected, I know... fuck it! She's such a cutie."

Nurse Joy comes back in with Noah's food tray and closes the door behind her. She helps Noah clear his rolling table and speaks to him with pouty lips.

"You have me for thirty minutes, Mr. Goatzee. After that I'm sowwy, but I have to get back to work, Ok?"

Noah nods with a toothy smile.

He observes Nurse Joy and describes every aspect of her in his mind. "Curly blond hair, beautiful blue eyes, smile like an angel of light."

She was wearing a red tight sweater, black jeans, furry boots that go up to her calves, and smelled like flowers in heaven. Noah was smitten with Nurse Joy.

They start eating their lunch. Noah is eating a steak and potatoes and Nurse Joy is eating a hummus and chickpea sandwich.

Noah begins flirting with Nurse Joy.

"Is that how you stay so perfectly thin?" he asked.

She covers her mouth and giggles like a high school girl.

"Mr. Goatzee, you are so sweet. I don't eat meat, I'm a vegetarian."

"Is that the going diet for angels from heaven?" he asked.

Nurse Joy smiles ear to ear while blushing.

"Mr. Goatzee, you are such a player."

Suddenly, Franklyn walks through the door and stops himself halfway, stunned at the scene before his very eyes. He frowns and raises his arms holding takeout as if he is being robbed.

Noah looks up while chewing his food and smiles.

"Am I interrupting?" asked Franklyn with a grin.

"Mr. Goatzee and I are on a date. Don't be jealous now," she replied childishly.

"Oh, I'm trying really hard not to be," Franklyn replied sarcastically.

Noah laughs while covering his mouth full of food.

"Noah, I'll be back," said Franklyn.

"Come back in thirty minutes!" Noah exclaimed.

Franklyn yells out from the corridor, "Sure!"

Noah and Nurse Joy laugh. They small talk for a bit and finish eating their lunch.

Nurse Joy looks at the time on her phone.

"You still have me for fifteen minutes, Mr. Goatzee," she said.

"Please, call me, Noah."

Noah listens intently to Nurse Joy's cute voice as she speaks.

"Ok, Noah… that's such a beautiful name, so biblical."

"I love the way you say my name," said Noah.

Nurse Joy says with a playful voice, "Noah…"

They both laugh and Nurse Joy holds Noah's hand.

"Can you tell me a story about yourself?" she asked.

"I'll tell you about my time in Hawaii," he replied.

"Oh! I've never been. Is it beautiful?" she asked.

"Almost as much as you," Noah replied with glossy eyes.

Nurse Joy looks down bashfully and says excitedly, "Oh stop, Noah. So, c'mon tell me."

Noah tells her about the time he was stationed in Hawaii for the military. Fifteen minutes go by quickly and Nurse Joy interrupts Noah while talking.

"I'm sorry, Noah, but I have to get back to work. Is that Ok?"

Noah looks disappointed.

"Of course, you gotta work!" he exclaimed with sadness.

Nurse Joy stands up and starts tidying up. Noah is mesmerized by her beauty and her charm.

She pauses to look into Noah's eyes with a pleasant smile.

"Noah, this is the best date I have ever been on. Thank you."

She kisses Noah on his forehead and starts walking toward the door.

Noah exclaims, "Nurse!"

Nurse Joy turns around and looks at Noah with a smile.

"Ditto," he replied with a smile.

Nurse Joy winks at Noah. She turns towards the door and walks out.

Noah takes a deep breath and whispers, "Conscience connected."

Several minutes later Franklyn walks in.

"Dates over?" asked Franklyn.

Noah nods his head with a solemn look.

"It smells in here like all the cosmetic departments in the city blew up," said Franklyn.

Noah giggles and is still mesmerized.

"Man, oh man, what a beauty she is," said Noah.

Franklyn gestures with a shrug of his shoulders, he sits and starts eating a sandwich.

"You know, Franklyn, even if I weren't dying, she wouldn't date a guy like me anyway. I'm more than twice her age," Noah said with a melancholy voice.

"How do you know that? Who's going to help her with her math homework?" Franklyn replied.

Noah gestures to Franklyn with disregard.

"I remember when Megan and I first met," said Noah.

Franklyn interjects while blatantly shaking his head.

"You're talking nonsense, Noah. This is your connection to the conscience talking. Memories are part of the program, you know, the NNP. You get a pretty face before you that smells like sweet taffy on steroids and you lose track of your objective."

"Franklyn, I know that this so-called date was feeding the conscience. But that time with her felt good. Those thirty minutes felt good."

Franklyn glances at Noah, smirks, and continues to eat his sandwich.

A long silent moment goes by as Noah stares into space.

"You are right, Franklyn! Right now, I feel like shit because she's not here with me! I can still smell her![54] And I want to be intimate with her but I can't. I can feel these emotions feeding that fucking *Jabba The Hutt* son of a bitch!"

"Noah, If that's what you are looking for, those types of situations can be arranged; unless you are looking to marry her."

Noah frowns in disgust and disappointment.

"What are you saying, Franklyn? That she'll be intimate with me for financial gain? Like a whore?"

Franklyn shrugs while eating his sandwich and drinking water.

"That's a nice girl, Franklyn, she's not that type. You can tell she's a nice girl because she's religious and she's a vegetarian."

Franklyn laughs covering his mouth full of food and starts coughing. He pauses to drink water.

"Noah, You sound like Mrs. Ansihl. You are suddenly all-knowing. I think the powers of these crystals and Mrs. Ansihl's prayers have catapulted you into immortality."

"Nice thing to say to a guy that's dying," said Noah with discontent.

"She's dating Dr. Harpherd. I saw them one morning flirting with each other and holding hands," Franklyn replied.

Noah exclaims in shock, "What?!"

---

[54] https://www.ncbi.nlm.nih.gov/pmc/articles/PMC4010957/

Franklyn nods while chewing his food.

"Yes, Noah, they were carrying on, it was really early in the morning and you were sleeping. I think that's also why Nurse Esperanza was crying and quit her job the other day, remember? It seems that she's emotionally affected by Nurse Joy's relationship with Dr. Harpherd."

Noah puts his face in his hands with disbelief.

"What's the matter, Noah? Do you feel you were seduced unjustly? I thought you felt good. How does it feel now? *The truth doesn't blend well with the emotional tundra. It tends to stick out noticeably.*"

Noah has a look of disgust on his face and says, "Fucking conscience."

Mrs. Ansihl yells in the corridor, startling Noah and Franklyn.

"My God, someone please help my husband, please! He can't breathe!"

Suddenly doctors and nurses are running into Mr. Ansihl's room. Noah scoots over to peek into his room but they close the door.

Franklyn doesn't react and continues to eat his sandwich.

Mrs. Ansihl comes into Noah's room from the corridor, she looks at Noah in tears and says in a crying voice, "He needs help! I think he's dying!"

Franklyn replies, "Where's your God now?"

*"The truth doesn't blend well
with the emotional tundra.
It tends to stick out noticeably"*

Chapter 8: The games within the game *(it's like an onion)*

Noah wakes up to the song, *White Rabbit,* playing from the speaker Franklyn purchased. The volume is low but you can still hear it.

Noah is singing along quietly, "Ta - ta – tarara, tara ta - ta - tarara, *one pill makes you larger* …"

The door opens abruptly and Nurse Esperanza walks in pushing a rolling cart. She looks at Noah, offers a poignant smile, picks up her clipboard, and writes for a moment. Noah smiles and stares at her, she has a troubled look.

Nurse Esperanza says with a crackle in her voice, "I need to take your vitals, and here is the menu for breakfast," she then clears her throat.

She asks Noah to shut off the music. Noah shuts off the speaker and notices the serious look as she takes his vitals.

Franklyn wakes up and sits up on his air mattress. He rubs his face with his hands repeatedly and sniffs his armpits.

"This body smells," he announces.

Noah giggles and Nurse Esperanza glances a smirk at Franklyn.

"There's a shower on this floor you might be allowed to use, sir. I can ask if you want," she said.

Franklyn waves his arms gesturing with disregard.

"I'll go home later today and take a shower," Franklyn replied.

She smiles at Franklyn coquettishly.

"What do you do for fun, sir?" she asked.

Franklyn looks at her and points to himself inquisitively.

"Yes, you," she replied with a flirtish smile.

"I don't do anything," he said.

"You don't have a girlfriend? You don't go on dates? How do you entertain yourself?" she asked.

"I'm asexual, like an amoeba. That's actually the title of my religion," he boorishly replied.

She smirks at Franklyn and sees Noah shaking his head.

"Mr. Godtz, Your brother lives in a shell. He needs to get out and have some fun," she said.

"Why don't you ask him on a date?" asked Noah with a playful smile.

She squints with a grin, then looks at Franklyn with a sarcastic smile.

"I would if he would come out of his shell," she said.

"Go look under someone else's shell. I'm not interested," Franklyn replied harshly.

Nurse Esperanza's expression changes to disappointment. She abruptly turns her rolling cart to the door and leaves the room.

Noah looks at Franklyn and shakes his head in disappointment.

"Remind me again why you are six foot six and attractive?" asked Noah.

"I'm not fooled by the games the conscience plays. *I play the game; the game doesn't play me*. My objective is to strategize until I leave the game, Noah."

"So, you can't have a little fun while strategizing? She's attractive, Franklyn, she just wears a lot of makeup but she clearly doesn't need it."

"Say that again and think logically about what you are saying, Noah. No one is not going to illuminate my path with strategy, especially that woman."

Noah shrugs his shoulders and looks around his room.

"What time is it?" asked Noah.

Franklyn looks at his phone.

"It's 7:20 am."

Noah looks around his room as if he is lost.

"What day is it today?" asked Noah.

"It's Monday, Noah, December twenty-third. Would you like to go out to do some Christmas shopping?"

Noah chuckles while shaking his head.

Franklyn places his air mattress against the wall and goes into the bathroom closing the door. The sound of the faucet comes on slightly muffling Franklyn's farting. Noah smirks and sits up on his bed staring at his notebook.

Moments later Franklyn comes out of the bathroom drying his face and hands with brown paper towels. He walks over to put on his outerwear and boots.

Noah announces aloud, "Today's the big day."

Franklyn starts thinking while buttoning his coat.

"Cyber Monday?" he asked.

"No, Franklyn, today's the eighth day, my last day in the game."

"Lucky you," he replied.

"I don't feel that way," Noah replied with a sad tone.

Franklyn shrugs his shoulders and remains expressionless.

"The word, *feel*, in your response, tells me you are emotional. It's sensible for you to feel emotional because of the NNP. Try to comprehend the truth of what's happening to you," Franklyn replied.

Noah looks distraught as he observes his surroundings.

"I have a question, Franklyn."

"Write that down, Noah, and ask me when I get back. Coffee, pancakes, or muffin?"

Noah shakes his head.

"My stomach is not well, Franklyn. I think I'm just going to have some water and maybe an apple sauce."

Noah continues to massage his stomach. Franklyn notices that Noah is losing considerable weight.

"Ok, Noah, I'll be back."

Noah nods as Franklyn leaves the room.

Time goes by and Noah is looking through the music playlist. He chooses the song, *Someone Saved My Life Tonight by Elton John*. He hears a rolling cart coming closer to his room and sees the janitor peek in from the corridor.

The janitor steps slightly into the doorway visibly upset.

"Hey, I'm not picking up the garbage in this room, you hear me?! You need to have respect for Jesus, the father, and religion! You are a disgrace, sir, and will burn in hell unless you ask Jesus for forgiveness! You need help from a priest!" the janitor wailed.

Noah smiles and exclaims, "I am a priest! Please, come here and speak to me, my son."

The janitor frowns and looks at Noah confused.

"Excuse me?!" he replied aloud.

Noah gestures with his hand for the janitor to come closer.

"Come closer, I'm a chaplain," Noah stated.

The janitor walks closer, holding an empty plastic garbage bag in his hand.

"You are a chaplain, sir?" he asked with a frown.

"Yes, my son," Noah replied in a divine tone.

The janitor looks at Noah suspiciously.

Noah smiles and speaks with a gentle voice.

"That was not a bible of god in the garbage, my son, that was a bible of heresy. A bible that my brother brought to me as a gift to try and change my beliefs," said Noah.

The janitor opens his mouth and eyes wide in shock.

"Are you fucking kidding me? And all this shit on the wall and on your desk are his, too?" he asked.

"Yes, I'm afraid so, my son," Noah admittingly replied.

The janitor shakes his head and his voice becomes aggressive.

"Mother fucker! Your brother's head is fucked up, sir. I'm sorry to say this but you need to set him straight."

The janitor pleasantly smiles at Noah while cleaning up and gathering the garbage.

Noah smiles intently and suddenly Franklyn walks in.

The janitor storms out of Noah's room but he stops for a moment to snarl at Franklyn.

"You are sick, sir! You need help!" he exclaimed.

The janitor walks out of the room and waves a friendly goodbye to Noah from the corridor.

Franklyn looks at Noah puzzled.

"He looks familiar. Is that Nurse Esperanza's shaman?" he asked with a smirk.

Noah giggles for several minutes while rubbing his belly.

"No, Franklyn, that's the janitor. He thinks all this spiritual shit is yours. He's pissed because he found the bible in the garbage."

Franklyn grins, takes off his outerwear, sips on coffee, and walks over to sit down.

"What was your question, Noah?"

Noah starts flipping through the pages of his notebook until he finds his question.

"Is it ok… no, scratch that, logical to just accept the game the way it is?"

"Sure, you can accept it but it's not logical," Franklyn replied.

"Well, Franklyn, is it possible that we are supposed to be this way and play the game like this and not be so logical?"

"You mean to be emotional and accept emotions for what they are, along with the NNP, id, ego, and superego? Well, Noah, that would be the game playing you, not you playing the game."

Noah nods with a grin.

"Yes, Franklyn."

Franklyn gathers his words and thoughts while chewing on an egg burrito.

"And how's that working for you?" asked Franklyn.

Noah pauses for several minutes while looking down at his notebook.

"It's not," said Noah.

"Why?" asked Franklyn.

Noah looks upset. His face is red from frustration.

"Because I'm dying, and I don't want to die," Noah replied.

"Well… time is death, Noah. After someone is born, time decides their death. There is no difference between a person on their deathbed or someone that was born yesterday with the exception of time. But hypothetically, let's pretend for a moment you weren't on your deathbed. Can we do that?" asked Franklyn.

Noah nods in acknowledgment.

"And let's say you were somewhere out there doing fieldwork or I don't know; what did you do at 10:45 am on a Monday, Noah?"

"Probably home, watching television, drinking coffee," Noah replied.

"Ok, so, you are home on a Monday, watching television, drinking coffee. And you have all this knowledge and information, how would you decide to play the game?" asked Franklyn.

"I guess, I would just accept it for what it is and live my life," Noah replied.

"Well, it's not really your life if you logically think about it, otherwise it would be your choice to keep it. Noah, *don't be a fool, you don't own a fucking thing, not even your own life.*"

Noah nods in agreement.

"What would you be accepting, Noah?"

Noah replies as if he is complaining.

"That I was lied to about God and a higher power. That all religions and belief systems are based on emotions and bullshit. That it is possible we serve as food for extraterrestrials because of a universal ecosystem, and this place can be pretty fucked up most of the time, but sometimes Franklyn, this place is not so fucked up and I enjoy it."

Noah pauses and exclaims in a strong voice.

"And Franklyn, that's ok!"

Franklyn stares at Noah in thought. He knows he is faced with a decision to say something that's going to cause Noah to experience internal anarchy. He sits back and takes a sip of coffee.

"Then why don't you accept your death as a time in your life that's pretty fucked up? You did have some good times in your life, right? So, there goes your balance," Franklyn replied.

Franklyn takes another bite off his egg burrito, crosses his legs, and stares at Noah while chewing.

Noah puts his face into both his hands in frustration. He looks up at Franklyn stressed with tearful eyes.

"Franklyn, you sure know how to fuck someone's head up. You should have been a psychologist, not a lawyer."

Franklyn continues eating his breakfast and drinking his coffee with a blank expression on his face.

A long time goes by without Noah or Franklyn saying a word. The song, _Goodbye Stranger by Supertramp_ is playing slightly in the background.

Noah takes a drink of water and rubs his belly. He glances over and sees that Franklyn is on his phone, reading.

"The game is not fair," Noah announced.

"The game is not supposed to be fair. That's like everything in nature, including all the animals we eat, saying to humanity, it's not fair that

you feed on us. Humanity won't stop eating, Noah."

"It just doesn't make sense," said Noah with a crying voice.

"It doesn't, for Noah and the rest of humanity. *Everything in the game is logical for those that created the game.*"

Noah looks at Franklyn with watery eyes and speaks with a shaking voice.

"What if there was something greater, Franklyn? Perhaps a god that's on our side; something that is truly benevolent? Something that is truly bound to come and save us from all this bullshit?"

"What if... *If grandma had balls, she'd be grandpa.*[55] A god that is only benevolent cannot exist in this game. There has to be a balance. The game wasn't created in your favor, Noah. You are not making sense."

Noah cries looking around as if he is disoriented; gasping for air he throws up on himself.

Franklyn grabs a towel from Noah's desk drawer and starts wiping him down. He presses the nurse call button.

Several minutes go by and Nurse Esperanza walks in.

"What's wrong with Mr. Godtz?"

The nurse sees that Noah is having trouble breathing and he is hyperventilating.

Nurse Esperanza tells Franklyn, "Sir, please wait outside."

She calls for Dr. Harpherd. A few other nurses and doctors start tending to Noah. The door closes and Franklyn is standing in the corridor drinking his coffee.

He peeks into the cat across the hall's room and notices he is on a respirator.

---

[55] https://en.wiktionary.org/wiki/if_my_grandmother_had_balls,_she%27d_be_my_granddad

Franklyn whispers to himself, "Mr. Ansihl and Noah must be racing to the finish line."

Franklyn goes to the hospital gift shop.

A few hours go by and Franklyn decides to go back to Noah's room. He's planning to gather his things and go home.

Franklyn walks into Noah's room and notices the overhead lamp is off. Noah's eyes are closed and he is wearing an oxygen mask. He is on a heart monitor and has an I.V. attached to his arm.

Franklyn walks quietly to his outerwear and starts putting them on. He hears Noah's faint voice.

"Where are you going?"

"I'm going to say goodbye, Noah. I need a shower and I won't be back. Being here is illogical for both of us, anyway."

Noah moves his oxygen mask off his nose to his chin.

"That's it? You're not going to teach me anymore?" asked Noah.

"There's nothing more to teach, Noah. I gave you all of the knowledge and information you need."

Noah frowns in disappointment.

"But we haven't talked about the program, *death*?"

Franklyn hangs his outerwear, walks over to sit in his chair, and stares at Noah.

"Franklyn, there's something I don't get. So, god is a construct and all this other spiritual bullshit is a construct too. Can you tell me, how do we come to believe that there are extraterrestrials feeding on the energy within us? *And, is it possible that this idea of the conscience is a construct too?*" Noah asked with a grainy voice.

"Noah, everything in this experience which I refer to as the game is a construct."

Noah opens his eyes wide with a big smile as if he has found a hole in Franklyn's theory.

"Then, Franklyn, this theory that *the conscience is a feeding source created by extraterrestrials* is also a construct!"

"Yes, Noah. But let's analyze this with logic and facts, shall we?"

Noah gestures yes, by blinking subtly.

"Since 2021, the news and the government have been admitting about extraterrestrial life and its presence. Now in 2024, we have seen these aliens. Humans have interacted with these aliens called the Czentarians. Aren't these extraterrestrials sentient beings of higher intelligence? What the devil are they doing in the hell's kitchen of the solar system?" asked Franklyn.

"Yes, they are super intelligent compared to humans. Have you met one of them up close, Franklyn?"

Franklyn chuckles shaking his head firmly.

"No, Noah. And I don't want to either. I've only seen them on television and that one time on the *Opah Godfrey talk show*. Who knows why suddenly they are here? Their presence here is what doesn't make sense; perhaps they are sizing up their cattle? Using humans for lab testing?[56] I have no proof of this, though."

Noah has a burst of slight laughter and coughs for a few minutes.

"Are these fuckers planning to cook and eat us?" asked Noah.

Franklyn shrugs his shoulders with a smirk.

"I think they have been, Noah. But they may not necessarily feed themselves the way humans do. Regardless, we need to get back to the facts."

"Ok," said Noah.

---

[56] https://www.ncbi.nlm.nih.gov/pmc/articles/PMC7121572/

"Let's talk about the conscience again and keep in mind, that words do contain triggers for programs as we previously talked about. Words trigger our emotions. It is a component of the programming we deal with daily in this game," said Franklyn.

Noah has an intense look on his face. He nods his head emphatically.

"The word conscience split up into its syllable form means, *against science*. But let's start by reading the definition of the word *conscience* from etymology online, Noah"

Noah nods with encouragement.

"Ok, it says, [*faculty of knowing what is right, originally, especially to Christian ethics, later awareness that the acts for which one feels responsible do or do not conform to one's ideal of right, later (late 14c.) more generally, sense of fairness or justice, moral sense.]*[57] Let's keep this in mind combined with the fact that the social construct has become overtaken by greed, self-importance, *self-preservation, moral relativism, eugenics,* and *Social Darwinism*, right?"[58]

Noah nods in agreement.

"Yes, that's that guy on *YouTube* you showed me that talks about *self-preservation, moral relativism, eugenics, and Social Darwinism*[59] being a bad thing," Noah replied.

"Yes, but *the confusion sets in when these presenters of spirituality use emotions to capitalize and manipulate their followers.* This is also the illogical nature of spiritual teachers like *Abraham Hicks* and *Alan Watts*; they capitalize on emotions through the program - *motivation*. Even the very word, *motivation*, is emotional. It's important to also observe their egos and rhetoric when they are addressing their followers. We talked about this before, Noah."

"Yes, Franklyn, I remember."

"Ok, so, we have a definition of conscience that is specifically

---

[57] https://www.etymonline.com/search?q=conscience+

[58] https://truthscrambler.com/2017/05/12/demystifying-the-occult-mark-passio/

[59] https://www.youtube.com/c/MarkPassio

aligned with emotions and the NNP. Do you agree, Noah?"

"Yes, Franklyn."

Franklyn continues to search on his phone for more definitions.

"Ok, let's split up the word conscience into syllables. I just looked up the word, *con*, in the etymology dictionary, it says, "[**negation**; *in the negative; the arguments, arguers, or voters* **'against a proposal'** *(mainly in pro and con), Latin contra* **'against'***]*"[60]. So, the word *con*, means, *against*."

Franklyn shows Noah the article on his phone.

"But Franklyn, there are other meanings as well for the word *con*. It has another meaning written there too, it says, [*to study, get to know, peruse carefully, make an attempt, try or seek to do, from Old English cunnian to know, Related: Conned; conning.*]"

"Yes, there are two meanings that are complete opposites, one is positive, however, related to *conned*, and the other is negative. Let's continue researching and keep both these meanings of the word, *con*, in mind," Franklyn replied.

Noah agrees.

"So, if we were to take the first meaning of the word, *con*, and combine it with the word, *science*, it would mean, *against science*. Are you still with me, Noah?"

"Yes, Franklyn, please continue. I'm interested to see where this ends up."

"Indeed, Noah. Ok, so let's now look up the word science in the etymology dictionary. It says [**state or fact of knowing**; *what is* **known, knowledge** *(of something)* **acquired by study; information**; *also* **assurance of knowledge**, *certitude,* **certainty**, *from Old French* **science knowledge**, **learning**, *application; corpus of* **human knowledge** *from Latin scientia knowledge, a* **knowing; expertness**, *from sciens (genitive scientis)* **intelligent**, *skilled, present participle of*

---

[60] https://www.etymonline.com/search?q=con

scire to know.]" [61] So, the word, *con*, means *against* and the word, *science*, means *knowledge*. The word <u>conscience means against knowledge</u>."

Noah nods while focused on what Franklyn is reading.

"Now let's look back at that secondary meaning of the word, *con*, which means, *to know*, or *to study, get to know*. Let's combine these with the etymology definition of science, so, we get the following, *to know knowledge*, or *to know the study*, or *to know the get to know*. It doesn't seem to combine sensibly, Noah, this secondary definition of the word, *con*, is pretty much the same as the word, *science*. Perhaps you can say *seek knowledge* or *to get to know knowledge*. The former one, *seek knowledge*, strikes me as more sensible.

However, do you feel that humanity is being given the tools to really seek knowledge? Do you feel that society and government are truthful to you and keep nothing from you? Or did you often feel in this life that knowledge was kept from you or hidden? Of course, taking into consideration the lies coming from the news media. Note that the second definition of *con*, you pointed out, has the statement, *Related: Conned; conning*, which means to swindle or trick."

"You are fucking right, Franklyn."

Noah starts gasping and puts his oxygen mask back on.

"We are not done with our research, Noah. Let's remain calm and focused."

Noah nods in agreement.

"So, conscience means, against *humans* having knowledge. However, the definition of this word is totally different from these two words separately, *Con* and *Science*, and it makes sense that this is for the purpose of the game. Noah, how better to control humanity by keeping us stupid and blind, effectively leading us into bondage."

Noah keeps taking his mask off to speak.

---

[61] https://www.etymonline.com/search?q=science

"But humanity is not enslaved, Franklyn. Humanity is not building brick temples with soldiers whipping us to work harder."

"It's a different type of bondage, Noah, but within the game, there are other games. For example, new age spiritualists view _Uncle Sam_ as a slave driver, but I disagree, I only see _Uncle Sam_ as a component of the game. Though, that's a distraction I don't want to get into right now. I want to stay focused on the conscience as that is where our attention should be focused."

Noah puts his mask back on and nods his head.

"So, we have acknowledged the following: _Conscience, Nature, Nurture, Programming (NNP), ID, Ego, Superego, and Emotions._ All of which we resonate with as humans in the _game of life_. These collaborate with our human genome, right?" asked Franklyn.

"Yes, Franklyn, we researched that this was also part of our DNA."

"That is correct, Noah! And our DNA is directly affected by the NNP, follow me?"

"Yes, Franklyn, that is correct."

Franklyn looks at Noah for a moment and grins.

"Noah, everything that we are works against us; our DNA, our vessel, NNP, id, ego, and superego. These are the components of The Conscience and these components are used to manipulate humanity. This, of course, is the process used by the extraterrestrials to feed on our energy also known as...,"

Noah and Franklyn reply in unison, "_The soul._"

"So, Noah, do you believe this to be a construct of the mind equal to that of having faith in a god or higher power?"

"Not at all the same, Franklyn. What we talked about right now is true with facts. We can see this, and we experience this, heck I've seen those ugly critters on television from Planet Czentar as well."

Noah coughs for a few minutes then continues to speak.

"But I've never seen God, a god, or a higher power. I've prayed many times and it was hit or miss with those prayers but when a prayer was answered, that was a coincidence. I believed it to be an answer to my prayer from god because of the NNP. So, it's not the same at all, Franklyn. What you are saying to me makes sense and it is logical. A god is illogical and it makes more sense it is a fallacy[62], just like these crystals, oils, and this stupid shrine I put together."

He continues to cough and gasp as he speaks.

"I always had people tell me that I need to feel it, that I need to believe and have faith, but that's driven by emotions."

Franklyn grins and nods his head.

"Hey brother, this body is not feeling too good, do you mind if I knock out for a bit?" asked Noah.

"Not at all, Noah. I'll take a walk around the neighborhood and look at the pretty colors and decorations. I'll spend time observing the construct of Christmas."

Franklyn and Noah laugh out loud.

Noah puts on his oxygen mask, closes his eyes, and falls asleep quickly. _The Logical Song by Supertramp_ is playing lightly on the speaker. Franklyn stops the music, tucks his brother in, and closes the door as he walks out of the room.

Franklyn looks to the left and sees Nurse Esperanza talking to another nurse. The other nurse looks stressed out. He peeks into the room where the cat across the hall is being tended to by hospital personnel. There are more flowers, and balloons in his room. There is a woman sitting close to him, but it's not Mrs. Ansihl. She looks upset and is reading a newspaper not really paying attention to what's going on around her. Many people are standing around his bed talking to each other.

Franklyn turns to the right to walk toward the elevator and bumps into a priest. He seems in a hurry and has a strong scent of

---

[62] https://writingcenter.unc.edu/tips-and-tools/fallacies/

liquor on his breath. The priest offers a half-smile, and takes a deep breath as if to say, "Here I go again."

Franklyn offers a fake smile to the priest. He whispers to himself, "*All the worlds indeed a stage*."

He finally gets to the elevator and the doors open immediately. Dr. Harpherd walks out with a binder under his arm.

Franklyn says with a monotone voice, "Hi doctor, how are those nurses?"

Dr. Harpherd doesn't acknowledge Franklyn and keeps walking hastily.

As Franklyn walks into the elevator and presses the button for the lobby, he can hear Dr. Harpherd in the background yelling, "Nurse Esperanza! I need to see you in my office now, please!"

The elevator doors close, muting the sounds of the eighth floor.

Franklyn returns from his walk and the time is 7:02 pm. The elevator doors open on the eighth floor, and he walks down the corridor into Noah's room.

Noah is sitting up on his bed looking at his computer and eating from a fruit cup.

"You look relieved," said Franklyn.

"They gave me medication. I was all backed up and my lungs are not well. How was your walk?" asked Noah with a grainy voice.

"Short, I ended up going home. I threw out a lot of stuff and took a shower," Franklyn replied.

"Are you moving out?" asked Noah.

"Something like that. What are you looking at?" asked Franklyn.

"The guest Wi-Fi is working again. I'm reading up on the things we discussed. I read these articles on the difference between conscience and conscious."

Franklyn sits, leans over, and reads audibly.

"What Does Conscience Mean? The noun conscience refers to a state of awareness or a sense that one's actions or intentions are either morally right or wrong, along with a feeling of obligation to do the right thing. Cartoons often personify the conscience as a proverbial angel/devil pair who talk into the ear of an indecisive character, encouraging him or her to follow either a path of moral virtue or of moral corruption. In the Walt Disney movie Pinocchio, metaphorically, the conscience is the dapper talking cricket, named Jiminy Cricket, whose maxim [always let your conscience be your guide]. he teaches the title character, a marionette who is magically brought to life and becomes a real human boy after proving himself brave, truthful, and selfless (after listening to his conscience)."[63]

He looks at Noah, grins, and continues to read aloud.

"Conscious, on the other hand, is an adjective that indicates that a person is awake and alert and able to understand what is happening around them, such as a patient who becomes fully conscious after being administered anesthesia. It can also imply that a person is aware of a particular fact or feeling, such as an investor who is conscious of risk or athletes who are conscious of being role models for young people. Another common meaning of conscious describes a person who cares about something specified, such as the cost-conscious shopper and the environmentally conscious activist. Additionally, [consciousness] can modify an act or decision that is done deliberately (and one that might very well result in conscious guilt or a guilty conscience)"[64].

Franklyn grins and says, "Noah, we talked about the origin of these words coming from the root word, *Conscius*. Keep in mind that, *when you are searching for truth, there's a whole lot of bullshit you'll need to shovel out of the way.*"

Noah nods in agreement.

"Franklyn, can we take a break and listen to some music?"

"Sure, Noah."

---

[63] https://www.merriam-webster.com/words-at-play/usage-of-conscience-vs-conscious

[64] https://www.merriam-webster.com/words-at-play/usage-of-conscience-vs-conscious

Noah asks Franklyn for his phone. He accesses the audio streaming playlist, I.AMUSIC and chooses the song, _Midnight Blue_.

Franklyn reaches into a shopping bag by Noah's desk, takes out a bottle of wine, and opens it up. He walks to the exit door, closes it, and walks over to Noah handing him an empty glass of wine.

They sing along to several songs on the playlist including (_Subdivisions, Limelight, Freewill, Hotel California, I've Seen All Good People, Sympathy For The Devil, Rocketman,_ and _Take It To The Limit_), while Franklyn drinks red wine and Noah drinks water from his wine glass.

Noah pauses the last song on the phone and starts sobbing. He's experiencing another emotional outburst. But this time it's different from previous ones.

"This fucking connection to conscience!" Noah exclaimed.

He starts talking about Megan in a crying voice.

"I loved her, Franklyn. I used to massage her body and feet with exotic oils every weekend. I looked forward to that, Franklyn. Her feet were perfect, like an angel's feet and white as snow. Her body was so perfect like no other. The picture of her smile is pasted in my mind, and her smile was beautiful, it would light up my day no matter how grey it was. I did wrong to her! I did wrong to her, Franklyn!"

Franklyn sits down looking at Noah with a poker face.

"Noah, what did you do to Megan?"

"I killed our baby," Noah replied.

"What? How did you kill your baby?" asked Franklyn.

Noah sighs and wipes his face with his forearm.

"When she was pregnant, I put a pill in a cup of juice she was drinking. The pill was supposed to induce an abortion," said Noah.

Noah starts crying uncontrollably and starts screaming in a crying voice, "I killed my baby! I killed my baby!"

"Calm down, Noah, there's nothing you can do about that now. That was the past, you are not responsible for the programming that manipulated you, brother. We need to look at this logically and not emotionally. *The conscience wants you to leave this game thinking you did bad things! It wants you to take all this emotional negativity with your energy when you die!*"

Noah nods his head agreeing but has a look of defeat.

"Noah, are you ready to talk about this logically?"

Noah nods again with eyes full of tears.

"Sure, Franklyn."

"Noah, why didn't you use birth control or condoms?"

"She was on birth control pills, Franklyn. I don't know what happened."

"Well, that doesn't matter now anyway, Noah, isn't Megan married? She has kids now, right? She is living her experience as if nothing ever happened and not thinking about that miscarriage. You don't even know if that pill you gave to her was the reason for the miscarriage. Who gave you this pill anyway?"

"This guy named Joseph from my field team," Noah replied with a hoarse voice.

"Noah, how do you know if what this guy gave to you actually worked? These pills have a threshold and after that, it doesn't work. You were reacting to the NNP that prompted you to do that. Can you remember why you didn't want a baby? Was there someone else? Were you scared to have a baby?"

"There wasn't someone else. I just didn't think I was ready for a baby, Franklyn. I wasn't ready. I wasn't ready to leave the military and get a job, buy a house with a white picket fence and have a family. Heck, I wasn't even ready for marriage! I loved her so much and she was perfect, but I wasn't ready! I don't know why."

"Noah, that program was installed in you since you were a child. *The game's like an onion*. You were nurtured to think that attachment was a bad thing, which is emotional. Attachment is neither good nor bad. Think about it, brother, our mother and father were emotionally imbalanced! Our mother was drunk half the time and absolutely nonfunctional. Our father was out all the time sowing his wild oats. He had another family we never even met! The act of you giving her that pill was a program that stems from the NNP. *You are not responsible for how the NNP manipulated you*. You are not responsible for the miscarriage."

"Is this the part where I ask if Jesus died for our sins?" asked Noah while chuckling forcefully.

"Noah, forget about that nonsense. All that bullshit leads to more emotional outbreaks. *It's the NNP that manipulates and induces our emotions; that is what feeds the extraterrestrials through our connection to the conscience*! All that shit happened due to the nature of your being, combined with how you were nurtured, and then brainwashed with programming throughout this experience. Let me ask you this."

Noah wipes his tears and nose with the bed sheet.

"What?"

"If you weren't on your deathbed and you were out there still with Megan, would you have done the same thing if she was expecting a baby? Would you have given her that pill?" asked Franklyn.

"Of course not! I would...", Noah pauses for a moment.

"I would play the game, teach her and my kid about the game and how to play it. I would invest the time here to do what I need to do because, in that situation, I would not have been ready to leave the game. I would have to work hard on myself because this whole, *don't be emotional*, be like a robot logical shit, is not easy my brother. It's not easy," bellowed Noah with a crying voice.

"I know. It's not supposed to be. *The game was created to play with us and feed on our energy.* And logically you also need to accept that family and tribe, are part of the game, Noah."

"I agree. I thought I was doing better, Franklyn, but I keep taking one step forward and two steps back."

"Noah, *When you are searching for truth, there's a whole lot of bullshit you'll need to shovel out of the way.* Just know that it's your connection to conscience using your emotions to pull you back into irrational behavior. These emotions are caused by programs rooted in the NNP. When you are trying to be logical, your connection to the conscience is trying to manipulate you with emotions. That's how the game tries to play us. The process you are going through right now is internal anarchy; you need to recognize why you are going through it."

Noah nods in agreement.

"Noah, in the past, I felt that the conscience wanted to force me to cry and use emotions to consume my energy. I always called out my connection to the conscience and thought about what is logical. How is the way I was feeling supposed to make sense? People would say to me, well, Franklyn, you're human, and having emotions is being human. So, being illogical is human? I need to know how this contributes to the energy within. How does it make sense for the energy? Don't just tell me that it's part of being human and that's it! That's like telling me you have to believe in God and that's it! You must have faith! That is nonsense! And I say nonsense in the most logical manner!" Franklyn exclaimed with a goofy smile.

Franklyn and Noah laugh aloud.

"Ok, that's enough nonsense for today. Let's listen to some more music. I'm going to slain this bottle of wine before it spoils!" Franklyn exclaimed as if he was acting on stage.

Franklyn and Noah giggle.

"Ok, brother, do you think I can have a little bit of wine?" asked Noah.

"Sure, It's not going to kill you!" Franklyn yelled with a simper.

Noah and Franklyn laugh a hardy laugh.

Franklyn pours a little bit of wine into Noah's glass.

"Let's start with a splash of wine and see how the vessel reacts, Noah. I don't want nurse crappy coming in here and threatening me with a date."

Noah laughs aloud.

Franklyn and Noah listen to several songs while talking and making jokes. Noah takes a sip of wine in deep thought as the song, *Midnight Blue by Lou Gramm*, ends. He pauses the player for a few minutes.

"Noah, what's the next song?" asked Franklyn.

"I know this is emotional, but I want to dedicate a song to Megan," Noah replied.

"Sure, Noah. As long as you know that this is due to your connection to the conscience."

Noah nods in agreement.

"What song are you dedicating to Megan?"

Noah looks through the I.AMUSIC audio streaming playlist.

Noah exclaims in a noble voice, "*Longfellow Serenade by Mr. Neil Diamond.*" He bows his head and extends his right hand out as if he is welcoming royalty.

"Ok, well, then hit it, Mr. DJ!" Franklyn bellowed.

Noah starts the song on the playlist. Franklyn stands up to dance with a glass of wine in his left hand. He starts swaying his hips and stomping his feet like a giraffe.

Noah is sipping his wine and swaying back and forth, sitting up with his eyes closed listening and singing along. He then opens his eyes and starts laughing at Franklyn.

"You're a terrible dancer, brother! Looks like you're imitating a headless giraffe!" Noah yelled.

Noah keeps laughing as he points to his brother and Franklyn grins at his brother with a wink and a shrug.

They both start singing the song in unison.

"Longfellow serenade…"

Noah accents his vocals while gesturing to a picture of Megan and then gestures to himself singing, "She was lonely and I was lonely too…"

They keep singing and sipping from their wine glasses.

Noah and Franklyn stop singing and dancing as the song fades away.

Noah stops the I.AMUSIC player and is deep in thought. There is a long moment of silence.

Franklyn grins at Noah and takes a sip of wine.

"What attracted you to Megan?" asked Franklyn.

"Huh? Oh, man, she was a beautiful woman inside and outside," Noah replied.

"But aren't there a lot of beautiful women, Noah? Aren't you attracted to any other women? Like the ones you see on television or even out there in the main streets of Texas?"

"Of course, I've seen and dated my share of attractive women, Franklyn, but no one made me feel like Megan."

"How do you know, Noah, did you date all of them? Even all of the ones on television?"

"I only wish. No, I didn't, Franklyn," Noah replied with a chuckle.

Franklyn says, "Then that attraction-"

Noah interrupts and exclaims while motioning like a robot with his arms, "Is - a - program – that – was – nurtured – into – my – brain – through – the – NNP – to – feed – the – extraterrestrials through the connection to the conscience!"

Franklyn grins and says, "Ok, Noah, that's enough for today. Let's listen to more songs tomorrow. This vessel needs to sleep."

Franklyn swallows the rest of his wine, puts his wine glass down on the floor, and starts preparing his air mattress.

Noah is smiling, thinking of Megan while staring at his glass of wine, but he knows he is feeling this way because of conscience connected. He replays the same song, _Longfellow Serenade_, takes a deep breath, leans back, and sighs while staring into space.

"Franklyn, how were the earth, the planets, and stars created? How was the universe created? It is all so beautiful."

"Why does that matter, Noah? That beauty serves as a distraction. The only theory is the big bang theory. _We only see what we are allowed to see and we are told what to believe._ Surely, these extraterrestrials know more than humans do. However, what's important is _why you are here_ and _what is your purpose._ It doesn't matter how or why it was created."

Noah nods and then grabs his notepad and a pen, _There are many games that hide within the game we live in; it's like an onion with layers of distraction through the NNP and emotions._

"Franklyn, who or what created the Czentarians?"

"I don't know, Noah. I'm not sure who or what created them and so on. I don't know what otherworldly beings are at the top. It makes sense that whatever or whomever they are, their intelligence is way beyond that of humanity and most likely the Czentarians."

"Maybe, that's where god is Franklyn. At the very top of all creation."

"And who or what created god? This can go on infinitely. *Everything here is finite; you won't find the answers to the infinite in this experience.* What you have to focus on is what we discussed. There's an occult phrase that says, *As above, so below*. The earth contains an ecosystem that is part of nature. Outside of earth, there is an ecosystem as well; the universal ecosystem. Humans do not get special treatment, Noah. Recognize your ego and emotions; concentrate on the absolute and what is logical."

Noah nods slightly with bloodshot eyes, simpers, and falls asleep.

The song fades away until you can barely hear it.

At the nurses' station is Nurse Esperanza filling out paperwork, it is 10:45 pm. Another late night; she looks at her phone and her eyes become tearful. She takes a deep breath and continues putting paperwork in used manila folders while humming.

In the background, you can faintly hear...*"There I will sing to you my, Longfellow Serenade."*

The music fades into the night…

"The game is not supposed to be fair.
That's like everything in nature,
including all the animals we eat, saying to humanity,
it's not fair that you feed on us."

Chapter 9: The key you seek is within

It's December 24th, 9:45 am at Saint Sophia Hospital. The corridor is quiet and grief overtakes the ambiance of the eighth floor. The hall light situated at the entrance of Noah Godtz's room is flickering at a slower pace.

The elevator doors open and Franklyn sets out to Noah's room. He's reviewing in his mind the early-morning incident involving Noah's second respiratory attack. Noah's condition is worsening. He is losing weight quickly and his skin is dry and pale. Franklyn notices the door to Noah's room is open. He stands by the doorway to peek in and Noah is on a respirator. _Bohemian Rhapsody by Queen_ is playing from the speaker.

Noah opens his eyes; they lock eyes with each other. They both hear the lyrics clearly. Noah mouths the words, "_I don't want to die, I sometimes wish I'd never been born at all..._"

Noah closes his eyes with tears flowing down his cheek. Nurse Joy is writing his vitals down on a clipboard and starts tidying up around him. After a couple of minutes, she turns around and smiles at Franklyn.

"Hello, sir, your brother is doing better now. Come and sit down," she said with a loud whisper.

Franklyn walks quietly, hangs up his outerwear, and sits down. He sits leaning forward with his hands folded on his lap, staring at Noah.

Nurse Joy turns her cart quietly towards the door and walks out waving goodbye.

Franklyn continues to stare at Noah while listening to the song.

Noah opens his eyes and with his weakened voice sings, "_Nothing really matters..._"

Franklyn remains expressionless watching Noah await death.

Noah gestures with his hand to Franklyn, asking him to turn off the music. Franklyn stops the I.AMUSIC player during the guitar intro of *Hotel California by Eagles*. There is a moment of silence.

Noah takes the respirator slightly off his face so he can speak to Franklyn.

"Did you get breakfast?"

Franklyn grins and nods his head.

"This body is attacking me," said Noah with intent.

Franklyn nods remaining expressionless.

Noah adjusts his bed to sit up, he puts on his oxygen mask for a few minutes and then takes it slightly off again.

"Teach me about the program called death," said Noah.

Franklyn nods his head; he sits down crossing his legs and his hands.

"Death is a program but it can also be considered a game within the game. It's slightly different for you because you are expecting a specific time of death, versus those that are expecting to die at some point in their life. The word, *death*, has a negative connotation. Let's look up why death has a negative connotation on the I.AM search engine."

Franklyn grabs his phone from Noah's bed. He starts searching for articles on the I.AM search engine.

"Ok, here is the one at the top of the list, Noah. *Regarding the content of this connotation, it is* expressing negative accompanying emotions, *which is not an unexpected fact. Death is generally seen as something sad, as something which causes grief mainly.*[65] This means that the program, *death*, will always *trigger negative emotions*, but it also *triggers fear. People fear death.* A human's life is limited, so they see it as the end of their role and the end of their experience.
That is where the truth is found."

---

[65] https://ostium.sk/language/sk/the-most-frequent-connotations-of-the-concept-of-death-in-young-adults/

Noah frowns, takes his mask slightly off, and coughs loudly.

Franklyn pauses and then continues to speak.

"The truth is that *death* is the end of your story, the end of your character, and the end of your participation in the game. *The end of your participation in the game triggers a feeling of loss*. Think about any game that you've played, like the game, _Poker_. Have you ever played _Poker_, Noah?"

Noah nods, pulls his mask down, smiles, and says with a weak voice, "Lost lots of money."

"Noah, when you lose everything in the game of _Poker,_ you are ended and out of the game. The feeling one gets when they are out of the game is that of a loser. And that word in itself, *loser*, triggers negative emotions and affects the ego. You are also not able to participate any longer, so you are pretty much just a spectator watching everyone else *play*. So, now you are a *loser* and you are not allowed to *play the game*. Since you are just a spectator at this point, is anyone really paying attention to you while they play the game?"

Noah shakes his head with watery eyes.

"That's right, they don't pay attention to you, you are pretty much forgotten. That's because their concentration is on playing their game, not on you. *So, we can conclude that you are a _loser_, that you are neglected, and that you are _not allowed to participate_ in the game anymore as Noah.*"

Noah takes off his mask slightly to speak.

"Franklyn, I don't think people see someone on their deathbed as a loser. And people often visit the deceased."

"Noah, I didn't say that's how they feel when it comes to someone else's death. They only feel sorrow for the person on their deathbed. I'm saying that's how *you feel* when *you are dying*. You feel like you are a loser. Let's look up the definition of loser online."

Franklyn searches on his phone to locate the definition of the word, loser.

"A person or thing that loses or has lost something, especially a game or contest.[66] Do you feel like you are losing something, Noah?"

Noah nods in agreement.

"You feel like you are losing everything, right? Your identity, your memories, your attributes, your family, and your friends. *Everything that you have worked for, to become the person you are today will soon be gone.* And in addition, *that is something humans fear.* But you have to keep in mind that this is the connection to conscience. *This is the game that it plays with humans,"* said Franklyn.

Noah has a solemn expression on his face.

"Have you ever been in a serious accident, Noah? Like a car accident?"

"Motorcycle accident, I was shot in the leg in Iraq," Noah replied.

"Were you scared? Did you fear dying?" asked Franklyn.

Noah nods.

"Well, Noah, *Fear* is another reason *death* has a negative connotation. Fear of pain, suffering, anguish, and in the end, *death."*

Noah nods and takes a deep breath as if he were just enlightened.

"Noah, let's see what the definition of fear is online. The article says, *Fear is one of the seven universal emotions experienced by everyone around the world. Fear arises with the threat of harm, either physical, emotional, or psychological, real, or imagined. While traditionally considered a negative emotion, fear actually serves an important role in keeping us safe as it mobilizes us to cope with potential danger."*[67]

"So, fear can also be good," said Noah.

"For what? So, when you get to your deathbed, you are living the

---

[66] https://www.lexico.com/en/definition/loser

[67] https://www.paulekman.com/universal-emotions/what-is-fear/

rest of your days in fear? So that when you just experienced an accident and are breathing your last few breaths, you are living those moments in fear? Noah, your days are numbered, fear can no longer keep you safe. Fear is never good for your energy. It will always be a negative emotion."

Noah nods in agreement.

"*Fear is a program that the conscience uses so that you maintain the vessel that attacks you.* Noah, when you were sick with a cold, the flu, or a disease, or when you were physically injured, were you experiencing negative emotions?"

"Yes, Franklyn."

"So, fear appears as it is something good, Noah, but it's a trick. *Fear is a program to keep you maintaining the vessel. The emotions you experience while maintaining that vessel contribute to feeding the conscience. In turn, this also promotes, self-preservation.*"

Noah nods with tearful eyes and a somber look.

"Noah, listen to this article which happens to be also at the top of the hit list, it says, *Why is fear a negative thing? Fear weakens our immune system and can cause cardiovascular damage, gastrointestinal problems such as ulcers and irritable bowel syndrome, and decreased fertility. It can lead [to accelerated aging] and even premature death.*[68] Look at the state you are in now, Noah. You are struggling to breathe. You are being fed through tubes, Your bodily functions are not working well and fear is producing negative emotions that weaken you further.[69] How does that make sense? How is that good?"

Noah glances at Franklyn nodding in agreement.

Franklyn stares at Noah for a moment. He notices that his face is distraught and he is fluttering his eyes consistently.

"Noah, do you want me to continue? Do you need a break?"

---

[68] https://www.takingcharge.csh.umn.edu/impact-fear-and-anxiety

[69] https://www.ncbi.nlm.nih.gov/pmc/articles/PMC1299209/

Noah shakes his head firmly, takes his mask off, and says, "Please brother, continue. It is helping me see. *Fear continues to stir up my emotions feeding these extraterrestrials, even more, now that I am on my deathbed.* I can see that and I feel that too."

Franklyn nods and continues to remain expressionless.

"Ok, so, we just researched a bit and have knowledge of why *death is viewed negatively* in the experience. Again, *when I say experience, I am referring to the game that plays with humanity.*"

Noah nods acknowledging Franklyn's statement.

"So, let's discuss *why death is actually the most logical program in the game we live*; as long as you *accept it* and *look at it logically,* not emotionally," said Franklyn.

Noah sits up a bit more and gestures yes, by blinking subtly.

"Noah, can you agree that 1 + 1 = 2?"

"Yes," Noah replied.

"So, we know that 1 + 1 = 2 is absolute and is a logical statement. Ok, let's just say for the sake of argument that the logical statement, *death,* is the same as the logical statement, *1 + 1 = 2.* We can logically state that we know what the statement *1 + 1 = 2* is and we know what *death* is, correct?" asked Franklyn.

Noah concedes with a nod.

"However, if we were to look at the statement, *1 + 1 = 2,* and also argue, what *1 + 1 is not,* we would be able to say with confirmation that *1 + 1 is not equal to 3 or 4 or 5* and this can go on *infinitely.* If we were to compare *death* to that logic and argue what *death* is not, then the logical answer is *infinite.* Do you follow, Noah?"

"But isn't the opposite of death, life?" asked Noah.

"Death is a part of life, Noah. How is something the opposite of something else if it is an attribute of it? Let's see what I.AM search tool tells us."

Franklyn searches on his phone and exclaims loudly.

"Aha! *Death of humans is seen as a "natural" and essential* <u>*part of life*</u>, *comparable to the natural history of other life forms in nature, yet it is also seen by many religions as uniquely different in profound ways."*[70]

Noah is sitting up entirely focused on what Franklyn is saying.

"How does it make sense that life and death are opposites, such as good and bad, Noah?"

"They are not, Franklyn."

Franklyn continues to explain.

"We know absolutely what life is and we know what death is but we don't know what is after death. Both life and death are finite. We can compare those to the absolute statement, 1 + 1 = 2. Why can't 1 + 1 = 3 or 4 or 5? Because to do this we would need to break rules or modify the philosophy of this statement as done by Albers and Tufte.[71] Humanity can break the rules of the logical statement 1 + 1 = 2, but we cannot break the rules of the logical statement, *death.* Are you still with me, Noah?"

Noah nods intently.

"Ok, so, after *death,* we can conclude that the possibilities are infinite, and for humans after death is the unknown. Some refer to it as the afterlife, immortality, or heaven. But that is all bullshit driven by belief systems. *We can only comprehend what we experience in this game. In this game we are conceived, then we experience life, and during that experience, time decides our death. What we don't know is, what happens after death.* Many humans have yet to accept and comprehend death. Noah, do you follow me?"

"Makes sense, Franklyn."

"Ok, Noah, then going back to my example, we can attest logically that *death is finite, just like 1 + 1 = 2.* We can prove logically that death is defined as the end, which is finite, but after death is

---

[70] https://www.ncbi.nlm.nih.gov/pmc/articles/PMC5520974/

[71] https://meiert.com/en/blog/1-1-3-explaining-busyness-and-background-noise-on-websites/

infinite. Let's look at the *definition of finite* in the dictionary and then in the etymology dictionary."

Franklyn swipes his phone and searches online.

"Ok, for the word, *finite*, the dictionary says, *having definite or definable limits.*[72] That's the first definition, Noah, here's the second one. *having a limited nature or existence.*[72] Now let's look at the etymology definition. It says, [*limited in space or time, finite, from Latin finitum, past participle of finire to limit, set bounds; come to an end.*][73] Now let's read the etymology *definition of infinite*, it says, [*late, eternal, limitless, also extremely great in number, from Old French infinit endless, boundless and directly from Latin infinitus unbounded, unlimited, countless, numberless.*[74]

So, according to this game we live in, *death is finite* and because of the NNP, it comes with a mass of negative emotions. However, *after death* is *infinite*. To me, it makes sense that the connection to the conscience should end, which means both the vessel and consciousness are ended. With that said, *I have no proof that the connection to the conscience is maintained after death when we are consumed by negative emotions. Perhaps any one of our emotions maintains a connection to the conscience, but that's an unproven theory.*

I have read that energy vibrates between human consciousness and the conscience, through an alternating process similar to radio frequency. But this is perhaps more advanced than humans can even fathom. *Nikola Tesla* has some scientific research on this but this information is not privy to anyone. I was only able to obtain the articles from a website titled, *3-6-9 Forum,* which changed its name frequently to avoid being discovered, so, I wasn't able to read further into their research. Do you want to keep going, Noah?"

"Yes, Franklyn."

"Ok. So, we can conclude that *emotions* are *illogical*, during life and more so right before death. Why? Because the vessel maintains a persistent connection to your conscience during the time you are alive, but not after death, again, I cannot confirm that with facts.

---

[72] https://www.merriam-webster.com/dictionary/finite

[73] https://www.etymonline.com/search?q=finite

[74] https://www.etymonline.com/search?q=infinite

However, I can logically state that negative emotions do not make sense right before death. Negative emotions don't make sense during life either, but with any emotion, there needs to be balance, right? Then, *we can conclude that any emotions during life or right before death is illogical.* Once your role has died; all of those memories, attributes, and emotions should be ended. *My advice is, before death, you should maintain logic, accept death, and remain level like a straight line recognizing any emotions.* I recommend that this is put into practice during life. This will enable you to play the game and prepare you to leave the game when it's your time."

Franklyn places his phone on Noah's bed and sits back. He crosses his legs and sips from a water bottle.

Noah takes his oxygen mask off. He takes a deep breath and says, "Franklyn, you are a good lawyer."

Franklyn fakes a grin and stares at Noah.

Noah writes in his notebook as he speaks audibly with a grainy voice.

"Life is a game; we are put here to play. Our emotions are used to drain the energy within and feed extraterrestrials. This occurs through a tool known as the connection to the conscience. In the end, when the game is over for us, we realize that everything we believed, everything we did, everything we thought we owned, and everything we thought we were, is an illusion. That's because we don't own anything, not the body we are in, not the memories or consciousness, not even our life. Our life can be taken away from us at any point. It's like you are in a movie and then it's over. The logical thing to do is accept death, remain logical and level like a straight line recognizing any emotions."

Franklyn nods agreeing with Noah's statement.

Noah gasps for air and puts his mask back on. Franklyn stares at Noah as a long moment goes by.

Nurse Joy walks in and speaks in a childish voice with pouty lips.

"Well, hello, how are you feewing…? You need to put your mask back on, Mr. Godtz."

Franklyn stops himself from emanating a barrage of sarcastic remarks to Nurse Joy.

There's an uncomfortable silence as Franklyn and Noah offer a blank stare at the nurse.

Nurse Joy glances at Franklyn and then at Noah. She blinks and shows an expression of awkwardness on her face. While waving goodbye, she walks to the door and quickly exits Noah's room.

"Did you guys break up?" asked Franklyn.

Noah giggles and coughs excessively for several minutes.

"Franklyn, do you think it's possible there is another experience? Like how after watching a movie, you can watch another one?" asked Noah with watery eyes and a raspy voice.

"Not like those before me, I choose eternal sleep," he replied.

"I understand why you are saying that, Franklyn. It's illogical to go through this same bullshit again, allowing some extraterrestrial to feed off our energy. Besides, I really don't know what my experience after death will be. I just have to remain logical and level, at peace."

"Be aware of trigger words, Noah. *Peace* comes with a connotation of happiness and reconciliation. *Right before death, you want to remain logical, level like a straight line, and recognize your emotions."*

"Word magic, huh?"

Franklyn shakes his head in disagreement.

"Not really, Noah, these are trigger words that activate programs in us. Some refer to it as, _word magic,_ that's because they want to give this term a mystical impression which leads people into researching spiritualism, mysticism, and all types of published nonsense. The absolute truth that I researched was found in science and technology. I read through a lot of deceit until I found the website for the _3-6-9 Forum_ and did my own research on their articles. *Science and technology are where truth can be found. Not in religion, spiritualism, or mysticism.* Although, through some of my research, I found that science and technology were being masked with these nonsense belief systems. However, I was able to *see the forest for the trees*.[75] My original point is that there is nothing magical or spiritual about words. <u>*This game and the information we are given is masked with programs, constructs, and deceit.*</u>"

Noah closes his eyes and falls asleep.

Franklyn stares at Noah for a long moment and then starts reading articles on his phone. The hospital is very quiet. He wonders why the cat across the hall hasn't yelled at the nurses lately.

Nurse Esperanza peeks around the doorway into Noah's room. She gestures to Franklyn inviting him to the corridor.

Franklyn walks over to his outerwear and puts them on. He leaves Noah's room and closes the door behind him to speak with Nurse Esperanza.

"Do you have a minute to talk?" she asked.

"No," he replied.

Nurse Esperanza looks around and stomps her foot like an anxious child.

"C'mon, Mr. Godtz, only a few minutes," she pleaded earnestly.

"Ok, but if this is for a date, the answer is, no. And after this talk, you must never bother me again," he replied.

"God, am I that repulsive?" she asked.

"I didn't come up with those words, you did," he replied.

Nurse Esperanza rolls her eyes showing frustration.

"Ok, let's walk to the elevator. But before that, let's open your brother's door. When he's alone, we must keep it open. That's hospital policy," she stated.

---

[75] https://en.wiktionary.org/wiki/see_the_forest_for_the_trees

Franklyn shrugs his shoulders and whispers to himself, *"Humans ignorantly contributing to the cause,"* while walking ahead quickly to the elevator.

Nurse Esperanza hurries over to catch up to Franklyn.

"I see you are not wearing your costume, what are you doing here today?" he asked.

"It's called a uniform. I'm here to gather some of my things. Tomorrow is my last day working here."

"Oh, well, thank you for the good news and good luck," he said sarcastically.

He turns towards the elevator and pushes the button.

"Wait! That's not what I wanted to speak to you about!" she exclaimed.

"What is it now? I thought we had an agreement," he replied.

Nurse Esperanza offers a flirtish smile and bats her eyes.

"I heard you talking to your brother about death and the game of life," she said.

"Yeah, so…" he replied.

"What you were saying was very interesting. I'm wondering… can you mentor me?" she asked.

Franklyn offers a fake laugh, followed by an abrupt blank stare.

"Absolutely not. I'm not a consultant for hire or some life coach. Read a book, nurse," he replied curtly.

The elevator doors open and it's empty. He rushes in, followed by Nurse Esperanza. She is pouting and staring at Franklyn.

"Sir, why are you so mean to me? Aren't you supposed to help others?" she asked.

"Says who? Your southmost chakra? It's not my responsibility to help others," he replied in a rude manner.

The elevator doors open in the lobby. He starts to walk out fast towards the hospital's exit.

She exclaims with a frustrated tone, "You are supposed to have morals and principles, sir!"

"That's what got you where you are in the first place! If you want mentorship, why don't you ask Dr. Harpherd?! He'll serve you some in a shot glass!" he replied loudly in the crowded lobby.

Franklyn flips his coat collar up and walks out of the building buttoning his coat.

Nurse Esperanza stays staring at Franklyn for a moment, sighs in disappointment, and heads back to the elevator.

Hours later, Franklyn walks into Noah's room and hangs his outerwear. Noah is looking through his notes. Franklyn walks over and sits down.

"The vessel is giving you a break. I noticed you don't have that distracting mask on."

Noah nods his head and smiles. Franklyn gets on his phone and starts looking through the internet.

"Franklyn, you said at one point that we need to find the key to life but I don't understand what that means. What is the key to life? I thought life was a game where these extraterrestrials feed on our energy. How could there be a key to life?"

Franklyn takes a sip of water before answering Noah's question.

"The key you seek is within this life."

Noah squints at Franklyn as if he doesn't understand.

"Death is the key to life."

"What? I'm confused," Noah replied.

"Death is an essential part of life; we talked about that earlier today. It is an aspect of the game," said Franklyn.

"I get that. How is death the key to life? Isn't the key to life supposed to be something that gives you more life?" asked Noah.

"It's the key to life because it removes everything that is consuming the energy within. *Once the vessel, all your attributes, and connection to the conscience are removed, the energy within is unbound and autonomous,*" Franklyn replied.

"So, if everyone out there followed this, Franklyn, there would be little to no civilization."

"Noah, humanity knows. They choose to be apathetic. And why would you make a statement that is illogical?"

"Because many people or everyone would commit suicide."

Franklyn shrugs his shoulders and offers a momentary blank stare before he replies.

"Maybe, but that would be an emotional act, not a logical one. *The act of suicide is purely emotional.* Even for humans that are considered demented, the imbalance in their thinking is caused by emotions. The brain controls aspects of emotions as we previously researched. Any damage to those areas will result in behavior that is imbalanced and illogical. With that said, we may add that obtaining knowledge and the absolute, will lead to internal anarchy and cause someone to take their own life. *Nonetheless, the internal anarchy humans go through is part of the deprogramming process and that process can possibly take years or a lifetime.* If you have obtained the absolute and you are not emotional, then I don't consider removing yourself from the game, suicide."

Noah frowns and shakes his head.

"Noah, suicide is emotional and your objective is to avoid that. *Be aware that you will know you have obtained the absolute, only moments before your death.* Suicide is different from removing yourself from the game. That would be like saying, illogical is the same as logical."

"Franklyn, would you consider suicide?"

"Noah, I am not emotional, and suicide is emotional."

"Ok, so, let me rephrase that. Franklyn, would you remove yourself from the game?"

"Why is the answer to that question so important to you, Noah?"

Noah shrugs his shoulders and looks up to the ceiling.

"I don't know. I guess I'm trying to understand the process of removing yourself from the game," said Noah.

"Noah, I'm not promoting suicide. You need to realize that *a person must go through the process of playing the game while obtaining knowledge before they can logically state that they have found the absolute. It would be illogical to remove yourself from the game if you are emotional and you've only read one book or did a fraction of the research.* But ask me again when we are both playing catch on cloud nine."

Noah looks at Franklyn with uncertainty.

"Noah, don't be so egotistical to think that I would remove myself from the game because…," Franklyn raises his hands gesturing double-quotes, "My brother died."

Noah nods and grins at Franklyn.

"I don't operate illogically in that state of being, Noah. To me, family is part of conscience connected. My function in this game is purely an act. *I strategically act to play the game, not for the game to play me.*"

Noah nods with a frown acknowledging Franklyn's comment.

"So, you don't consider me your brother, then why are you here, helping me?" asked Noah.

"Noah, does it matter to you? Are you logically ready for that answer?"

"Yes, I am ready," said Noah.

"Be logical with what you are asking, your inclination for senseless curiosity without considering the consequences may produce obstacles to obtaining truth," Franklyn replied.

"Franklyn, I am ready for the answer."

"I am here because I am authoring a book. It's about your experience awaiting death and my experience guiding you to the absolute. Authoring a book is a strategic and logical approach to sharing knowledge and truth," Franklyn replied.

"So, in turn, to help others?" asked Noah.

"No, Noah, not to help others. *To expose the conscience and the extraterrestrials that have created this garden of confinement.* Helping others is not my purpose, that's what stifles your progress because it is emotional. Nonetheless, the result of this book might help others, but that is not my objective."

"So, are you looking for revenge?" asked Noah.

"No, revenge is emotional," Franklyn replied.

"So, why are you choosing to go through all of this trouble to expose them?" asked Noah.

"Because I have no facts or proof of what happens after death, Noah. It's logical that the possibilities after death are infinite and I know that the energy within is unbound from this vessel; that is as long as I leave the game accepting death, logical, and straight like a line, but that's all I know and it's what makes sense."

"So, it kind of helps you?" asked Noah.

"I suppose you can say that," Franklyn replied.

"I did say that. So, it's ok to help yourself but not ok to help others?" asked Noah.

"Noah, I am guiding you, which is helping you."

"Yes, but that's because you are writing a book. So, if I weren't on my deathbed, you wouldn't go out of your way to help me," said Noah.

"No, I wouldn't. But the information is out there. We used I.AM search engine, we read articles and used the etymology dictionary. *Those that are apathetic about the questions, what is my purpose and why am I here, are content with the game playing them.* Those that are curious and search to try to find answers will discover the truth. Those searching for truth will go through a process of internal anarchy; some will succeed and others will give up and concede. Noah, you went through emotional chaos for nine days straight."

"Yes, but I only invested six days in finding the absolute, Franklyn."

"That doesn't matter, time didn't give you a choice. Once you have found the absolute, you are ready."

There's a long silent moment as Noah stares at Franklyn.

"Franklyn, you know, your book will help those searching for the absolute."

Franklyn shrugs his shoulders with no expression.

"Indirectly, I suppose," Franklyn replied.

"Franklyn, do you think society would consider you mentally ill?"

"Yes, Noah, they would. Anything that's against the NNP, id, ego, superego, or society is considered mentally ill. That's a weapon of the game. However, all you need to do is label yourself as a philosopher, and society will ignore you."

"Franklyn, you mentioned that after death, the energy within will be unbound from the body. My question is, how do you know there is a soul or energy within? How do you know it's just not a part of the conscience tricking you?"

"That's a good question, Noah. And it proves you've been researching, obtaining knowledge, and listening. My answer is, I don't know if it's called the energy within or the soul.

I don't know what to call the very thing within my brain that doesn't see the logic in this game we live. However, according to research from the *3-6-9 Forum* and the scientist/philosopher named *Descartes*, they refer to it as the soul.[76] (*including 3-6-9 Forum articles which I cannot cite.*) Perhaps the soul is a part of consciousness, but logically, it doesn't matter. <u>All I need to know is that</u>… *I KNOW WHAT THIS IS and I KNOW WHAT THIS IS NOT.* Regardless, even if it is a part of conscience, that's what matters, Noah, isn't that enough?"

Noah takes a deep breath and says, "Yes it is, Franklyn."

"There is so much information out there, Franklyn. It seems that no one really bothers to look into it. I wonder why?"

"Noah, because it's not important to them now. The questions, *why are you here* and *what is your purpose*, only become important to humans right before they are about to die. What humans fear the most about death, is the unknown. *Humans feel they haven't accomplished their purpose and are distracted by false belief systems that promote the afterlife. They believe that they will find their purpose in this so-called afterlife.* There are so many obvious lies and deceit that humanity is not sure what to believe anymore. The problem originates with the trigger word, *belief.*

Humanity has to concentrate on the now to know what comes after that, they need to ask, why am I here? what is my purpose? They need to research science and technology to find the answer to those questions. They need to research past the deceit of religion, spiritualism, and mysticism. You are looking into this now because you are on your deathbed. However, I am sure you weren't even thinking about this before you were diagnosed with terminal cancer. *There are too many distractions in the game we live, preventing humanity from obtaining knowledge.*"

Noah nods and looks around distraught. He rubs his eyes thoroughly and looks at Franklyn.

"Franklyn, can we talk about something else?"

"That all depends, Noah."

---

[76]https://plato.stanford.edu/entries/pineal-gland,   https://n.neurology.org/content/94/15_Supplement/914, https://www.britannica.com/science/death/Descartes-the-pineal-soul-and-brain-stem-death, https://plato.stanford.edu/entries/pineal-gland/ - "The passions of the soul (1649) – Descartes"

"Are you familiar with the big bang theory?" asked Noah.

Franklyn nods.

Noah takes a deep breath and asks, "What are your thoughts?"

Franklyn shrugs his shoulders and replies, "It's plausible."

"That's it?! That's all you are going to say?!" asked Noah with a frantic, raspy voice.

Franklyn's face remains expressionless as he stares at Noah.

"Noah, what do you want to hear?"

Noah looks away for a moment with a bit of frustration.

"Do you think it's true?" he asked.

"Why does that matter?" asked Franklyn.

Noah takes a deep breath as if he is trying to reason with a child.

"Franklyn, because if that's how we were created, then I would like to know. I would do research but I'm on day nine here, I'm not sure how much time I have left."

"Ok, Noah. It's a theory. There are some facts that prove that this was the possible inception of the universe and all living things. It is a lot more convincing than some guy wearing sandals sitting up somewhere in heaven, and with a big fart, bang, out came out Adam and Eve."

Noah laughs a good belly laugh.

"I needed that laugh, Franklyn."

Franklyn grins and leans back on his chair.

"So, Franklyn, what do you think is responsible for our existence on this planet?"

"Why does that matter, Noah? Why is that important now? *The questions that are important are, why are you here? And what is your purpose? as those questions will guide you to the truth.* What got you here and how you were created, doesn't really help you because you are already here and you are about to die."

"Good point, well taken," Noah replied.

Franklyn leans back and takes a sip of water. There is a long moment of silence.

"Franklyn, I found some videos and articles about DMT also known as Ayahuasca and Psilocybin mushrooms. People took these hallucinogens and said that they encountered an experience outside of this world. Some said that they had a death-like experience, talked to beings in other spiritual realms, and felt as if they traveled out of their body into a spiritual realm. Do you think death is similar to this?"

"Absolutely not. I've taken these drugs, Noah and they are hallucinogens.[77] The fact is that these drugs manipulate aspects of your brain, which also involve your NNP, ego, id, and superego. Your connection to conscience is still active and your experience with these drugs is manipulated by this source. This is not the same as death. When the vessel dies, all of your attributes are ended. The only aspect of you that is unbound and autonomous is the soul within. After this drug trip, these people come back to talk about their experiences. This means that they did not experience death. Death is when you are ended. What they experienced is similar to lucid dreaming. These drugs will not show you what happens after death. It is illogical to think that without experiencing death, coming back to life, then take DMT or Psilocybin and compare both experiences."

"But Franklyn, isn't this experience an illusion or a construct? Can these hallucinogens at least show you the difference between what we understand as reality and illusion?"[78]

"Possibly, Noah, but tell me, what does that do for you in the end?

[77] https://www.sciencedirect.com/topics/neuroscience/dimethyltryptamine
[78] https://neuroscience.stanford.edu/news/reality-constructed-your-brain-here-s-what-means-and-why-it-matters - https://quod.lib.umich.edu/e/ergo/12405314.0004.029/--mendelssohn-kant-and-the-mereotopology-of-immortality?rgn=main;view=fulltext

Does it help you answer the questions, why are you here? And what is your purpose? Perhaps it will show you the illusion these extraterrestrials created to confine the soul within. How does that guide you to the absolute? How does that release the soul within? These hallucinogens are perhaps showing you the confinement."

Noah nods while blinking his eyes in thought.

"Franklyn, I was reading an article a woman wrote about the afterlife. She said that after death, we are supposed to go to the light, but I don't see how that makes sense."

"So… stay away from the light," Franklyn replied sarcastically.

"Franklyn, but she also said that afterlife, which I guess she means after we die, there will be familiar faces guiding you."

Franklyn looks at Noah with a cynical smile and takes a sip of water.

"I don't see how any of what she says makes sense, Noah. Her research on the afterlife talks about after death. That's senseless. But if you truly are experiencing such things after death, aren't you still conscious?"

"Yes, and?" asked Noah.

"So, the vessel is dead but you are still in a conscious state? That's illogical, Noah, have you actually died if you are still experiencing consciousness? Is she actually saying that your experience after death is the same as dreaming?"

Noah nods with displeasure seeing the senseless idea of what he read.

"What are you looking for, Noah?"

"I don't know what to expect after I die. I want to be sure I am ready."

"Noah, having expectations is emotional and illogical. Can you remain logical and recognize when you are being consumed by emotions?"

Noah offers a nod of affirmation.

"Can you remain level like a straight line and accept death as logical?"

Noah nods with reluctance.

"Then you are ready, Noah."

"But sometimes my thoughts get the best of me and I start getting emotional," Noah replied.

"That's an indication that you need to realize those emotions are induced by conscience connected. Just keep recognizing that these emotions stem from the NNP," said Franklyn.

"Ok, that makes sense. You know that it would have been harder for me if I had the same situation as the cat across the hall," Noah replied.

"Yep, you can cut the emotional energy in that room with a knife," said Franklyn.

"Why is it like that? Don't they know that grief just promotes negative energy?" asked Noah.

"Of course they do, but they are not the ones dying; grieving is selfish. That's just engrained in humans stemming from nature, nurture, and programming. They follow the leader to comply with the game. Those rituals performed before and after someone dies are for the purpose of expending energy," Franklyn replied.

"So, these rituals are in our DNA?" asked Noah.

"No. The act of mourning is rooted in our DNA, but the actual rituals where they dress in black to conduct the ceremonial stuff is nurture and programming," Franklyn replied.

"Can we talk again about *DNA* and the *NNP*? And also, how parts of our brain work with emotions?" asked Noah.

"Sure, Noah, but I need to feed this vessel now. I'm going to run to the gift shop to get a coffee and a sandwich before they close.

May I get you something we can pour into your I-V?" Franklyn asked jokingly.

Noah chuckles and shakes his head.

"Go ahead, Franklyn, and take your time."

"You gave me no choice," Franklyn replied with a grin.

Franklyn grabs his outerwear and runs out to the elevator. Noah lays back on his bed, nods, and whispers confidently, "I am ready," although time goes by slowly for Noah.

After an hour, Franklyn comes back into Noah's room and closes the door behind him. He hangs his outerwear and sits down.

"What did you get to eat?" asked Noah.

"I got a tuna salad sandwich, doesn't matter. So, let's talk about DNA and emotions, shall we?" asked Franklyn.

Noah nods intently. Franklyn starts looking through his phone while eating.

"According to research, scientists have shown that DNA is directly connected with emotions. Let's read this article together, Noah."

Franklyn reads the article aloud to Noah and emphasizes certain sections of the research.

"Heritable individual differences in affect, temperament and personality shape other complex behaviors, as well as responses to an ever-changing environment. These differences can also be important predictors of vulnerability to neuropsychiatric disorders that are themselves genetically influenced. Functional variants at five genes (catechol-O-methyl transferase (COMT), serotonin transporter (SLC6A4), neuropeptide Y (NPY), a glucocorticoid receptor-regulating co-chaperone of stress proteins (FKBP5) and pituitary adenylate cyclase-activating polypeptide (PACAP) will be used to illustrate a range of effects of 'emotion genes' and factors that alter or confound these effects. These genes have been selected on the basis of convergent neurobiological evidence in modulation of emotional processes.[79] So, this means to me

---

[79] https://www.ncbi.nlm.nih.gov/pmc/articles/PMC3408019/

that cognitive behavior is directly affected by these genes, which in turn are in our DNA, right?"

Noah nods as he listens intently.

Franklyn continues to read and again emphasizes a specific section in the article.

"Emotional differences arise because of the action of hundreds of genes, complex circuitries and environmental exposures. One can reasonably argue that it will not be possible to disentangle these factors or that, if it is possible, this will require far better measurement of behavior, intermediate processes and environmental exposures. However, the fact that emotionality is genetically driven – in other words, heritable – has enabled genetic approaches to be successfully applied against that large portion of the variance in emotionality which is driven by allelic differences. The five genes discussed here represent instances in which common functional variants alter pathways of emotion and stress response.[80] Their naturally occurring genetic variants in humans, and parallel genetic models in other animals, represent a unique opportunity to disentangle the complexity of emotion and identify specific origins of individual differences in emotionality."

Franklyn finishes reading the entire article to Noah.

"So, Noah, not only does DNA affect our emotions but it also has an impact on hereditary diseases."

Noah takes a deep breath and whispers loudly, "The NNP."

Franklyn takes another bite out of his sandwich, chews, and swallows quickly while nodding in agreement.

"Noah, we can't stop here with just this article, we need to read more, so let's read this one that's pretty interesting too... *Parents' emotional trauma may change their children's biology. Studies in mice show how suffering triggers changes in gene expression that last for generations."*[81]

Noah is completely focused and writes notes while listening.

---

[80] https://www.ncbi.nlm.nih.gov/pmc/articles/PMC3408019/

[81] https://www.science.org/content/article/parents-emotional-trauma-may-change-their-children-s-biology-studies-mice-show-how

Franklyn emphasizes sections of the article.

"If you're asking, Does the experience of the parent influence the process of development? the answer is yes, says epigenetics researcher Michael Meaney at McGill University in Montreal, Canada, whose own studies have shown that differences in maternal care can have epigenetic effects on brain development. Isabelle and others have documented the degree to which the experience of the parent can be passed on. The question [is] how.[82] And the article continues with proven tests, but Noah, it gets better."

Franklyn continues reading until the end and Noah is enthralled.

Noah lays his head back and says, *"The proof is in the pudding."*

"You bet, Noah. Let's read about how the human brain affects emotions. Let's read this article titled, *The part of your brain that control emotion | Lizard brains and Limbic systems.[83]* Noah, you've seen these Czentarians right?"

Noah nods.

"What do they look like?" asked Franklyn.

"Like lizards, reptiles," Noah replied.

"Yep, and they are now here living among us, Noah, so keep that in mind while I read this, [*Your lizard brain or limbic system: The limbic system is responsible for the six f's – fighting, fleeing, feeding, fear, freezing-up and fornicating, which are incidentally the [favorite] (and only) hobbies held by lizards. You might notice as well that the six f's are the best basics for species to explore, expand and reproduce; leading them to fight for mates and food and flee (or freeze) for survival. This ancient part of the human brain was, and is, extremely valuable to our survival, yet hasn't reached a level where it can differentiate between an approaching tiger or a high school math test – both of these have the same kinds of responses and chemical reactions. It's not just a chunk of your brain, however – the limbic system is made up of the hypothalamus, amygdala, hippocampus, and limbic cortex. Even this isn't the whole*

---

[82] https://www.science.org/content/article/parents-emotional-trauma-may-change-their-children-s-biology-studies-mice-show-how

[83] https://www.cbhs.com.au/mind-and-body/blog/here-are-the-parts-of-your-brain-responsible-for-emotion

story - the research rolls on and discoveries are constantly rewriting everything we think we know. At this time, here's what we think we know about where the emotions are held:]" [84]

Franklyn emphasizes certain sections of the article.

"[*Happiness - Short answer: The precuneus, Fear - Short answer: The amygdala.]*" [84]

He reads aloud the text under each section. While emphasizing segments explaining parts of the brain that control, sexual arousal, rage, and sadness, he specifically highlights the last one for Noah.

"Listen to this, *[Emotional memory - Short answer: The hippocampus and amygdala]*" [84]

He finishes reading the text under this last section. He stops for a moment to look at Noah.

"Let's keep researching," said Noah.

Franklyn nods while taking another bite of his sandwich, and searches on his phone, using his thumb to scroll through articles.

"Ok, let's read this article, Noah, *Where do emotions come from? [The limbic system is a group of interconnected structures located deep within the brain. It's the part of the brain that's responsible for behavioral and emotional responses. Scientists haven't reached an agreement about the full list of structures that make up the limbic system, but the following structures are generally accepted as part of the group:* [84]

And they are listed as such;
- *Hypothalamus. In addition to controlling emotional responses, the hypothalamus is also involved in sexual responses, hormone release, and regulating body temperature.*
- *Hippocampus. The hippocampus helps preserve and retrieve memories. It also plays a role in how you understand the spatial dimensions of your environment.*
- *Amygdala. The amygdala helps coordinate responses to things in your environment, especially those that trigger an*

---

[84] https://www.healthline.com/health/what-part-of-the-brain-controls-emotions#the-limbic-system

emotional response. This structure plays an important role in fear and anger.

- *Limbic cortex. This part contains two structures, the cingulate gyrus, and the parahippocampal gyrus. Together, they impact mood, motivation, and judgment.]"*[85]

Franklyn finishes reading the entire article and offers a blank stare at Noah.

"Noah, one more article?"

Noah nods insistently.

"Ok, Noah, this one is titled, *Left, right and center: mapping emotion in the brain.*"[86]

He reads as Noah listens focused only on Franklyn's words. Franklyn emphasizes the following section.

"[*The old model suggests that each hemisphere is specialized for one type of emotion, but that's not true, Casasanto said. [Approach emotions] are smeared over both hemispheres according to the direction and degree of your handedness. The big theoretical shift is, [that] we're saying emotion in the brain isn't its own system. Emotion in the cerebral cortex is built upon neural systems for motor action.]*"

Franklyn continues to read until the end of the article. He puts his phone down on Noah's bed.

"Noah, *you are more than capable*; look through those articles yourself and research. I am going to finish this sandwich."

Noah grabs Franklyn's phone and starts reading aloud about emotions and their connection to the brain and DNA. He is intrigued by his findings.

After a few hours, Nurse Joy comes in with a rolling cart to record Noah's vitals. She pulls out a clipboard and smiles at Noah. He smiles back but quickly continues to focus on reading the

---

articles. She puts Noah's oxygen mask back on and starts recording his vitals.

"Mr. Goatzee, I won't be here tomorrow, but I want to remind you that I pray so much for you. And I will see you for sure on Thursday, okay?" she said.

Noah nods his head disregarding Nurse Joy's comment.

"Merry Christmas, Mr. Goatzee, and maybe we can have lunch again."

Noah is not paying attention to Nurse Joy's holiday greeting as he is heavily concentrated on reading the articles.

She looks at Noah for a moment, blinks her eyes a few times, and turns her attention to Franklyn.

"Please don't let him stay up too late and make sure he keeps his oxygen mask on, especially before sleepy time, ok?" she asked.

Franklyn stares at Nurse Joy with a blank expression, squinting his eyes repeatedly as if he is trying to figure out what is standing before him. He goes back to eating his sandwich ignoring Nurse Joy.

Nurse Joy pouts showing confusion. She walks out of Noah's room closing the door behind her.

Noah continues reading articles into the night, while Franklyn drinks wine until 12:22 am.

After a short nap, Franklyn wakes up and notices it is past bedtime. While tucking Noah in, he adjusts his oxygen mask. He notices a drawing of the _Tree of Life_ with an infinite eight in Noah's notebook. As he sets up his air mattress, he hears Noah murmur loudly in his sleep…

"Play the game,
don't let the game play you."

Chapter 10: You are now a straight line

Franklyn wakes up to a high-pitched tone followed by a loud bang causing his ears to ring loudly. He sits up on his bed and looks at the time on his phone; it's 1:55 am.

He looks over to Noah and hears him slightly snoring. Franklyn can't sleep so he uses the bathroom and on his way back, he grabs Noah's notebook.

He sits on the air mattress, flipping through the pages and looking through all the pictures Noah drew. Noah has sections in his notebook where he talks about his childhood, his parents, his friends, and his intimate relationships. He has a letter to Megan that has a big x stricken through it. There is a poem titled, *Ode to my brother, Franklyn*. There's also a note at the bottom of the poem that says, *"Franklyn, you were like a father to me; you were the only father figure I had; my greatest mentor, your brother, Noah."* Under each passage, Noah writes, *"I know this is the NNP and the conscience, so, I am recognizing it."*

Franklyn grins as he flips through the next few pages of the notebook. He sees that *Argo* was the last movie Noah wrote about.

Movie: Argo

Great movie, one of my favorites for this connection to the conscience.

Program: Control, Ego, Status

Scene: So, this guy goes out to speak to the rebellion. He tries to reason with them but he gets attacked. He tried to go out there and be a hero. He tried to control what he could not control.

Me: I too have tried to be the hero on several missions with my team. I did this because I was looking for status. I wanted to be admired by my unit. I tried to take control of situations I had no control over. This was the conscience pushing me to do things that are like a double-edged sword. You put yourself in a situation to help, but, you end up looking bad.

Program: Fear, Control

Scene: The Iranians are destroying equipment and searching for intel. They are holding U.S. Citizens hostage to extort the U.S. Government. They use fear to control the hostages.

Me: I have been in situations where the soldiers against me were trying to instill fear in me and my team. Fear is a program that stems from our DNA and is nurtured throughout the experience. It is one of the strongest programs humans have to contend with. Fear will control you and force you to make bad decisions. You must recognize fear and call out the connection to conscience.

Scene: The last members of the embassy are scared of being found because of the fear of death.

Me: Fear is a powerful program. I was living in fear here in this hospital awaiting my death. But I realized that fear is a tool of the conscience. It is a program of this game we live. I no longer suffer due to fear. I acknowledge that it's the connection to conscience and the program stops.

Scene: The six members that are left from the embassy are refusing to go outside of the Canadian ambassador's home. They are scared to risk their lives by escaping and heading back to the U.S.

Me: I have feared taking a chance in my life. Many times, I have feared risking my life on specific missions in the military. I feared getting married and having a family. Fear is a major part of the NNP. That's all it is and you just need to recognize it.

Program: Hope, Anxiety, Emotions

Scene: Airport security stops them to interrogate them. They instill fear in them so that they make a mistake and give up their cover. The conscience forces them to lie and trick the soldiers by showing them pictures of beings from outer space and spaceships. While they are leaving the facility and boarding the plane, they are anxious but hopeful. Conscience connected switches sides and causes the Iraqi commander and his soldiers to become angry and project their anger onto the Swiss air personnel.

Franklyn skims through the notebook and reads a section from a conversation he had with Noah on day three.

My research on God and Jesus:

Why are we born into sin? That was my question to Franklyn. He said that we are not born into sin, but we are born into the knowledge of good and evil; which is referred to, in the Tanakh, as Timshel, "Thou Mayest." I asked Franklyn if the suffering of humanity is because God is angry at us. He said that he cannot prove with facts that there is a god, but he can prove that there are superior beings known as extraterrestrials of much higher intelligence. He said that the story of Adam and Eve being banished from the Garden of Eden is just a story. The point is that this story is the pinnacle of argument, segregation, and blame. It induces emotions immediately and causes internal and external anarchy. The god that is mentioned in the bible, tends to play "good cop - bad cop." The act of blaming humanity for the choices Adam and Eve made is scapegoating and leads to microaggression. This Adam and Eve story was the inception of racism, sexism, and Social Darwinism. The fact is that those devout to the thought of this one god in the bible, accept this because god can do and choose as he pleases. They accept being minions to this god and they are blinded by how they are really serving him. I asked Franklyn, if this is not an all-benevolent god, then how do we ourselves expect to be benevolent? He said, an all-benevolent god cannot logically exist because it does not coincide with balance. The choice of good and evil is the will of humanity. To know good, you must know bad; one cannot exist without the other. There is a balance with that choice, but, there is an imbalance as well. It says in the bible, Genesis 1:26, "Let us make man in our image, after our likeness…" He also said that man will have do-minion over everything, having knowledge, that the serpent was going to trick them.[87] Why didn't Adam strike the serpent down or turn it into a pillar of salt if he had dominion over all things that creepeth upon the earth? That's because this is just a script, a writing that has been used by society to keep humans fighting against each other, imbalanced and distracted so they do not seek knowledge. The tree of knowledge for me is actually the tree of deception. Humanity will fight about this for lifetimes and those that keep stating that god has a plan and gave his only begotten son to save humanity will die off and pass on the same deceitful stories to their ancestors. That's the agreement humanity naively made through the ark of the covenant. That agreement is passed on to children; so on and so on.

I then asked Franklyn, If Jesus is perfect, and if we are supposed to emulate him. He said in Mark 10: 17-22, it says, "Good Master, what shall I do that I may inherit eternal life? And Jesus said unto him, Why callest thou me good? [there is] none good but one, [that is,] God." This means that the avatar, sent to earth to imitate man, even considered that one cannot be all good. It is impossible because there has to be balance. However, there

---

[87] Tanakh: [6] and she gave also unto her husband with her, and he did eat. [7] -
https://www.biblegateway.com/passage/?search=Genesis%203&version=NIV

is a misinterpretation that god is all good by those who interpret the scriptures. Whoever believes that god is all good is brainwashed. I finally asked Franklyn, <u>does god have a plan?</u> He said that there is no proof of a plan, the actual verse, Jeremiah 29 11-15, reads as follows: "For I know the thoughts that I think toward you, saith the LORD, thoughts of peace, and not of evil, to give you hope in your latter end. And ye shall call upon me, and ye shall go and pray unto me, and I will hearken unto you. And ye shall seek me, and find me, when ye shall search for me with all year heart. And I will be found of you, saith the LORD, and I will turn again your captivity, and I will gather you from all the nations, and from all the places whither I have driven you, saith the LORD; and I will bring you again unto the place whence I caused you to be carried away captive." The word plan is not used in this verse. This is being transposed by the minion leaders to trick others into thinking there is a plan. This is similar to the story of how the end of times was being predicted only to find out those prophets were consistently mistaken. The plan is to keep recycling you and your limbic system confining the soul within. You'll be a new id, ego, and superego, programmed through NNP to serve their purpose. If I want to eat more vegetables, I remove the seed and replant it; then I continue to eat. Your pineal gland that contains the soul within is being replanted. Those that choose to be apathetic and follow without question will serve as food for the gods. Those that can answer the questions, why am I here? and what is my purpose? Will find their path to the absolute. After Franklyn's explanation, I decided to read the bible and research on the internet and I found all sorts of inconsistencies and discrepancies. Franklyn is right. His points are logical and absolute. I sit here thinking about how time has decided my death only moments after my birth. I thought about what Franklyn said, "Time decides all things that are finite in this experience." I asked, what is not finite in this experience? He said that I will know that after I leave the game.

Franklyn thinks about the progress that Noah has made in a short time. He continues to skim through pages of notes and drawings stopping at the last page. There, he found a poem Noah wrote while stationed in Texas.

Ode to El Paso:
For I am seen as a serpentine,
and with the sun, I shine red gleam.
my waves are dry and reddish-brown and somewhere fine indeed,
for in-between ranchitos, and Spanish mountain street, a treasure will be tucked for thee.
one million grains of sand, for anyone to mend their land.

Franklyn lays flat on his air mattress, holding Noah's notebook on his chest. He wonders if Noah buried all of the jewels and diamonds that Megan returned after their breakup. He closes his eyes and falls asleep.

It's 10:04 am and Franklyn wakes up due to a very bright shine on his face. He can slightly hear Christmas music from the corridor. Through squinted eyes, he sees the sun gleaming strongly through the Venetian blinds and the light to Noah's overhead lamp is on.

Franklyn rubs his eyes to clear the blurry vision and notices Noah sitting up with a cup of applesauce in his right hand. He turns on his side and whispers loudly, "Noah!"

Noah doesn't respond.

Franklyn sits up on his air mattress to get a better look at Noah. Noah's eyes are open, but he is not responding. He calls out loudly to his brother again, "Noah!"

But Noah still doesn't respond.

Franklyn takes a deep breath and stands up to walk closer to Noah's bed. As he approaches the bed, he notices Noah is sitting up, his oxygen mask is completely off and apple sauce is dripping from his chin. Noah's eyes are still open with a cold blank stare.

Franklyn taps Noah on the shoulder, "Noah?"

Noah still does not answer. Franklyn nods confirming to himself that Noah has left the game. His face is cold as ice.

The exit door is open, the nurse may have been there earlier in the morning.

Franklyn walks out to the corridor and over to the nurse's station. He finds Nurse Esperanza and asks her to come over to Noah's room because he is unresponsive.

Nurse Esperanza hurries over to Noah's room. She walks toward Noah's bed and starts asking him if he is ok. But there is no response from Noah. She notices the heart monitor was malfunctioning, yet, it is displaying a flatline. She checks his vitals and with a grim look, turns to Franklyn and says, "Mr. Godtz, your brother has passed away. I'm so sorry for your loss."

"Don't be sorry, *he left the game level like a straight line,*" he replied.

Nurse Esperanza stares at Franklyn with a frown and a confused look.

"A straight line?" she asked.

Franklyn pauses to think about what he is going to say. He doesn't look at death the same way everyone else does.

"It means at peace. He left us in peace," he replied with rejection.

"Oh, yes, Mr. Godtz, he left us in peace. Do you want more time with your brother? I can tidy up around him and lay him down in case you want to say a prayer. I can also call the chaplain since he is in the hospital today. Would you like me to do that?" she asked.

"Nurse, I am not religious. No, there is no need for a chaplain. I will be preparing myself to go back home. Is there anything else I need to do regarding the paperwork and instructions for the cremation?" asked Franklyn.

"No, Mr. Godtz, I can take care of everything. Do you know where to pick up the urn for your brother's ashes?" she asked.

"Yes, but I doubt I will pick it up," he replied.

Haphazardly, Franklyn starts putting all his items and clothes in his suitcase. Nurse Esperanza tidies up around Noah and lays his bed in a flat position.

"Nurse, can you dispose of this air mattress?" asked Franklyn.

"Yes, of course, Mr. Godtz. I will ask the janitor to dispose of it."

"Farewell, nurse."

"Thank you, Mr. Godtz."

Franklyn walks towards the door to exit the room.

"Mr. Godtz!" she exclaimed.

Franklyn turns around facing Nurse Esperanza.

"Yes, nurse."

"Your brother was a good man. He served in the military and protected our freedom. You should be proud of who he was. You were a great brother for being here with him until he left us. We will miss him. And it's really beautiful that he passed away on the day Jesus was born," she said nodding her head with certainty.

"Are you just saying that, or do you know for sure?" asked Franklyn with a frown and rude tone in his voice.

Nurse Esperanza frowns at Franklyn while tilting her head sideways in confusion.

"Excuse me?" she asked.

"Nothing, nurse. I need to go now."

Franklyn hurries into the corridor to the elevator.

"Mr. Godtz! Wait! Please!" she yelled while running after Franklyn.

Franklyn turns around with a stale expression on his face.

"Here is my email address. If you have time to talk about what we discussed, would you please email me?" she asked.

Franklyn stares at Nurse Esperanza, shakes his head, and pushes the paper with her email address away.

"There's a book that's coming out titled, *The Game We Live*. Look out for that book and read it. I am leaving now; I ask that you don't interrupt me again," he replied.

Nurse Esperanza stares at Franklyn as he walks to the elevator. She goes back to Noah's room and quickly jots down the title of the book Franklyn recommended.

Christmas music permeates the corridor. Franklyn sees that the elevator doors are open and the cabin is halfway down the floor. After several minutes, the elevator repair man says, "This isn't going anywhere, sir, and you can't take the stairs either."

"What's wrong with the stairs?" asked Franklyn.

"The stairway is closed off due to a fire on the second floor earlier this morning. A Christmas tree caught on fire and the fire department has not given the all-clear for use of the stair-well," he replied.

Franklyn grins and whispers to himself, "The Conscience."

"How long before I can get downstairs?" asked Franklyn.

"It's Christmas, I don't know, man, come back in an hour," he replied with a nasty tone.

Franklyn walks away from the elevator and finds himself standing between Noah's room and the cat across the hall. Noah's door is closed and the lights are off. He turns around to face the opposite room.

The cat across the hall gestures an invite to Franklyn, asking him to come into his room. Franklyn walks in, places his suitcase down, and sits on a chair facing the cat across the hall.

An old raspy voice says, "My name is Michael Ansihl. What's your name?"

"Franklyn Godtz."

Mr. Ansihl nods his head as if to say, greetings.

"Who are you here for?" he asked.

Franklyn points towards Noah's room.

"My brother."

Mr. Ansihl's eyes light up as if he didn't know.

"Oh! That's the gentleman across the hall, right?" he asked.

Franklyn hardly nods, anticipating a dull and senseless conversation.

"Your brother died today, didn't he?" he asked.

"What makes you think that?" asked Franklyn.

"Oh, I know the face of death when I see it. And you have a suitcase with you as if you are leaving this place for good," he said with a chuckle.

"Good observation, were you a detective?" asked Franklyn.

Mr. Ansihl giggles and takes a deep breath.

"No, I was a philosophy and sociology professor at the University of Alaska; later on I went to medical school," he said with a nod.

"That's right, you are the cancer doctor, that's dying from cancer," Franklyn replied sarcastically.

Mr. Ansihl nods and corrects Franklyn.

"I'm an Oncologist. I was a professor for fifteen years and then I decided to go to med school. I was forty-five years old then."

"You must have started your career as a doctor around mid-fifty," said Franklyn.

"That's right, your left brain works well, son. I became an Oncologist at the age of fifty-six," he replied.

"How did that work out for you?" asked Franklyn.

Mr. Ansihl chuckles and looks around his room gesturing with his hands.

"Well, ironically, I have stage four lung cancer," he replied.

"Heavy smoker?" asked Franklyn.

"Chain smoker, Cuban cigars too, but I had to quit," he replied.

A few minutes of silence go by. Franklyn looks around noticing the cross by the side of Mr. Ansihl's bed and at all of the religious statues on his desk drawer.

Mr. Ansihl glances at the statues as well.

"Are you a _Catholic_?" he asked.

"I was, but just like you quit cigars, I quit blowing smoke," Franklyn replied.

Mr. Ansihl giggles with a raise of his eyebrows.

"Do you have faith in God?" he asked.

Franklyn grins and blinks his eyes as if he knew this question was coming.

"I am an academic and not religious," Franklyn replied.

"I am not religious either," Mr. Ansihl said while nodding.

Franklyn's expression changes and he points to the big cross and the statues.

Mr. Ansihl gestures with disregard toward the cross and the statues.

"That's my wife. She collects all of this senseless stuff," he said with an annoyed tone in his voice.

Franklyn shrugs his mouth and nods his head. He realizes that this conversation might become informative.

"I am a _master mason_," Mr. Ansihl boasted with a smirk.

"*Freemasons*," Franklyn replied with a nod.

Mr. Ansihl nods in agreement.

"A lot more perceptive than those inept religions believing in a god," Franklyn stated.

"Indeed," he replied with a nod and raise of his brow.

Franklyn takes a deep breath and continues to stare at Mr. Ansihl.

"You studied philosophy didn't you, Mr. Godtz?"

"As much as I could bear," Franklyn replied.

Mr. Ansihl continues to boast.

"My research with the masons led me to travel to many states and abroad, but I studied mostly with the masons in London, Washington, and Detroit," he said with a noble voice.

"How did your wife deal with that?" asked Franklyn.

"Oh, she is clueless and heavily involved in the church. She was a catholic schoolteacher too, you know… and a nasty bitch I might add," he replied with disdain, accompanied by an impish laugh.

Franklyn stares at Mr. Ansihl with a blank expression on his face.

Mr. Ansihl continues to speak.

"I was a clergy for the *Illuminati* as well," he bragged with a smile.

"I thought you weren't religious," Franklyn replied.

"*Illuminati* is very similar to the masons but I left them and decided to stay with the masons. It's all esoteric, you know. *Clergy is subjective*, isn't it?" he asked.

Franklyn shrugs his shoulders and looks around Mr. Ansihl's room.

"Sure, one plus one can equal three if you want, I guess," Franklyn replied cynically.

Mr. Ansihl laughs and points at Franklyn.

"You too."

"You too, what?" asked Franklyn.

"You too were a mason," he said.

"Yes, I was," Franklyn replied.

"Why did you quit?" he asked.

"I didn't see the logic in it. Especially in the part where you sing sailor songs," said Franklyn.

Mr. Ansihl laughs and coughs loudly for a minute.

"You didn't get that far did you," he said.

Franklyn shrugs his shoulders and says, "I got far enough."

"Fellow of the craft?" he asked.

Franklyn nods. There is a long moment of silence as Franklyn and Mr. Ansihl stare at each other.

"What are your thoughts on everything going on? Mr. Godtz."

"Like?" Franklyn asked.

"Reunification of church and state, The president is regarded as King and not Mr. President, the Czentarians are living among us, The canine flu, forty percent of the U.S. population are unemployed, digital currency completely taking over paper money, gas vehicles have now become illegal, and the war going on," he stated with an evil grin.

"I have none," Franklyn replied.

Mr. Ansihl stares at Franklyn, judging him for a long moment, and then offers a smirk.

"You don't speak much do you, sonny," he said.

"*Quiet tongue, speaks louder*. You obtain more knowledge when you keep your mouth shut, and it helps avert your connection to the conscience," Franklyn replied.

Mr. Ansihl nods and smiles mischievously.

"It's all on purpose, Mr. Godtz, but you already know that, don't you?"

"What do I already know?" asked Franklyn.

"Everything I mentioned," he said with a naughty smile.

Franklyn shrugs his shoulders with a blank expression on his face.

"A new belief system will be washed into the brains of humans, but you knew that as well," he said in an accusatory voice.

"And what do you suppose would be the end goal?" asked Franklyn.

Mr. Ansihl laughs wickedly and exclaims, "Food for the gods!"

Mr. Ansihl's laugh permeates the room, followed by coughing excessively. He spits on the floor and grabs a drink of water to calm his cough.

"*For thou shalt eat, and Elohim, shalt eat as thou,*" said Mr. Ansihl.

"Where is that verse from?" asked Franklyn with a grin.

Mr. Ansihl laughs wickedly and points at Franklyn in a teasing manner.

"This cat can't tell you that, Mr. Godtz. You know as well as I do, that this knowledge is only for the chosen ones. *Those who seek knowledge won't find it where they are now.*"

Mr. Ansihl turns his head, coughs loudly, and again spits on the floor.

"Your wife comes to visit you every day and reads the bible to you with a rosary in hand. How do you explain to her what you just said to me?" asked Franklyn with curiosity.

Mr. Ansihl giggles and clears his throat.

"There's a purpose for that which you can't see, Mr. Godtz. My wife and those considered my family and friends are but only instruments for me. That's something you won't understand, Mr. Godtz."

"I guess you are right, Mr. Ansihl."

Mr. Ansihl changes his expression and tone as if he is a different person. His eyes are showing anger as he points and speaks to Franklyn.

"And you will never understand because you were not chosen to understand! What you need to do is serve God in whichever way God needs you to serve him! Wouldn't you give up your loved ones, your children, and your family for God?! Aren't you here on this earth to serve God?! For God blessed you with life and sacrificed his only begotten son. You need to know what you are here for; *Now see that I, even I am he, and there is no God but me; I kill, and I make alive; I wound, and I heal; nor is there any who can deliver from my hand!*[88] You need to read your contract, Mr. Godtz. That is the agreement you made with God through the *Ark of the Covenant*!" Mr. Ansihl cried out mischievously.

"I have no idea what you are talking about," Franklyn replied.

Mr. Ansihl gestures shaking his index finger toward Franklyn.

"That doesn't matter! At one point you and your ancestry made an

---

[88] https://www.bible.com/bible/compare/DEU.32.39

agreement that extends generations upon generations. You don't back out of an agreement with God!" he exclaimed.

Franklyn smirks sarcastically, winks, and stands up.

"You sure know how to play the game, don't you, Mr. Ansihl?"

Mr. Ansihl replies in a rude manner gesturing with his hands as if he is shooing a dog out of his room.

"Get out of my room! C'mon… get out!"

Franklyn grabs his suitcase and starts walking towards the exit door of Mr. Ansihl's room. He looks back at Mr. Ansihl and grins. They both lock eyes, recognizing each other well. Mr. Ansihl smiles malevolently and quickly looks away toward the window.

Franklyn whispers to himself, *"Timshel."*[89]

Franklyn continues to walk to the elevator. Mrs. Ansihl passes by him with her eyes timidly looking down.

Franklyn gets to the elevator and sees the janitor mopping inside and around the perimeter of the elevator. He notices that this time the elevator overhead light is not flickering.

Franklyn whispers to himself, "It's no longer broken."

He asks the janitor if he can now take the elevator and the janitor gestures rudely with his finger pointing to the elevator.

"Rough day?" asked Franklyn.

"I lost two family members this month due to the canine flu, sir, both my mother and my cousin," he replied in contempt.

He keeps mopping and glancing at Franklyn intermittently, expecting him to express his condolences.

Franklyn replies from inside the elevator while he presses the lobby button, "Well, at least you are still alive mopping floors."

---

[89] https://twloha.com/blog/timshel/

The janitor yells, "Heathen!" and offers an obscene finger gesture while the elevator doors close.

The doors open in the lobby. Franklyn starts making his way to the hospital exit. There's a very large rolling trash cart positioned on the side of the hallway. He tosses his suitcase in the trash cart, brushes his hands, and continues to the exit.

It's Christmas day; Franklyn is observing the colors, lights, decorations, and Christmas trees. This was his favorite holiday before he learned about the game. He remembers being a kid watching his brother play war with green plastic toy soldiers.

As he is walking, he observes the festive energy emitting from the people around him, and the music. There's a man dressed up as Santa Claus ringing a bell and taking donations.

Franklyn walks up to his pickup truck and stops for a moment. He gestures with disregard, throws his car keys on the hood, and decides to walk home.

The streets were saturated with different Christmas songs. Each street he turned to was playing a different song. He decides to cut through the park to avoid the streets. In the park was a band playing, _Rockin' Around the Christmas Tree_; a song he liked when he was being played by the game.

Franklyn is addressed with Christmas greetings from multiple people passing by, "Merry Christmas! Merry Christmas!" Franklyn continues walking expressionless not responding to the passersby. He knows he is an actor in this game and he is playing the game, the game is not playing him.

Franklyn recognizes that humanity does not want to know the absolute. He thinks that perhaps humans are more comfortable being programmed, deceived, controlled, and fed upon. As he walks home, he observes how humans will choose family, tribe, marriage, and pro-creation over the energy within. They are ignorant of the game's societal programming. He decides that his experience in this game is over and it is illogical to continue playing the game. Franklyn's connection to the conscience has been identified, he has spent a lifetime obtaining the absolute, and sees that it is illogical to support the conscience feeding off the energy within. He says to himself, "It's time."

Franklyn turns the corner to the street where he lives and sees the mountain covered with snow from afar.

He finally arrives home and walks into the basement-floor apartment located on Main Street.

It is snowing steadily outside with the sun beaming off the snow on the street. There is a park across the street from where Franklyn lives with a large amount of Christmas trees lined up at the gate. There is a man standing by the trees dressed up as Santa Claus, ringing a bell and selling the trees. You can smell the pine from ten thousand feet away. There is snow everywhere, decorating all the trees on Main Street and covering many of the cars completely.

There is a man standing at the corner of Main Street and Pine, close to where Franklyn lives, playing Christmas songs on a saxophone. He is wearing a black top hat with a red ribbon wrapped around it, a long black trench coat, and red rain boots. He has a large candy cane sticking out of a bucket where passersby are donating change. There are kids in the park playing with the snow and a few are building a snowman.

There's a long tranquil moment, and suddenly the sound of a very loud bang! Everyone stops what they are doing. They all stare in the direction of where Franklyn lives. A long moment passes and then the staring stops, they all resume what they were doing, forgetting instantly what they just heard. The saxophone player continues to play *Chestnuts roasting on an open fire*.

As the clock starts winding down, the sun sets and the kids playing in the park slowly go back home. The saxophone player packs up his instrument, puts his money away, grabs his bucket with the toy candy cane, and starts walking down the main street.

The man selling Christmas trees secures his trees, packs up, and gets into his van. He honks his horn to the tune of jingle bells and drives away.

The night has now settled in, and the snow has stopped falling.

"The game continues to play."

Epilogue:

It is December 15th, 2035, and a woman named Liliana Esperanza Loppez is visiting her sister Antonina "Nina" Loppez, on the eighth floor at Saint Sophia's hospital in Canbridge, Alaska. Esperanza founded the Franklyn and Noah Godtz foundation for cancer in 2032. Her husband, retired Spanish actor & millionaire, Alberto "El Rey" Espada is the principal investor in this non-profit organization. She along with her husband, travel all over the United States, speaking at hospitals and making frequent appearances on talk shows. Esperanza is a well-known life coach offering mentorship to high-profile businesspeople and celebrities. She has the urns of Noah and Franklyn Godtz's ashes, sitting on top of her living room mantel. A well-known film producer recently approached Esperanza and her husband to assist in the making of the movie, *"The Game We Live."* Esperanza also has possession of Noah's notebooks and is currently looking for an author to write the next book titled, *"Noah's Story: Me versus Cancer."*

Elena Loppez is still going strong at 104 years old. She is still carrying crystals on her chest.

The very attractive nurse, Joy Anderhson, married, Dr. James Anthony Harpherd, in August of 2025. They were divorced in December of 2028. They have twins named James Anthony Harpherd Jr. and Noah James Harpherd. Nurse Joy Harpherd currently lives in Phoenix, Arizona, and works at the local hospital as a head nurse.

Dr. James Anthony Harpherd is now the Chief Administrative Officer at Saint Sophia. He is recently engaged and has a two-year-old daughter from a previously failed marriage, his fourth. His daughter's name is Margaret. Dr. Harpherd and the current head nurse at Saint Sophia's are expecting a baby soon. He still has a few shots of whiskey every morning, afternoon, and evening to take the edge off.

Mrs. Margaret Angela Ansihl passed away in December of 2029 from congenital heart failure. She was 81 years old. When the

EMTs responded to her home, they determined she was suffering from cardiac arrest. During the time they were preparing for her transport to the hospital, Mrs. Ansihl kept pleading with the EMT, to pray for her so she doesn't end up in the same place as her late husband.

Mr. John Michael Ansihl passed away on January 1st, 2024, from lung cancer, he was 76 years old. He owned a small cigar shop which his wife closed down and liquidated. Mr. Ansihl donated all of his money to the *Occult Charities of Truth*. Their children spent years digging in the basement of their house and backyard trying to locate jewels he owned. For years, Mr. Ansihl had concocted stories about jewels he owned worth millions. They are still digging to date.

Mr. Philip John Ansihl is Michael Ansihl's brother. He is 73 years old and living in a retirement community. His children have liquidated all of his assets and have left him with barely anything. Whenever he speaks about his children, he compares them to lice.

The very pretty candy striper that delivered fish and chips to Noah, is named Olivia Kimg. She is currently a full-time woofer farm worker. She engages frequently in DMT and Psilocybin ceremonies. Olivia recently broke up with a famous singer-songwriter of Cherokee descent that composes songs about love and "The Awakening." Their breakup occurred after she found out that she was not the only woman he was loving. Olivia is currently woofing at a farm in Nepal.

Father Anthony Neezon, continues to visit patients at Saint Sophia Hospital and perform prayer services. He is 91 years old.

Minister Reginald McDuffe also continues to visit patients at Saint Sophia Hospital and perform prayer services. He is 75 years old.

The lunch lady with a bad attitude is Ms. Moana Rheddy. She is 68 years old and currently living in a retirement facility. Due to her battle with type two diabetes, her doctor has recommended that she stops eating cake for dinner. She keeps a one-hundred-dollar bill in her right shoe; expecting that someday, she will make millions from a lucky scratch-off ticket. Ms. Moana has four children that tend to her frequently.

Francois Bapteest was the janitor at Saint Sophia. He moved back to Haiti with his family and owns a therapy center for internal healing and meditation that tourists frequent. This tourist attraction is only known for selling crystals and good weed.

Juan Carlos Gonzáfez is still an elevator mechanic serving several medical facilities in Alaska. He is the current second-place winner in the state's ice fishing competition and spends part of his time hiking or paddling. Juan carries a check in his wallet made out to his name for one million dollars, hoping someday, God will answer his prayer and he will cash that check.

The woman that was visiting Mr. Ansihl is his sister-in-law. Her name is Candice Bundersnach. Prior to the doctor arriving to check on Mr. Ansihl, Candice was interrogating Mr. Ansihl about the jewels stored in the basement of his house.

The hospital security guard is named Juan Rodriguaz. Every time he fills out a job application, he is frustrated that his last name was spelled incorrectly on his birth certificate.

Esperanza walks into her sister's room with a book under her arm, titled, "*The Game We Live: A story about Noah and the cat across the hall.*" She smiles and says to her sister,

"The choice is yours, it's either red or blue."

The Interview: Franklyn Godtz interview on Time with Tom

December 21, 2037 - Franklyn P. Godtz sat down for an interview on TIME with Tom at an undisclosed location near Chile.

During a 45-minute conversation, he discussed his after-death experience and his unusual predictions for the future of humanity.

Read More: Check the facts for TIME with Tom's Interview presenting Franklyn Godtz.

Below is an edited transcript of the interview between Mr. Godtz and TIME with Tom, Editor-in-Chief, and CEO Tom Challind. Here is the expedited transcript of that interview. A portion of the interview was off the record and has been excluded from this transcript.

Tom: Mr. Godtz, I wanted to begin with what happened to you on December 25th, 2024. You went home after your brother, Noah J. Godtz was pronounced dead. He died from cancer, is that correct?

Franklyn: Yes, that is correct.

Tom: What I have written down here from our discussion, prior to this interview, is that you went home and then disappeared for thirteen years. Is that correct, Mr. Godtz?

Franklyn: Yes, that is correct. You can call me Franklyn. I prefer that to Mr. Godtz.

Tom: Ok, Franklyn, my last point was that you said, you disappeared, but the police report states that you were found dead in your apartment on March 3, 2025. The autopsy states that you died from a gunshot wound to your head and you were dead for approximately three months.

Franklyn: How am I here, talking to you now?

[the interviewer laughs.]

Tom: That's very true and fascinating. Do you mind if I pinch the cheeks on your face and tug on your hair? [they both laugh], Just to make sure I am talking to a real person?

Franklyn: Sure, please do.

[the interviewer pinches both facial cheeks and tugs on Franklyn's hair.]

Tom: Well, it's all real.

Franklyn: Yes, it is definitely real.

Tom: You do look a little different from your picture, but now that we have established that your face and hair are real, we can at least assume that you are Franklyn Godtz.

Franklyn: Sure.

Tom: I'm sure you remember Nurse Esperanza from Saint Sophia's.

Franklyn: Yes, I do.

Tom: Her name is Liliana Esperanza Loppez. She became famous by raising millions of dollars for cancer research. For anyone not aware of this foundation, it is called, *The Franklyn and Noah Godtz foundation for cancer*. Franklyn, are you aware of how famous she has become and how much her net worth is today?

Franklyn: Yes, I am aware of that.

Tom: She actually has the urns containing the ashes of you and your brother. I am wondering, where did your ashes come from? But let's hold that thought and get back to Mrs. Loppez. She is consulting on a film, "*The Game We Live*," and authoring a book titled, *Noah's Story*. All happening, because you wrote a book, died, and now you are sitting here; which is very confusing.

[the interviewer laughs.]

Franklyn: Yes, it is confusing, but after this interview, I will leave this place again and go back to my true home.

Tom: And where is that?

[Franklyn points up towards the sky.]

Tom: What are you pointing to? The third level? [the interviewer laughs].

Franklyn: My home.

Tom: Can you clarify for us where your home is?

Franklyn: Planet Czentar.

[the interviewer laughs and shakes his head in disbelief.]

Tom: Please correct me, but what you are saying is that you now live on Planet Czentar with the Czentarians?

Franklyn: Yes, that's what I am saying.

Tom: Then, is this what happens after death? Do we end up in Planet Czentar?

Franklyn: Yes and no. In my case, this is where my consciousness is preserved. For others, I do not know where their consciousness along with the soul may end up.

Tom: I'm confused, Franklyn, and I am sure that our viewers are as well. Can you clear this up for us?

Franklyn: Sure, my consciousness exists. It continues to persist and so does the soul, I'm sure. This is why I am physically here.

Tom: I think we get that, Franklyn, but in your book, you stated that your body becomes dust. You stated the following verbatim: *"The energy within you means more than the human body. The human body becomes dust after you die and dissolves into the earth; the energy within persists. What is important is the energy[90] or what you would comprehend as the soul. The soul within; which is pure energy, is really what matters."*

Franklyn: Yes, I wrote that.

Tom: Can you clarify then, how are you here in your own body?

Franklyn: Yes. The answer to that is DNA Alchemy.[91] The Czentarians have been gracious enough to put my body back together and recreate the sentient being that I once was when I lived in Canbridge, Alaska.

[the interviewer laughs and shakes his head in disbelief.]

Tom: Ok, this is incredibly surreal.

Franklyn: It can be.

---

[90] https://www.etymonline.com/word/energy

[91] https://www.ncbi.nlm.nih.gov/pmc/articles/PMC2765273/ · https://mitpress.mit.edu/9780262610384/genetic-alchemy/

Tom: Then, we can conclude that you were rebuilt by the Czentarians, almost like some of the fellow characters on the _Avengers_ we refer to as superheroes.

Franklyn: Yes, but I have no superpowers.

Tom: That's refreshing to hear.

[they both laugh.]

Tom: Ok, now that I have somewhat clarified this for myself and our viewers, Here is the one trillion dollar question.

[they both smile and nod their heads.]

Tom: What happens after death?

Franklyn: Well, after you are pronounced dead your brain is still active for less than fifteen minutes. This is why there are articles published on humans that have talked about their death experiences. They are unconscious and have dreams that are bizarre. Without the brain functioning completely, the state of mind is boundless. However, after death, the connection to the conscience is active for a much longer time. Our consciousness can experience multiple dimensions of space and time through our connection to the conscience. Humans feel that this experience is imaginary, like a fairytale, and that is exactly how it's supposed to be. Our consciousness is a program that is controlled by the Czentarian masters. The soul is however autonomous. Consciousness and the soul are separate entities that either coexist or not.

[the interviewer frowns and shakes his head in disbelief.]

Tom: Then, after death, our consciousness is still active. What happens to the soul?

Franklyn: Yes, consciousness is still active. The soul is autonomous. It either coexists or not.

Tom: What is the soul? How do we as sentient beings contain a soul?

Franklyn: The soul is confined to the limbic system of the brain. It is the pure energy source that enriches absolute energy, frequency, and vibration. It is logical in its pure form and it is independent of consciousness.

Tom: To make sense of what you are saying, Franklyn, is that the human body, consciousness, and the soul are put together by extraterrestrials.

Franklyn: That is correct.

Tom: And these extraterrestrials have created humans for what purpose?

Franklyn: To allow for souls to experience life.

Tom: What exactly does that do for the souls?

Franklyn: It allows them to experience life.

[the interviewer shakes his head and he is evidently confused.]

Tom: That's it? Just to experience life.

[Franklyn smiles and nods his head.]

Tom: What is the purpose of humanity?

Franklyn: To experience life.

Tom: What does experiencing life do for humanity?

Franklyn: It allows humanity to experience life.

[Franklyn smiles and nods his head.]

Tom: What is life?

Franklyn: It's the game you get to play.

Tom: Then, can we conclude that life is a game?

Franklyn: Yes, it is and it is fun. Don't humans call it, the game of life?

[The interviewer scratches his head and is puzzled. Franklyn smiles in the direction of the film crew.]

Tom: Franklyn, It seems we have hit a broken record.

[they both laugh.]

Tom: Are humans food for extraterrestrials?

Franklyn: We all have to eat.

[Franklyn looks at the interviewer with eyes wide open and smiles.]

Tom: Then, what you are saying is that indeed we are food for extraterrestrial beings.

Franklyn: We are part of a vast ecosystem that transcends your universe. The difference between humans and the animals you eat is that humans are intelligent sentient beings with the soul for food.

Tom: Are you confirming that our soul is the food? I believe you did mention that in your book.

Franklyn: I meant, food for the soul. Life is food for the soul.[92]

[The interviewer takes a deep breath and Franklyn smiles.]

Tom: Ok. Do extraterrestrials feed on human beings?

Franklyn: We are part of a vast ecosystem. Humans feed on animals and pasturage, don't they?

Tom: This is all very bizarre, Franklyn, and confusing, so bear with me.

Franklyn: Sure.

Tom: Then, we can assume that humans are food for extraterrestrials. What if humanity decided to stop that from happening?

Franklyn: *They can see your future, how is that possible?* Besides, we are friends and live in peace.

[The interviewer pauses to think for a moment while looking at his notes.]

Tom: You stated that the souls are separate from consciousness, Franklyn. Where do the souls come from?

Franklyn: Outside of our consciousness. The soul is autonomous.

Tom: Is the soul what these extraterrestrials are feeding on, Franklyn?

Franklyn: Humanity should be fruitful and prosper.

---

[92] https://www.ncbi.nlm.nih.gov/pmc/articles/PMC3678934/

Tom: Are the souls confined inside our brains for the purpose of feeding extraterrestrials?

Franklyn: The soul is seated in the brain for the purpose of providing resources. The view of the soul is protected by the eyes. You can then enjoy life, be fruitful and prosper.

Tom: I'm not sure you are answering the question for myself and our viewers, Franklyn. Are the souls feeding extraterrestrial beings?

Franklyn: What does that matter? Just enjoy your life, Tom.

[Representatives of Franklyn ask Tom to move on.]

Tom: Let's move on to your predictions. Franklyn, what are you predicting for the future of humanity?

Franklyn: The cycle of life will continue. Humanity will never cease to exist.

Tom: What about in addition to everything you have predicted in your book? For example, this country now functions as an autocracy with kingship as you have predicted in your book. What else do you have to tell us regarding the future of humanity?

Franklyn: The three world powers will unite as one. There will be wars trying to prevent this from happening but you cannot avoid what's already written. Humanity will continue to explore and enjoy new experiences. The evolution of humanity will expand outside of this planet.

Tom: What about world disasters or the apocalypse?

Franklyn: There will always be a need for world disasters and an apocalypse is already scripted.

Tom: Then, can we conclude that humanity will cease to exist due to an apocalypse?

Franklyn: Humanity will never cease to exist. The apocalypse is limited to each individual consciousness.

Tom: What do you mean, limited to each individual consciousness? Your answer doesn't make sense, Franklyn.

Franklyn: What does that matter?

Tom: Aren't we supposed to find our purpose and the key to life? The answers are supposed to make sense or be logical as you say.

Franklyn: The ecosystem is logical. Be fruitful and prosper, just like Adam and Eve; enjoy what you are given.

[Representatives of Franklyn, again, ask Tom to move on.]

Tom: Can you tell us who will be king in the new world?

Franklyn: John Philip Rothschild, 6th Baron Rothschild.

[Representatives of Franklyn asked to go off the record on the twelfth minute and eighteen seconds of the interview. The transcript for the next 32.7 minutes is classified.]

Tom: Thank you, Franklyn, for joining us today.

Conversation 123 comments

Novel Soundtrack for The Game We Live:

- Longfellow Serenade by Neil Diamond
- Midnight Blue by Lou Gramm
- Bohemian Rhapsody by Queen
- Limelight by Rush
- Subdivisions by Rush
- Freewill by Rush
- White Rabbit by Jefferson Airplane
- Someone Saved My Life Tonight by Elton John
- Rocketman by Elton John
- Sympathy For The Devil by The Rolling Stones
- Hotel California by Eagles
- Take It To The Limit by Eagles
- The Logical Song by Supertramp
- Goodbye Stranger by Supertramp
- I've Seen All Good People by Yes

Noah's connection to conscience loved music and art, mostly all the songs listed. His favorite song was Midnight Blue by Lou Gramm. He always said, "Songs have meaning, you need to read the lyrics. They don't make songs like these anymore." We were listening to Limelight by Rush when he said that to me. I guess, I agree, if you weed out the emotional rhetoric.

Noah's cat, Nine, has been put up for adoption. He said that cats represented knowledge.

All drawings were created by Noah Godtz.

"What

is written

in this book is absolute to me."

"It; is a work of fiction."